TRUE BLUE

Trudy Nixon

A True Communications book
Copyright © 2024 Trudy Nixon

eBook First published in Anguilla in 2024 by True Communications Ltd.

The moral right of Trudy Nixon to be identified as the author of this work has been asserted.

All rights reserved. No part of this publication may be reproduced, distributed or transmitted in any form or by any means, including photocopying, recording or other electronic or mechanical methods, without the prior written permission of the publisher, except in the case of brief quotations embodied in critical reviews and certain other non-commercial uses permitted by copyright law. For permission requests, write to the publisher, addressed "Attention: Permissions Coordinator," at the address below.

Any references to historical events, real people or real places are used fictitiously. Names, characters and places are products of the author's imagination.

Front cover image by Esme Mackenzie https://esmackenzie.wixsite.com/illustration
Instagram: @illustratesme
Book cover design by Andrew Fleming
Editing by Alex Mackenzie https://alexmackenzie.uk/
Book design by Polgarus Studio

First printing edition 2024

DEDICATION

To my beloved Aunty Dorothy and my dear Aunty Gemma

A note about UK English versus US English in *True Blue*

Dear readers, please understand that this book (and the others in the series) is written in British English, which is very similar to US English except for some very slight (and potentially to you, annoying) differences. Please know these are not typos and Trudy's editors are fully in control – as far as any human can possibly be.

If you are a word nerd or grammar girl and would like to know more about these differences and the style choices we made, please feel free to reach out to Trudy via her email, info@trudynixon.com, and she will attempt to answer any of your questions!

PROLOGUE

MYKONOS, GREECE

Why am I in Greece when I should be in Wiltshire? thought Charlie miserably.

She tried to keep a pleasant expression on her face as the charming young Greek woman introduced her to the many delights of the magnificent accommodations she'd be staying in until … well, until she could fix that which had been broken. If it could be fixed.

She managed a wan smile when the woman opened a door to reveal Charlie's own private balcony, replete with two blue chairs, a little table and an even-better version of the spectacular view of the Aegean and the islands that ringed Mykonos. According to her, the sunset was legendary. It was an incredible view, one that should inspire awe, excitement and the desire to take a million selfies, but which left her cold. And what use were two chairs anyway when she had no one with her to share the moment?

All she could think was, why? Why did I come here? Why am I looking at that flat blue water and hot white rock, smelling the cloying sweetness of figs when I should be at home in Puddlington taking my dog for a walk – breathing in sharp, clean air under a canopy of russet, red and gold chestnut leaves? Momentarily she imagined herself walking along the bridle path – wellington boots squelching through wet green grass and soft brown mud, with Teddy and the others puffing and panting beside her, then racing off to chase rabbits they would never catch. The thought hurt, so she concentrated instead on what the woman was saying now, about the white marble bathroom with its matching indoor and outdoor showers and designer amenities, the daily maid service and the mini fridge stocked with cold water and fruit, until the woman left with a puzzled look on her face, evidently unused to such a lack of enthusiasm from the villa's guests.

I'm ungrateful, Charlie thought, embarrassed by her bad manners, as she dropped her handbag on a white cotton comforter that was so crisp and bright it looked like fresh snow. But there's a limit to how grateful you can be when you're somewhere you just don't want to be and when the person you'd always thought you could trust had let you down.

PART ONE

FEBRUARY 2015
ENGLAND

CHAPTER 1

Sitting pretty in the luxurious speedboat, Charlotte Pierce, Charlie to her nearest and dearest, watched Zephyr disappear, getting smaller until all that was visible was a thin, deep aqua line atop the endless turquoise of the surrounding Caribbean Sea. She felt no regrets as she wished a fond farewell to the small island nation that had become one of her favourite places in the world.

She'd done the right thing – owing it to herself to explore the instantaneous connection she had forged with a wonderful man she'd met and made friends with on her last trip to the island. Now she knew for sure their destiny was to be friends, not lovers – good job really as a long-distance relationship with someone who lived in the Caribbean wasn't ideal. Her next boyfriend needed to live closer to her home in Puddlington, she thought, and then looked at her phone to read the text she'd received that morning for the umpteenth time; she smiled in satisfaction. It was nice to know that someone was as excited as she was about her return home.

Twenty hours and an overnight transatlantic flight later, Charlie spotted her best friend Ali waiting on the other side of the barrier. The pretty diminutive lawyer was impossible to miss. She was easily the most colourful person in the dreary lineup of taxi drivers holding hand-written signs alongside anxious looking family members in dark winter coats. She drew the eye like an iridescent hummingbird in a flock of monochrome pigeons.

Charlie squealed and ran in for a hug as the crowd watched their reunion. The friends always attracted attention when they were out together. Perhaps it was because of how different they looked. Or maybe it was the squeaks of excitement and buzz of animated conversation, creating a positive energy field around them, that drew the eye. This dark and icy late-winter morning at London's busiest airport was no exception.

"Thanks for picking me up, darling. What a treat not to have to schlep home on the train."

Ali grinned. "No problem, me lover. All part of the Super Ali package," she said, substituting her usual, cut-glass 'Queen's English' accent for the over-the-top West Country accent she liked to use occasionally. She returned to her normal voice to drawl, "Besides, I just adore getting up at stupid o'clock to drive along a rainy M4 with all the lorry drivers and desperate commuters. Especially when the alarm interrupted me in the middle of a hot, and I mean scorching hot, like, so bloody hot I didn't need my electric blanket on, sex dream."

Charlie laughed, secure in the knowledge her friend would do anything for her, including getting up at stupid o'clock. "Aw babe, appreciate you."

With their welcome-home hugs over, Charlie, tall, model slim and elegant in butter soft jeans and an oversized navy-blue hoodie, glossy dark hair spilling over her shoulders, and Ali, almost a foot shorter with bouncing red curls and wearing a fitted ultramarine down jacket that failed to cover up her generous heart-shaped bottom, made a dash to the short stay carpark.

"You bloody well should, especially as you've been living it up in Zephyr while I've been working on *the* most complicated deal known to lawyer-kind in wet, cold, miserable Bristol." Ali sounded slightly breathless as she scurried along trying to keep up with her friend's leggy stride. "Your payment, as soon as we get in the car and on the road, is full disclosure. I want to know everything." The women kept their heads down as they picked up speed, trying to avoid the icy winds that whistled through the concrete corridors and parking bays. "You know I hate running but we've got no choice, it's bloody freezing," Ali moaned.

"I know. I don't know which is harder to believe – that you missed out on the chance of a holiday with *moi* or that yesterday I was in a bikini. Winter sun holidays are a bit discombobulating, to be honest. I'm really tanned underneath all these layers, but no one would know because all you can see is the tip of my nose!" she whined piteously.

Ali snorted, then chanced a look sideways, removing her face from the warmth of her snood, to give her friend an admiring glance and said, "I think you look *amazing,* Charlie. Fabulous. You are one gorgeous, bronzed beach babe." Then with a voice heavy with relief. "Oh, thank God, here's the car." Her friend had a penchant for strong, vibrant colours, and her lime-green beetle – nicknamed 'the slug bug' – was hard to miss even in the Stygian gloom of the multistorey carpark. Ali popped the boot and the two of them worked together to haul the luggage into it. "So … was it as good as you look?" She pulled a mischievous face and said lasciviously, "To look *that* good, you must have got up to no good. Did you? Did you get up to no good?" Not bothering to wait for a response, Ali carried on, "You did, didn't you? I hope you didn't break the poor guy's heart."

Charlie shrugged bashfully and giggled at the way Ms Impatient had answered her own barrage of questions. Ali, her best friend forever, always made her laugh and, as Charlie's self-proclaimed number one fan, often overestimated her charms. She loved her back equally. From the moment they met, the two of them formed a mutual-appreciation society of two. She admired her friend's confidence and intelligence and basked in her support and loyalty. But sometimes even Ali got it wrong, Charlotte Pierce – who for a painfully short time had been Charlotte Browning – break someone's heart? Chance would be a fine thing.

"I assume you are referring to my friend Chix?"

"The gorgeous older man you travelled to Zephyr to see to find out if he and his golden locs could ignite a fire down there." Ali drooled, as if she was describing the world's most tasty morsel seasoned to perfection and sizzling on the grill.

"Sorry to disappoint you, but I can confirm that when I left Zephyr his heart was completely unbroken," adding primly, "and please don't drool when you talk about him he's not one of one of your Tinder hotties."

Ali's face vividly showed her feelings without having to spell them out in words. Disappointment.

"Don't look at me like that. I know we both thought something might happen, but it didn't, and I promise that I'm OK about that, truly. Chances are that *you're* a lot more upset about it than *I* am."

"Seems like a waste to me," Ali muttered.

"Not at all. I had a lovely, lovely time. I got a great tan," she dug under her layers and lifted her white tee-shirt to demonstrate, "and, you will be happy to know, I laid some ghosts to rest."

Ali growled. "I'd like to lay bloody Graham to rest. Permanently. And what use is being all bronzed and gorgeous if no one apart from me gets to see your white bits?"

She smiled indulgently at Ali's Pavlovian and protective response to anything to do with Charlie's husband of less than a month.

It's sweet though, she thought, that these days Ali was far more outraged by her ex's behaviour than she was. Another thing to add to the long list of reasons she loved the girl.

She reached over and put her arms around Ali's shoulders and gave her an affectionate squeeze before moving to the other side of the car to let herself in. As she folded her long legs into the passenger seat she said carefully, "I know that everyone, well, you, Simon and Mummy and Daddy, of course, think it's a bit weird that I went back to Zephyr after what happened, but I did want to see Chix again and as Marvel invited me …" She paused. "And she's been great – so kind during a truly horrid time, and honestly, Ali," she said, willing her to understand, "she is *such* a laugh. I wish you'd come with me. I know you would love her, and Zephyr, too."

Ali grunted, neither agreeing nor disagreeing, as she fastened her seatbelt and checked her mirror. Charlie sensed from her muted response and a few other choice comments over the months that Ali was a teeny bit jealous of her new American friend. Which was a pity as she really did think the two of them would get on. Even though they were both alpha females for sure. She hoped that wasn't the reason her friend hadn't come with her. She'd blamed work, but maybe there was another reason.

She pressed on, shivering as the little car took its time to warm up, hoping Ali would warm up too. "O-M-G! Her parents' villa is a dream." She couldn't stop herself from gushing. "I had a gorgeous bedroom which opened out onto their pool and, in the morning, I just flopped out of bed and into the water, which was lush. And when we'd enough of that, we explored a lot of Zephyr itself. I saw a different side this time. Not just the hotels and the typical tourist traps. It's beautiful … and the people are so nice, and the food is so yummy and Chix…"

"And what happened with Chix exactly?" asked Ali. Even though the engine had been running for some time and she could have reversed out, the car had remained static; she was staring at Charlie with the beadiest of eyes.

"Well, it *was* wonderful to see him and we hung out a lot, but as friends – usually the four of us, Marvel and I and 'the boys'." She emphasised her pet name for them in air quotes and said laughingly, "It's hilarious really that we call them the boys when they are both on the wrong side of forty, but honestly Ali, the two of them, Chix and Dwight, they are just big kids. Dwight is *such* a playboy. I didn't really get to know him last time. He was too busy chatting with Graham about building bloody hotels, but he's hilarious and a brilliant host." She enthused, trying to capture the specialness of what she'd experienced over the last few weeks. "Oh. My. God, Ali. His yacht! You would absolutely love it. Champagne and rum punch on tap." She paused and smiled in satisfaction. "And Chix, well, he's just Chix. I've never met anyone quite like him. He's cool. Very clever, very funny too. But warm and kind with it. Basically, a great person. Honestly, the three of them were excellent company – I had plenty, plenty laughs and good times."

Ali, who had finally hit the accelerator, was now reversing out of the snug parking space, and said in a voice dripping in disbelief, "So you're telling me even with all that sun, sea and rum punch – and hanging out on a mega yacht – you weren't tempted? By a man who sounds amazing and who, judging by the pics I've seen, is bloody gorgeous to look at too?"

Charlie nodded. "He *is* gorgeous. And if I didn't like him so much, or was more of an old slapper like you …" She grinned at her to lighten the tone, adding, "Maybe I would have … but …"

Ali snorted and said nothing, remaining quiet as she carefully negotiated the car, which was nearly as wide as it was long, around the extreme bends of the multistorey carpark. As she did so, Charlie, snug in the car with jet lag surfacing, almost dozed off as she thought back over the last two weeks in Zephyr. The island was indeed a picture-perfect paradise with endless turquoise waters, sugar-white sands and a sultry tropical temperature that warmed your blood and made your body ache to be with the person you loved … or desired. But sadly, she'd concluded, that wasn't Chix. She realised she had better tell Ali why, or she'd never hear the last of it.

"There was this one night, Ali, one night when if it was going to happen it would have. The four of us were hanging out on Dwight's boat *Big Ting*, and we'd all had a little too much to drink. I can't remember whose idea it was to go to the prow of the deck and look for shooting stars, but somehow Chix and I ended up lying side by side on the deck gazing up." She paused, lost for a moment in the memory of the exquisite, infinite beauty of the starry sky above them. How the air was warm and fresh, and the boat was rocking so gently, the only sounds were waves lapping against the bow and the distant voices of Marvel and Dwight rising and lowering in animated discussion about God knows what at the other end of the boat. "So we're lying there, and he's pointing out the constellations, and I find my fingertips brushing against his and all of a sudden I become conscious that our heads are really close."

"Wow. That sounds like super sexy. Go on," Ali urged.

Charlie was getting into her groove now. "We were so close that my hair and his locs were intertwined, I could smell this spicy scent that always hangs in the air around him."

"And?"

"I knew that if I turned my head just an inch towards him our lips would be … well, the most natural thing would be to kiss, but I didn't do it and neither did he. Instead, literally at the same time, we moved away from each other and sat up – looked at each other, like 'well, that's that then' and smiled. And all I felt was relief and I believe he did, too. And then I said let's join the others, and he said good plan, and we had this friendly hug and that was that. And we were just cool for the rest of the time."

The car jerked and the bite of the seatbelt raised her from her reverie. Shaking free all thoughts of starlit nights in Zephyr, she dragged herself back to the now. While she'd been talking Ali had negotiated the pay station, a multitude of roundabouts and filtered through the busy airport traffic and now the sporty car was racing away from Heathrow, heading west to join the old Roman road that would take them home to Puddlington. Her driving style spoke to her feelings about Charlie's lack of romantic action.

"I know you're disappointed with me. And that Chix, on paper, is exactly the sort of no-strings-attached sexy type I should go for to get myself back in the game, Ali." She looked at her friend's rather stern profile but wasn't to be put off. She'd made the right choice. "But I don't like one-night stands and I figure that I'd rather be his friend for life than have a quick bonk. You get that, right?" She wanted Ali to understand.

"I guess. But I really thought you might. Because you should—" She let out a deep sigh, finally giving in. "Never mind." Her frustration was evident. They were very different from each other – especially when it came to men. Ali had lost her virginity much earlier than her. She'd had more boyfriends and tonnes more lovers. She was upfront about enjoying sex and was miles more adventurous and confident than Charlie, a fact supported by her track record of loving and leaving a bunch of panting bad boys in her wake and never seeming to want to settle down.

"I just wanted you to …"

Charlie reached over and squeezed her knee reassuringly. "I know you did, sweetie, and I love it that you want me to have someone, but Chix was never really a serious contender, living where he does. I'd really like to meet someone who lives closer to Puddlington. Plus, he's too old for me. I've never really fancied older guys."

"Haven't you? Well, I think you're missing a trick. All that experience." She gave her a knowing look. "How many times do I have to tell you to experiment a little before you settle down again?" Then with a grin, she said. "Life is like a box of chocolates, Charlie." In her best Sally Fields in Forrest Gump impression.

"It is indeed, my lovely, and don't give up on me quite yet because I have some news for you … chocolate selection-wise." She was eager to share her latest romantic update.

"What? Tell me." Ali said, darting an expectant look at her.

Charlie beamed back proudly. "I've been texting with Ryan the whole time I've been away."

"Texting with Ryan? From my office? Body-to-die-for Ryan?" And then she thought of something. "But you hate texting! You didn't even text me," she said with a touch of petulance, which Charlie chose to ignore.

"Yep."

"I knew he was back from the U-S-of-A, but I didn't realise *that* was back on."

"Yes, he called just before I left for my holidays wanting to meet up and was *very* sad to hear I was going away. Apparently, he's been counting the days until he could get back to Bristol and take me out."

The hunky American had taken her number months ago, and they'd gone out once, for a drink, before he had to go back to the States because of a family emergency. He was tall, good looking, a bit of a Leonardo de Caprio lookalike, and Charlie had fancied him as soon as she'd set eyes on him.

"We've been messaging while I was away and …"

"And?"

"I'm going on a date with him, finally!" she squealed triumphantly.

Ali made an approving noise. "Good. Where? When? Dinner or lunch? You could go to …"

Only half listening to her friend's suggestions, she looked out of the window at the rolling green countryside of her beloved Wiltshire and felt her spirits soar – happy to be close to home. She had relished the turquoise waters of Zephyr for two weeks, but the bucolic beauty of the English countryside never failed to fill her with contentment.

Charlie had a date to look forward to. And she couldn't wait to go to work tomorrow and catch up on all the gossip over a nice cuppa. She had the best job in the whole world ever: working as a secretary-stroke-animal-wrangler at Brown's, aka Kimble Veterinary Practice. She adored all the animals *and* the people that worked there: Ed and Kitty, the volunteers and the other vet, Ali's brother Simon Hobson, who was a terrible tease but a really good laugh.

Two weeks away from what you love was a long time.

CHAPTER 2

She didn't like lying to Charlie, but she didn't have any choice *and* it was fib by omission rather than a full-on porky, Ali reasoned as she waved goodbye. She sped out of the Pierce's gravel driveway, displacing a spray of stones in her haste.

Ali had chosen to ignore the disappointed looks on the faces of all the Pierce family members when she refused Helen's offer of 'your favourite, beef casserole and some lovely new potatoes' for lunch in the cosy kitchen she'd spent so much time in when she was growing up that it felt like a second home. She gave her 'other parents' Peter and Helen a quick kiss on the cheek, and Charlie a quick hug, then made her excuses, blaming a business meeting in Bristol later that afternoon, which it was. Sort of. She *was* meeting someone from work. She just wouldn't be doing the kind of business any of them thought she would be doing.

She sighed. Life moved on. Back in the day, she told Charlie everything – but that had changed when she'd left the flat they'd shared in London and moved to Spain to complete her last training seat in her journey to become a lawyer. Charlie, who at the time was in the first flushes of her relationship with her ex Graham, had been preoccupied by him and, although she and Ali had spoken often, most of their talk revolved around the budding and fated romance. Ali hadn't minded. She'd been having the time of her life. With both of them so busy in their own ways, they'd lost track of each other a little and the reality was that Charlie didn't know half of what had gone on during Ali's time in Madrid.

Driving her back from the airport, listening to Charlie's blow-by-blow account of all the wonderful experiences – the lobster lunches and empty beaches, the boat trips her friend had enjoyed in Zephyr – she'd found herself, if not jealous, a little envious of Charlie's time in the Caribbean. She would love to hang out on a mega yacht and whizz over to St Barth's to enjoy 'endless champagne' at the famous Nikki Beach.

The multiple mentions of what a caring and brilliant host Marvel had been, and how amazing the American's parents' villa was, had also grated. She knew it was irrational and ungenerous to feel irritated as Charlie had invited her to come on holiday with her, but she couldn't help herself.

Listening to the stories made her nostalgic for her own holidays with Charlie. They would go to places in Europe like Ibiza or Corfu, stay at a cheap little hotel, drink and club too much, having a lot of fun – but they hadn't done anything like that for a while. Too long. And her excuse was always that she was studying or working. She worked all the time. She was always working. In fact, she had worked so hard, studying for and gaining a first in her degree and acing her law exams, then getting taken on by one of the top international firms to do her training contract, that she'd forgotten how *not* to work hard. And now she was qualified, and she found herself working even harder.

Charlie and her family assumed Ali was excited about her fantastic new job and moving back to the UK. But they had no idea how much she had loved living in Madrid and what she had left behind. They didn't have a clue about the challenges of her new position in Bristol and what she did day to day. Ali specialised in corporate law, specifically mergers and acquisitions, and she loved what she did, for which she was recompensed handsomely, but it was a big, stressful, important job. And the responsibility sometimes weighed heavily on her.

She was up to the challenge; she was sure of it. Learning had always come easy; Ali had a gift for languages. She could remember things (she didn't tell many people that she had a close-to-photographic memory, otherwise they started testing her and she'd feel like some sort of circus trick). She was in the right profession for her; she loved the complexity of law, and the cut and thrust of negotiation. But, taking up a new position as a young woman, the expectations put on her coming into a position with glowing references, figuring out the office politics and getting presented with huge targets to meet was nerve wracking and stressful when she hadn't found anyone at work she could talk to about it yet. And though Charlie would offer to listen, dear sweet Charlie, she had the career aspirations of one of the Shetland ponies at the rescue sanctuary, and didn't understand half of what she did.

"That said," she said out loud, turning up the windscreen wipers to full speed and squinting through the driving rain that was making the busy motorway even more unpleasant than usual, "having a couple of weeks away somewhere beautiful with my undemanding, sunny-natured best friend and forgetting work and all the surrounding drama is just what the doctor would order – if it could be put on a prescription – but it ain't gonna happen." And she shook her head in frustration.

In her business, there were unwritten rules about taking time off – especially when you were still proving yourself. She hadn't taken a full day off in months – let alone a whole week or two. It didn't look like it was going to change anytime soon, as their biggest client had last week instructed her office on another huge deal and she was a key member of the team. And, then, of course, if she went away, she might lose out on the chance to spend time with her love, who had sprung a surprise visit on her and who she was, at this very moment, rushing to meet.

In the way life does sometimes, when you're picturing someone so vividly, you conjure them into being and her phone rang. His name lit up her screen. "Speak of *el diablo*," she said and chuckled, checking her mirror and indicating left, before easing into the lane that would allow her to exit the motorway and drive into the city. As soon as it was safe to do so, she punched a button on the dashboard and her lover's deep, sexy, heavily accented voice filled the car. "*Cariño*! I'm here! At the apartment. Where the hell are you?" He sounded put out.

"Mi amour, be patient. I'm about 15 minutes away if the traffic behaves. You made good time. How was your flight?"

"OK. But why are you not here to greet me?" his voice whined. She smiled.

How could such a macho guy be such a big baby? "You know how difficult it is for me to get away. I made a big effort because you said you wanted us to have more time together."

She responded patiently, her heart brimming with happiness because he was so eager to see her, even if he was behaving like a spoilt brat. "Of course I do, silly. It's such a treat you're here. I can't wait to see—"

He interrupted her, "But I'm here, and *you* are *not* and you know I don't like to be kept waiting." She could picture the arrogant pout on his face. She should be turned off, but it was the reverse. God, she loved that face. He kept complaining, "I would have gone straight to the hotel, but you said to come here."

"I know," she soothed. "And I promise that I will be there in just a few moments." She hated missing even a precious minute of their limited time together, but she had promised Charlie. She couldn't help herself from reminding him why this situation had occurred. "I did tell you I was meeting Charlie from the plane this morning and it was too late to cancel her as she was already in the air. This wouldn't have happened, Antonio, if you had given me some notice—"

"Eh," Antonio cut her off dismissively, "you ask the impossible, Ali. It's only because they called a last-minute meeting in Bristol tomorrow morning for the new deal and there's no flight from Palma early enough to get me in on time, it's lucky I could fly in today and see you."

"I know, and I'm grateful. It's a real bonus," she said, placating him.

Something struck her, and even though beggars are not normally choosers, she knew there was something off with this scenario.

"Did you say you flew in from Palma? Were you in Mallorca, then? You told me you were staying in Madrid this weekend to work."

"Something came up. You know how it is." His voice came in and out of focus, like he'd tucked the phone under his chin and then she heard him opening the fridge door. "Don't you have any wine?" he questioned, abruptly changing the subject. Like he always did when the subject of Mallorca came up. "I can't find anything."

"Plenty, you silly," she soothed. "Everything you like, just nothing cold.

Check the drinks cupboard in the dining room. There are some bottles in there. You can open a red now or choose a white and put it in the freezer to chill. And there's gin on the side and some tonics and ice. Why don't you mix me one, please? I'm nearly there."

"OK, *cariño*, but you'd better hurry because I need to see you," suddenly playful, "we only have a few hours together and I want to make the most of it."

"A few hours?" Anxiety barrelled into her like a runaway train – forcing the excitement and anticipation that had been making her body thrum off the tracks. She tried to control her voice and sound cool – they both hated it when she sounded clingy. "I thought the plan was for you to stay over?"

"I can't, *mi amour*," his voice softening to a conciliatory tone as he explained, "Christopher wants to meet me at my hotel at seven to figure out a strategy for tomorrow's meeting. Then the client will join us for a working dinner later. You know how it is. I couldn't say no." Antonio never apologised. It simply wasn't in his makeup, but he was good at buttering her up. "I don't want to go. I wish the whole evening was for us to enjoy doing the things we do best," he finished sexily.

Her heart sank. It was close to three in the afternoon already. "But I want … I really want …" she trailed off. She was going to say I want to wake up with you tomorrow. She wanted to say lots of things to him – like she missed him every day. And that she loved him so much it hurt. And she couldn't stand their separation any longer. But she didn't.

He pounced on her unfinished sentence, deepening his already husky voice, coaching her to speak to him. "You want what, baby? You want your Antonio? Eh?"

His voice, as always, was like catnip to her. She managed a breathy uh, huh.

"He wants you too, baby, and he's been saving something special for you."

He sounded a bit like a seventies porn star when he spoke to her like that, but it worked! She just wanted to roll on her back and purr for him. It was so easy to slip back into their old ways, and she responded equally flirtatiously.

"He knows I want him. Has he missed me?"

"He has missed his sexy little *pelirroja* very much." Her cheeks burnt and her body tingled in anticipation as he described the delicious things his 'little friend' wanted to do to her if she would only just get home.

Her car filled up with the rich timbre of his voice taking dirty – an aural aphrodisiac of the highest order. She drove faster, beyond impatient to see him. Needing to inhale his citrusy cologne and to taste every inch of his skin. A year on from when they first met, and he still made her melt inside. Forget cocaine or ecstasy, Antonio Garcia Fernández was her drug of choice.

She raced the final few miles with a heightened awareness of her body, keenly noticing how her thighs rubbed together as she braked, and how her inner arms brushed the sides of her breasts as she steered. She was struggling to concentrate on her driving but needed to so she wouldn't get into an accident.

Reaching home at last, she parked the car, locked up and ran-walked into the converted warehouse building where her apartment was located. The lift took what felt like forever to come and then, when it arrived, she had to wait for the charming but talkative elderly lesbian couple that lived on the floor below her to get out. She held the lift door open as they exchanged pleasantries until she couldn't stand it anymore; she cut their conversation short, missing their slightly hurt expression as she punched the buttons to close the doors and begin her ascent in a swift and familiar move. Her rapidly pounding heart stopped for a moment as the vintage lift stalled, then jerked as if it was broken, before ticking back into its regular thumping pattern and continuing its slow progress to the top floor.

I yearn for him, she thought savagely as she rushed out of the lift and through her door. Like one of those soppy, silly heroines in a 'bodice-ripping' romance – ready to be ravished.

"About time." His voice rang out across the space between them. Antonio, her lover, stood, proudly shirtless, his bottom half hidden by the kitchen island – deep brown eyes locked onto hers, hooded and impossible to read.

She moved around the island and was rewarded with a full view of him; her throat tightened. She looked down, drinking in every delicious inch. He was completely naked and, true to form, entirely comfortable with that. His thick legs were planted firmly on her dark grey slate floor and his strong, tanned arms were wide open, ready to embrace her. As she stepped towards him, he followed her gaze downwards and, clearly content with what he saw, smiled devilishly.

"Mi amour, come say hello to my little friend – he has missed you very, very much."

CHAPTER 3

Charlie shrugged off her old navy Puffa jacket and shivered as she hung it up on 'her' brass hook, one of the many that lined the back porch and boot room of Brown's.

She eased out of her long, dark blue Barbour wellies, placing them between Kitty's tiny, short red rubber ankle boots and Simon's enormous green Hunters. She felt a thrill of pleasure – it was so good to be home. Ed's boots were missing from their usual spot next to Kitty's, so he must be out on call. No sign of the dreaded Sandy's riding boots either, she noted with relief.

Toes already burning with cold from having only a woollen sock between them and the ancient flagstone floor, Charlie grabbed her indoor shoes, a battered pair of sheepskin UGG boots, from the wooden shoe rack and hastily slipped into them. She lifted the old cast iron latch and shouldered open the huge heavy and creaky oak plank door that led into the Brown family's 17th century farmhouse.

She stepped into the kitchen, looked around and inhaled gustily; the room was as warm as the toast of which it smelt. Brown's had a unique and unmistakable aroma. Sandy, Simon's Aussie girlfriend, always turned her nose up at the light undertone of cow manure and wet dog that was ever present in the kitchen and porch, but Charlie didn't mind it. It was a country smell – honest, homely and familiar. The only bad thing about coming home and going back to work, was getting her body acclimatised to the cold British weather after two weeks of Caribbean sunshine – but a nice cup of coffee and a few minutes in front of the old Rayburn range that kept the scruffy room warm would soon sort that out.

"Woo hoo! Anyone want a cuppa?" she shouted as she made her way towards the kettle. She lifted it out of its base with one hand and discovered it was still warm but empty. No doubt Simon had made himself a cup of tea and not bothered to refill it. Typical.

She placed the duty-free bag she had with her onto the kitchen table and then picked up the kettle to refill it. As usual, the huge Belfast sink contained breakfast debris: crumb covered plates and knives smeared with butter and marmite which she washed up as the kettle boiled. The door right behind her, the one that led to the office, creaked open and a small, slim woman with a short grey bob haircut, ruddy cheeks and an oversized, navy-blue fisherman's jersey with a big hole in the elbow, walked through the door with an expectant look on her face.

"Oh goodie, it *is* you," said Kitty Brown, owner of Kitty's Kennels and loving wife of Ed Brown, the senior vet at the practice. "Welcome home. I thought I heard someone rustling around. Lovely to have you back. How was your trip to the Caribbean?" she gushed excitedly.

"It was lovely, Kitty, really lovely."

"Glad to hear it and you certainly look well. All tanned and relaxed. Was it hot?"

"Super hot. I went swimming and sunbathing every day."

Kitty sighed and said dolefully, "How wonderful. You know I've never been to a tropical place like that in the winter or in the summer. In fact, Ed and I have never even gone to a place where the sea is any warmer than it is in bloody England. Are you making me a coffee?"

Charlie nodded and reached for Kitty's favourite mug, a stained old white one that was adorned with a Thelwell pony eating an irate child's rosette. She put in an inch of full fat milk, a teaspoon of Nescafe and two heaped teaspoons of sugar, just the way she liked it. The older woman beamed gratefully.

"Sweet girl." Then carried on with her grousing, "You would think that Ed, mucking around on farms, in the cold most of the time, would want to go somewhere like your lovely Zephyr to relax. But oh no! It's always some blinking bothy in the Scottish Highlands so he can shoot or a little cottage up a Welsh mountain where we can take the dogs and look at bloody birds and animals and farmland all day! Not a palm tree or golden sandy beach in sight. Only time he ever took me to Spain, we went to Asturias to check out a breed of cow he liked the sound of."

Charlie had no idea where she was talking about. She was crap at geography and her puzzlement must have shown as Kitty explained.

"Northwest Spain. They call it 'green Spain' and it is stunning, by the way. We rented a gorgeous converted barn with views of the Picos de Europa and there was a river at the bottom of the valley. Actually, quite romantic …" Her words drifted off while she took a sip of her coffee and, Charlie assumed, judging by the gleam in her eye, took herself back to the delights of the cosy barn for a while. Charlie cleared her throat and Kitty, brought back to earth, smiled wickedly then carried on, "Delicious food, too. Lots of yummy, fishy rice things and octopus and this lethal cider which we drank far too much of. As we went in May I had to light a fire most days. It was super, but a bit like going to the Lake District with much better food," she finished gloomily.

Charlie smiled supportively and let Kitty grumble on. She wrapped her hands around her cup to warm them up and took a tentative sip of hot coffee, happy to listen and to be back in their familiar pattern. Kitty was always complaining about Ed, her husband of over forty years. And Charlie saw it as part of her daily duty to lend an ear, nod her head when necessary but never venture an actual opinion. Because though Kitty professed that he drove her mad, she adored her husband and would rush to his defence at the slightest whiff of criticism. Charlie loved them both and admired their marriage. Her heartfelt desire was to be in a relationship just like theirs one day.

As she was talking, Kitty moved closer to the big yellow and red plastic bag, emblazoned with 'Duty Free', that she'd been darting ever more curious looks at. Reaching for it but not delving inside it, she glanced at Charlie with an expression as hopeful as a child on Christmas day – waiting for the moment their parents said it was OK to open their presents. Charlie chuckled and said encouragingly,

"Go ahead, you can dive in. I got gifts that everyone can share."

Kitty put her hand in the bag and drew out its contents: a huge bottle of Zephyr's potent vintage rum, a gaudy, cocktail-shaped magnet for the fridge that said 'It's rum punch time somewhere' and a round silver cake tin decorated with a hand drawn picture of a Rastafarian holding out a slice of cake and rough yellow lettering surrounding it saying, 'Zephyr black cake: dark and delicious'.

"This looks good. Should we have it now or at teatime?" Kitty said, holding the shiny tin out in front of her.

"Probably tea time, if we want to get any work done at all today. It's lethal."

"Ooooh, how exciting. Has it got some of that *marry due wanna* in it then?" said Kitty innocently, sounding as posh in her pronunciation as the queen she adored.

Charlie spluttered out a response. "No, it hasn't. I doubt it would have made it through customs if it had. However, it has …" she paused before she pronounced the next two words in a passable Zephyr island accent, "plenty rum in it, though."

The door swung open as she was speaking and Ali's brother, Simon Hobson, Ed's partner and the other, younger vet in the practice, walked through the door just in time to hear what she said.

"Plenty rum? You trying to get my Pony Posse pissed again, Charlie Girl?"

'The Pony Posse' was Simon's pet name for three local ladies who made up the SPuRS volunteer work force. SPuRS, which stood for the Small Pony Rescue Sanctuary, was a not-for-profit foundation based at the practice and was the brainchild of Lady Clarissa Hodge, the former neighbour of Ed and Kitty. When she passed on to the great paddock in the sky, she left her considerable fortune in trust to SPuRS so they could carry on her work rescuing and protecting Shetland ponies who'd been abandoned, treated cruelly or bought by 'the wrong sort of person'.

SPuRS's stables and paddocks backed onto the practice and, as neither Ed nor Kitty wanted to see the little sanctuary shut down after Lady Clarissa died, they carried on its work. The trust covered most of their costs and paid a little towards the office space. Unable to do all the work themselves, they recruited a team of volunteers who were *supposed* to do most of the work.

Simon was leaning against the ancient door frame, his tall broad form taking up most of it. He cocked his eyebrow at her inquiringly. She giggled.

"They better eat it under supervision. This cake is lethal – they soak the fruit in rum first and then pour loads more rum over the top after it's baked. To preserve it, apparently," she deadpanned.

"Yes, ration it then. Remember that time you brought in cake and some bottles of prosecco for Christmas and the three amigos polished the lot off before any of us got a look in?"

"And then they decided to go to the Lamb to carry on celebrating—"

"And you got a call from Sammi to come and pick them up because they were saying they could drive home and she wouldn't let them—"

"And I drove Gloria home and her husband was furious because she hadn't told him she was going out and he'd been calling her for hours."

"And he was all funny with you because he was jealous, because she kept stroking your arm and saying what a wonderful way you have with the animals!"

"And you had to take the other two back to their houses."

"That was awful. O-M-G, Amanda could *not* find her keys, and I had to break in and open the door for her because I couldn't let her climb through the kitchen window."

"Well, not to put too fine a point on it, I don't think she would have fitted through the window!" Simon snorted and carried on the story as Charlie was laughing so much at the memory that she couldn't speak. "And then, when you'd got her sorted, you took Jeanie home, and *she* set off her bloody alarm!"

"And then," Charlie said, "I had to stay there and deal with the security company because she was so out of it."

"Lightweights!" they scoffed in unison.

"They can't hold their drink," said Simon at the same time as Charlie said,

"No 'plenty rum' for them." And they grinned at each other.

"Listen to you two. I've missed hearing your banter around the place,' Kitty interrupted, looking from one to the other fondly. "Glad to have you in a better mood Simon." She turned to Charlie and said slyly, "He's been a *bit* of a grump while you were away."

"Only because I had to make my own coffee, Kitty," Simon whined defensively, but with a barely contained smile on his lips.

"Ha! I knew it! You missed me! You can't do without me," Charlie crowed, looking into Simon's grey eyes, which were twinkling with good humour. It was so good to be home.

"Sorry to interrupt the joyous reunion," a strident Aussie accent rang out across the room, alerting them to her presence. Sandy (only ever called Sandra one time by those brave enough to use her full name and then never again), Simon's diminutively gorgeous, Kyle Minogue lookalike Aussie girlfriend, was watching them closely, a hint of steel in her baby blues. Her comment successfully accomplished just what she said she didn't want it to: stopped their jokey conversation dead in its tracks.

She walked into the room, reminding Charlie just how stunning she looked in her work clothes. Sandy pulled off the horsey/practical/professional look with aplomb. Her long, blonde bob was as sharp as always and her tiny, curvaceous figure was shown off to best advantage in a tailored jacket, skintight jeans and long brown leather boots. Her style was perfect for the large stable in posh Lamborn where she worked as a secretary for a very successful horse trainer. Charlie's normal work wear, old jeans and a ratty sweatshirt accessorised with ChapStick and a scruffy ponytail, fell somewhere between office junior, land girl and stable hand as befitted her multifunctional role.

As Sandy moved closer to the table, Charlie could swear that the temperature in the room dropped. She watched with interest as Simon's teasing manner and ready smile disappeared and was replaced with a look of resignation.

"Hope you had a good time in the Caribbean, Charlie. Assume you are tanned up under all those layers?" She glanced over, a perfectly shaped eyebrow arched in enquiry.

"Great, I—"

"Sounds fabulous. We must catch up later." Finished with small talk, she moved on to the reason for her visit. "But right now, I'm going to have to break up this little reunion party and drag my boyfriend away. There's a situation at the stables and I told our vet I'd get Simon to give him a second opinion."

CHAPTER 4

The dim lights and cavern-like quality of her 'local', the Blind Pig, provided the perfect atmosphere for Ali to lick her wounds and drown her sorrows with copious adult beverages.

She watched the arrivals from her regular spot, close to the till. After having had the speakeasy-style bar to herself for the last hour, it was beginning to fill up with a fresh wave of late-night drinkers. The bartender, Kris, who she'd been chatting with, had furnished her with a fresh drink then hurried to the other end of the bar to present two middle-aged women with a cocktail menu. They chose their drinks quickly and were now enjoying his best Tom Cruise in *Cocktail* impression. Some new arrivals, two post-theatre couples by the look of it, were headed towards the bar. They took the three remaining free bar stools and she watched as Kris managed the situation by asking the only other person at the bar – a single guy in his thirties she would guess – wearing a fitted black polo shirt and lots of hair product, to move to another stool so the group could sit together.

A few minutes later, the guy moved to sit on the barstool beside Ali. He was now so close she could smell generously applied cologne mixed with a heavy dose of fabric softener.

"Evening, love," he said in a heavy Welsh accent.

"Good evening," she said politely, deciding it might be nice to talk to someone. Her new neighbour was passably attractive and, as she didn't have anyone to go home to, it was better than sitting there brooding. Especially as Kris was now fully occupied, pouring drinks and making cocktails at top speed for guests at the bar, as well as for the cocktail waiter who was looking after the people occupying the banquette seating that lined the dark and cosy room.

They exchanged names, and she forgot his immediately. She sipped her drink and made the occasional encouraging noise while he did most of the talking. After what felt like the longest fifteen minutes of her life, she came to the conclusion that he was so dull he could bore for Wales and if being dull was ever introduced as an Olympic sport, he'd win the gold medal. She only carried on listening to him because she had a soft spot for the Welsh accent, if he'd been droning on in a Brummie accent for example she'd have cut him off ages ago.

Ali loved Wales. She had fond memories of family holidays in Llandrindod Wells at her godfather's house. Uncle Michael had gone to boarding school with her dad and was a 'gentleman farmer'; he and his wife Aunty Violet always welcomed the Hobsons with open arms and homemade cakes. She'd adored all Mick and Vi's children, who were older and treated her like a second sister, teasing her affectionately but unmercifully. And to make things even better, she sometimes got the chance to cuddle baby lambs and gorgeous little sheepdog puppies. Her brother Simon loved going there too and became obsessed with riding the quad bikes around the hilly terrain and, as a result of those family holidays, developed an ongoing fondness for animals and farming that had resulted in him becoming a vet.

"Fancy coming back to my hotel for a nightcap? It's close by and I've got a minibar," her neighbour rudely interrupted her reverie.

Bloody cheek of him, Ali thought. What gave him the right? If she'd been flirting, that comment might have been acceptable, but she hadn't encouraged him at all! And yet, despite the fact he hadn't asked her one question, or found out anything about her, and there being zero chemistry between them as far as she was concerned, this boring dude thought he was in with a chance! She decided she could do one of two things: tell him to go away, or take her frustrations out on him and piss *him* off. She decided on the latter.

"Are you single, then?" she said, arching an eyebrow to add emphasis to the question.

"Em…"

"It's OK, I guessed you weren't," she said blandly as she watched him try to figure out what to say next.

"Well, I am, like, but you know how it is."

Oh, she knew. She knew firsthand exactly how it was. He was looking at her with nervous expectation, not sure how to take her.

"I bet your wife doesn't understand you, right?" she said in a voice so saccharine sweet and dripping with an empathy so fake, she couldn't fathom how he'd fail to notice.

But he didn't. Instead he seemed encouraged, and said earnestly,

"She a smashing girl, you know. The best. I love her to bits, but well …"

Ali moved her head in a tiny nod of encouragement.

"We married young. I was twenty-one and she was nineteen. I love her but I'm not *in* love with her, if you know what I mean?" He was angling for her approval with a hopeful puppy dog look in his eyes. "We've grown apart."

Ali could barely hold back a derisive snort at the expected cliche and reached for her glass for support. She took a deep gulp of her vodka, stopping herself from blurting out a chilling retort and scaring him off. Listening to him try to wheedle sympathy out of her about his dull marriage as he hit on her was gruesomely fascinating – she wanted to hear how this would pan out. He didn't disappoint.

"I need more, you see. I want to travel. Go somewhere exciting." He moaned on, "She just wants two weeks in the Canary Islands every February. And I can't get her out of Wales in the summer. Wants to go to Barry every weekend with our—"

Although he was in full whiny little bitch mode, Ali noticed he still was cunning enough to cut himself off before he'd admitted to having kids. She fidgeted on her bar stool and reached for her drink again, hiding her face as she struggled to maintain control of her reaction.

"You alright? Your face looks a little funny." It was the only question he'd addressed to her (outside of the invitation to sample his mini bar) since they started talking, or rather, he'd started talking at her. Had he finally cottoned on to the fact that she wasn't exactly hanging on to his every word? She gulped at her drink again, then nodded and smiled tightly, unable to speak because her face muscles ached. Satisfied she was still enthralled, he continued. "I want to go somewhere more adventurous, like…." His eyes sparkled as he confided his dearest dream. "I want to go to America for the NASCAR racing, spend some time following the circuit. But she's not that interested."

She didn't blame the poor woman. She couldn't imagine anything worse than endless days at a NASCAR track with this guy. He probably had a wardrobe full of those trucker hats, which she knew he would proudly wear back to front. Most likely paired with a tee-shirt, leather vest and tight denim cutoffs – she nearly shuddered at the thought.

Ali realised that he was inching closer and, in an attempt to stop him encroaching any further into her personal space, she leant as far back on her stool as she could and crossed her bejeaned leg over her thigh. This allowed her to angle her boot heel in his direction, effectively creating a barrier between them. The unwanted approach had finally brought her to her senses. What on earth was she doing chatting to this idiot? Why had she let this happen?

But she knew why, because otherwise she'd have to sit and think about how Antonio had only given her four hours of his precious time. Four amazing hours, four hours she'd take over not seeing him at all, any day, but four hours were nowhere near enough time to satisfy her need for him.

She jumped as Kris thumped a drink down in front of her with a heavy hand and brought her back to the here and now.

"I've got this one, darling," her next door neighbour said proudly.

She had almost forgotten the bore was there for a few blissful minutes. Despite her growing dislike of him, or maybe because of it, she decided to accept the vodka because, well, why not? She'd earned a drink for listening to him for all that time. Anyway, nothing else made sense at the moment, so she might as well drink too much and pass out when she got home.

Kris was giving her what her nana would have called an 'old-fashioned look' from the other side of the bar. *I like Kris a lot, but he better not be judging me*, she thought, then took another deep swallow of her drink. *It's up to me if I want to let a bloke buy me a drink, even if he— for fuck's sake, he's soooo boring, he's telling me how much he loves paintball now!* The man's voice droned on, as relentless and irritating as a mosquito on the prowl. She tried to blank him out. She'd made a mistake encouraging this idiot. She wanted to be left in peace to drink and chat shit with her friend Kris about the other characters at the bar. To stay here till closing and help him lock up because she couldn't face going home. Not to an empty flat. Not when she knew Antonio was just a few miles away.

I can deal with it when he's in Spain, she thought bitterly, because I'm used to it. That's all part of the agreement when you fall in love with a married man. But this is torture, actual physical torture, to know that he's here in the same city, but not with me. She took another slug of the drink in front of her and grimaced, then glared at Kris's back. She couldn't taste the booze. Either she was so drunk the alcohol didn't register or he'd made it light.

She did feel a bit woozy to be honest, and the room had got uncomfortably warm and stuffy. Picking up a coaster, she started fanning herself ineffectively as she looked around the room. The bar had emptied out and only a few stragglers remained. She'd been there too long and she knew she should leave, get away from the guy, but she was powerless to move. Stuck in place by the thoughts that were driving her crazy. She kept picturing Antonio lying in a hotel bed just a few miles away.

An idea occurred, a dangerous one. What if she just got in a taxi and went over there and surprised him? She dismissed the idea; he hated surprises. But she really wanted to go! She would go. But message him first and tell him she'd be very careful and just sneak in. No one would see her. She went to grab her phone, fumbled and it slipped out of her hand, falling to the floor.

"Arrghh." The anguish of her situation refused to stay quiet. This should *not* be happening. Without meaning to, she spoke rather than thought the words she'd been worrying over all night: "Why couldn't he have come back to mine after the meeting?"

Her neighbour, predatory as a jackal, picked up on what she said and misconstrued it to suit his purpose.

"Say that again, love. You want me to come back to yours?" As he spoke, he moved in on her, attempting to put his arm around her shoulders and pull her towards him.

His breath, sour from the lager he'd been drinking, invaded her space and made her gag. Instinctively she recoiled in disgust and went to shrug him off, but his arm was clamped around her neck and, inconceivably, given her reaction, he seemed to be angling for a kiss. How had he got so close? Fuelled by revulsion, she found the strength to unwind the unwanted appendage and push him away.

"Don't get your hopes up, boyo. It's not going to happen," she snapped.

The guy put his hands up in mock defence and said,

"Alright, Ginge! Keep your knickers on." And then added with a nasty sneer on his face, "Don't act all innocent, woman. Why else would you be sitting at a bar on your own, taking drinks off blokes you don't know, and getting wasted if you didn't want to meet someone?" And then, to add insult to injury said, "And there's no need to be racist."

All the frustration she'd been repressing for the last couple of hours came bursting out of her in a torrent of icy, received pronunciation English.

"Oh, bugger off, you absolute tool. I'm not being racist. I bloody love the Welsh – apart from you, that is. How dare you try to make out I was 'asking for it' by sitting here?" adding air quotes for emphasis. "You're the type of archaic, misogynistic imbecile that still believes only men and whores sit in bars alone." Pleased with her putdown, she thought, *I may be tipsy, but I can still make a case.*

Visibly irate, he got up from his stool and loomed over her, but Ali wasn't intimidated, she had dealt with bigger bullies than him over the years: in boardrooms, classrooms and bars. She may be a pussy where her boyfriend was concerned, but she was a lioness in life the rest of the time.

"Back off," she snarled, then turned her back to signify she expected him to do just that. She looked down at her drink and chugged the last inch, but stiffened in shock when she felt him grab her shoulder in an attempt to get her to face him. How dare he touch her!

"Do NOT put your hands on me," she said witheringly in a very loud voice and Kris, who'd been loading the glass washer, looked up and caught her eye, assessing the situation.

The man, shocked at her tone, stepped back a pace.

"Well, don't insult me then. I can't believe I bought you a drink," he whined. "That vodka cost me twelve quid."

Ali shook her head in disgust and turned round to look at him.

"Did they cut your expenses? Are you experiencing hard times in the industrial cleaning product world?" she said faux sweetly.

Ali noted the signs of his escalating humiliation and anger as he paced beside her – his hands now tightly furled, his jaw clenched and she wondered, absently, if she should be worried, but the amount of booze she'd drunk had numbed her senses to the point where she actually didn't care. His next words were delivered slowly and with menace.

"You are such a little bitch," then, shaking his head in disbelief, said, "a snobby, drunk little bitch. I wouldn't have fucked you anyway – bloody ginger." He spat out the last word.

"Yes, you would," she responded, laughing bitterly and treating him to a look of purest disdain, "of course you would."

"No, I wouldn't," he spluttered, chest out like a fighting cock, zinging with anger and frustration. "I've got much better at home." He stilled, then seemed to come to a decision and moved towards her as if to grab or hit her, only to find his way blocked by Kris's impressive presence.

Ali watched the two of them face off. Her friend was roughly the same height as the annoying Welsh salesman, but a lot fitter looking. Weightlifting and circuits, combined with stocky genes meant Kris was as solid as a brick wall and just as unbending in his defence of her,

"That's enough, sir. You have had your say. Now please leave the lady alone."

"Lady. She's not a lady. She's a bloody—" But before he could finish the insult, Kris stepped towards him – close as could be without touching the angry man – and said commandingly,

"I am asking you, once again, to leave now, sir." Ali watched on, trying not to giggle as the two of them engaged in a staring contest. It was so … macho.

A few seconds later, it was all over. The Welsh guy was the first to break eye contact and, as he looked away, his shoulders slumped in defeat. He was down but not out, though, because he had to have one last word before he left.

"Don't think I'll come back to this shitty bar. And don't think I'm paying for my drinks – or hers, either." He walked to the bar, lifted the lid off the black ceramic box Kris had earlier placed before him with the unpaid bar tab, removed his credit card and put it in his wallet.

"That's fine by me sir," said Kris blandly.

Having made his point and slightly mollified by having drunk for free for the night, the man headed towards the door with a little swagger, leaving without a second glance. He was the last person to leave the bar apart from Ali and as soon as he was outside, Kris locked the door and started cleaning the few remaining tables with glasses on them.

Desperate for the loo, Ali slid off her stool and nearly fell over but righted herself just in time, then wobbled over to the ladies on numb legs. By the time she came back, Kris was unloading the glass washer and although no words were exchanged, his body language gave her the distinct impression that her bartender friend was mad at her.

"My hero," she purred, wanting to win him over. "Wasn't that fun? You put that idiot well and truly in his place."

"No Ali, it was not fun. I dislike having to throw a customer out. And it was not enjoyable watching you get yourself into a situation like that."

"Oh, I could have handled him. You didn't need to get involved."

Kris looked at her with disbelief and said in an exasperated tone, "Ali, what am I going to do with you?"

"Oh, don't be a spoilsport, you loves me really!" She batted her eyelashes.

"Did you tell him where you live?" Kris wouldn't let it drop.

"Course I didn't, silly. Anyway, that would have meant him asking me a question or listening to my answer. Which he didn't. That guy was seriously on broadcast, not receive."

"Good. What does broadcast not receive mean?"

"It means he just droned on about himself and had no interest in learning about me. A character trait many men suffer from. Any chance of another drink while you close up?"

CHAPTER 5

"So, then Simon said, 'Charlotte', he always calls me Charlotte when he's attempting to boss me around, 'Charlotte, it's best if ponies only leave the paddock if you're there to supervise, because we can't afford to have another incident like we just had with the village allotment.' Which means even more bloody work for me!"

Ali murmured supportively down the phone. The two friends had been chatting for a few minutes. It was four in the afternoon and Charlie, who had been making a cup of tea when Ali called, was now enjoying a refreshing cuppa and a couple of chocolate fingers, sitting on a lichen-covered oak bench, under a fabulously blooming cherry tree at the bottom of her parents' garden. It was a sunny spring afternoon, warm enough for her to be outside in only a jumper and jeans and all was right with her world.

Her dog Ted, the newest member of the Pierce family, a black and white rough-haired Jack Russell, and Muffin, her parents ancient, mainly toothless, but still feisty tan and white version of the same breed, were both lying close to her feet in the lush, green grass, having a snooze. Charlie gazed lovingly at her pets. She never tired of looking at them. Muffin was whimpering and twitching, most likely chasing rabbits in her sleep. Ted was lying spread-eagled on his back, his furry tummy on display. Her heart literally melted every time she saw him. She was so happy to see him completely and utterly relaxed.

Having a pet of her own had been a dream for ages and the reality had exceeded her expectations. Ted was a sweetheart, loving, fun filled and well behaved for a JR. She'd got him from the rescue centre not long after she got back from Zephyr. At fourteen months of age, he was out of puppyhood but still youthful.

According to the kind people at the shelter who had been on the lookout for an abandoned Jack Russell for her for months, his previous owners hadn't been cruel, but had handed him in because he 'didn't fit their lifestyle anymore'. He had been physically healthy – well fed, crate and potty trained – but neglected emotionally. And when she'd first met him, his behaviour was subdued and shy. Not any more, she thought. Look at him with all his bits on display. Not a care in the world because he knows he is loved very, very much.

She had learnt that when the previous owners purchased him (she suspected he'd come from a puppy farm) they had thought Ted was 'perfect'. When their cute little puppy grew up to have a slightly deformed jaw – which resulted in an underbite that meant his bottom teeth were permanently on display, they decided Ted wasn't pretty enough for them anymore. Their loss was Charlie's gain. Ted (she'd decided to keep the name as she didn't want to confuse him) was exceptionally handsome and she thought his underbite added great character. In fact, when she'd first taken him for a walk around Puddlington to introduce him to the village, she'd met a local farmer who loved Jack Russells, too, and who'd said, after giving him a thorough inspection, that she'd found herself a very good dog, praised his looks saying, "Well, 'tis 'is deformed jaw what makes 'im so appealing" in his broad Puddlington accent. A statement which had been repeated so often at Brown's that it was now enshrined in legend. Simon thought it was one of the most hilarious things he'd ever heard, and used the expression in as many situations as possible.

Ali, in great contrast to Charlie, was talking to her from the pub, a dive bar called the Blind Pig. Ali seemed to spend all the few hours she wasn't at work there, and Charlie was looking forward to visiting her friend's favourite hangout. Even though it was the weekend, Ali had taken her laptop to the bar to do yet more work. From the background noises it sounded like was also enjoying an afternoon drink, so it wasn't all work. Thank goodness she's having some fun, Charlie thought, then carried on with her story about the naughty ponies invading the allotment.

"It was a close call, to be fair. Luckily, Old Stan was there, and he was able to grab Bumble and Bee and drag them back to the paddock in the nick of time, just before they pulled up his prize carrots or did too much damage to his or anyone else's plots. Could have been a village disaster of epic proportions. Eh?"

"Epic."

"Imagine what would have happened if they had polished it all off! The show would have been cancelled for the first time in a billion years!" she concluded dramatically.

"What indeed. A tale of disaster to be retold throughout the years," Ali concurred, "ahh Bumble and Bee – the fluffy piebald pair? I think they're my favourites. Too cute," cooed Ali, who'd been sent pictures of all the SPuRS rescue ponies.

"I know. Those two are adorable – on the outside. But inside? Monsters. Simon calls them the Evil Furbies – because they look so cute with their big brown eyes and furry round bodies but are capable of random acts of evil and terror." Ali laughed from the other end of the line. "Did I tell you that Bumble had a bit of a problem with biting when he came to live with us?" she confided.

"No."

"Probably a result of being mistreated. And he's been so much better since he came to SPuRS. Although he took a nip out of this woman the other day. I swear it was because she said that Bee had squinty eyes. He doesn't like anyone insulting his girlfriend. I was quite glad he did bite her though because she'd come to see about fostering them, but I didn't take to her. Simon didn't want her to have them, either."

"So where were the famous Posse when the siege of Kimble allotment was taking place? I assume they were supposed to be in charge."

"Supposed to be. It's their job to walk the ponies on the road, so they grind their hoofs down a little – one of the few things they don't mind doing and don't usually muck up. But they said that this time, the new lady vicar heard them coming down the road and invited them in for coffee and 'it would have been rude not to', so they tied them up outside. To a tree. They swore they did it properly, ate their lemon drizzle cake, had a nice chat with the vicar who apparently is 'really nice' and were 'deeply shocked' to find them missing and had 'absolutely no idea' how they could have got loose." She sighed. "Simon said he'd give them a talking to, but they absolutely refused to take any responsibility. Said someone else must have let them off. Honestly Ali, I can't believe he is such a wuss. He *never* tells them off. He's putty in their middle-aged hands," she finished, her tone a mix of affection and frustration.

The Pussy Posse, aka Simon's fan club, had him wrapped around their little fingers. She'd grown fond of them and it was sweet how kind Simon was to them, but they were volunteers and she really needed them to do the work they'd volunteered for. She was tired of taking up their slack.

"So, I've put up this roster and explained that I want them to come in on different days and they all have a specific job to do, but it's an uphill battle. All they really want to do is come in every morning and drink coffee and gossip until it's time to toddle off for lunch."

"And who makes the coffee?" said Ali, teasing her. "Let me guess…"

"Yes! Me mostly," replied Charlie.

"You mug. You have always been too nice." Ali laughed. "So it's not just Simon taking advantage of you – sounds like you're running around after all of them."

"I know, but I don't mind, really. It's just a lot to do, and it's just going to get busier as Kitty and Ed are getting ready to go away for a month now, so he can recover properly from his knee op. Basically, Simon's flat out, so I really don't mind stepping up."

"How *are* my brother and his charming girlfriend? I haven't seen either of them for ages."

"Well, you haven't been to Puddlington for ages. Not since you dropped me off after my trip to Zephyr at the beginning of February, and that didn't really count. When was the last time you were here and properly spent time with your family?"

"Those few days at Christmas, I think. Which is quite a long time ago, I guess."

"Four months! Which is ridiculous, considering you're only an hour's drive away!"

"I know. But I'm so busy with work and … no one's been up to see me either to be fair," Ali added, sounding a touch defensive.

"True that. Apart from me."

"And that's only because you fit me in before or after a date with the lovely Ryan, then rush back to Puddlington to walk your new best friend Teddy, or muck out one of your animal dependents. I hardly see you either."

It was true. Charlie had thought she would see loads of her best friend now they were living close to each other again, but they didn't get together in the flesh that often. She was dating Ryan and it was going really well. They talked all the time but due to various commitments they'd only met up three times in the flesh: twice for lunch in Bristol and once at a country house hotel midway between Puddlington and Bristol. She'd driven each time and had consumed one modest glass of wine on each occasion, as had he. She liked him very much, and she liked the pace of their relationship. She'd rushed into love before. She'd thrown herself into a hasty marriage with Graham and look how that had turned out! Not again. Ryan was handsome and thoughtful, and she enjoyed his company. She wanted to get to know him more, which (she congratulated herself on being so mature) was a successful start. No major fireworks yet, on her side at least, but she could tell he really liked her, and she hoped there would be rockets galore when they finally took it to the next level.

As if she had read her mind, Ali asked, "How's that going, by the way? Any progress on the rooting Ryan front?" she teased. Enunciating rooting with gusty roll of the 'r'.

"Aliiii! Honestly. A little respect, please. And not yet." She heard a theatrical sigh of despair at the other end of the line. "But soon. I like him a lot. I love hearing about how he was 'raised'. That's how they say it in America – so different from us. Did you know he comes from a vast family? He's one of ten kids and his family has a town named after them in Connecticut?"

"No I didn't. Not that interested to know the man's background at this stage. Much keener to hear if there's been any action at all?"

She knew her friend wouldn't rest until she got what she wanted, so she gave her the best update she could.

"There was some very nice kissing on our last date. And he asked me to come for the weekend and stay over in Bristol and I want to but ..."

"But?"

"Well, like I said, we are so busy at Brown's, Ali ... it's hard to plan to do anything as we are so short staffed. I just want to be there for ... well, for everyone."

She wanted to be there to support Simon when Kitty and Ed were away, because he needed her. They worked well together. In fact, the other day he'd told her that he didn't know what he would do without her. And then when she'd checked to see if he was joking, because he teased her all the time, he'd looked at her and said carefully so she knew he wasn't: "I mean it, Charlie Girl, you're amazing", which had made her feel pretty darn good.

Ali scoffed at the other end of the line, effectively bursting the bubble of her reverie.

"Do not let my charming git of a brother con you into working too hard, Charlie. He's always known how to get the most out of people and he's always known how to push your buttons."

Charlie winced. She had worked hard to blot out her past mistakes with Simon, to have a normal friendly working relationship, but Ali was always there to remind her that once he'd meant more to her. Even though she didn't want reminding.

True to form, Ali carried on in a tone that combined a hint of hectoring with a touch of patronising.

"I warned you about this from the beginning. My only problem with you working there is that I don't want you getting all moony over him again."

Off she goes, Charlie thought with a twinge of irritation. *I wish she would just forget about that chapter of our lives. I have.* She rolled her eyes in frustration, happy that Ali couldn't see the expression on her face, then taking the higher ground, said lightly,

"No chance of that, my lover. He's a mate. And unlike my hunky, fragrant, handsome Ryan, he stinks of horse poo half the time."

Ali snorted; she was always happy to slag her older brother off and joined in,

"And pig's piddle."

"And cow dung," said Charlie, playing along.

"And don't forget possum juice," trilled Ali in an awful Dame Edna Everage voice as a not-very-subtle insult.

"Yuck. Don't want to think about Sandy's down under," parried Charlie, happy they'd got back to their normal bantering selves. Ali guffawed on the end of the line.

"God. I'm sorry, but she's truly awful. Do you think he really will marry her?" Ali had never mentioned it before, but it was a subject that Charlie and Kitty had frequently talked about while Simon was out on calls. "Mother is trying to be fair and says she's not all bad, but I think she's fibbing and that she hopes he will dump her. Hold on …" Ali paused the conversation and Charlie heard her order another drink, then continued, "I think he will probably stick with her. She's quite bitchy and men like that."

"Oh Ali, that's a bit of a sweeping statement."

"Well they do. The nicer you are to them the more they treat you like shit in my book. She's also a strong woman and he can be a bit of a wuss where women are concerned, hence the Pony Posse and the way he always gives in to Mater. I think he likes the fact she takes charge. Lots of men do."

Charlie wasn't enjoying this conversation one bit. She didn't think Simon was a wuss. She distracted herself by rubbing Ted's furry tummy with the toe of her trainer. Ali had more to say on the subject and went on to ask and answer her own question.

"If they were going to break up, it would have happened months ago. You know when she made such a mess of working at Brown's."

Charlie remembered it well. Simon returned to the UK following a successful stint working as a vet 'down under' to take up a partnership offer at the Kimble practice and brought his girlfriend, Sandy, with him. They'd expected that she would work with him at Brown's. However, within a week, she had clashed with Ed, antagonised Kitty and upset the volunteers, so, to maintain the status quo, he had found her a more suitable job working for a horse trainer in Lamborn. Where, according to everyone, including her, she had effortlessly integrated herself into the posh racing community. Around the same time, on a drunken night out in Bristol, Ali suggested to Simon that Charlie, who was at a loose end post-divorce, would make the perfect veterinary assistant. And to everyone's pleasure, including her own, Brown's had taken her on and she had found her niche. It was the perfect example of how Ali was always looking out for her, and how her friend often knew more about what was best for her than she did herself.

Not wanting to talk about Simon and his girlfriend anymore, Charlie changed the subject.

"What about *your* love life then? Any tattooed Lotharios to tell me about ? Are you breaking hearts in Brissssstolll?" The last word was deliberately pronounced in the thick Bristol accent.

Ali seemed to hesitate before she answered, and Charlie's ears pricked up, hoping to be entertained by a recent dating escapade. Ali was much braver than her sexually and was a big fan of dating apps – Charlie loved hearing about the guys she met, even though she'd never wanted to try hooking up that way herself.

"No, nothing to report at the moment."

"What? I don't believe it. No one? Sexy Ali suffering a dry patch?" she teased, to be met by silence at the other end of the phone. She carried on regardless. "Drunk the Tinder well dry, then?" Not a giggle in return. "What about the guy from your bar? The one that rescued you from the awful Welshman that time?" she finished.

"Kris?" Ali paused, then said, "Kris is just a friend. Not my type. At all."

"Ahhh too nice a guy for you, is he? The type you bring home to Mummy?"

Charlie teased. She knew the type of love-'em-and-leave-'em men Ali usually got with. She had a soft spot for the type of guy you would *not* want to introduce to the parents.

"Har, har, very funny. Kris is cool. But I don't, you know … want to …" Words had failed Ali for once.

After a bit of a pause, she tried to coax an answer out of her and said gently.

"I don't know unless you tell me."

"I've already …" Charlie's ears pricked up. Ali sounded like she was going to reveal something juicy, but then changed her mind. "Kris is just a friend and we want to keep it that way."

Charlie who had heard several stories featuring Kris over the last few months, all of which had endeared her to the barman even though they had never met, imagined him to be a younger version of Chix, possibly with a Bristol accent.

"What does he look like?" Charlie pressed on undaunted.

Ali sighed, then recited a bullet point list of attributes: "Muscular, dark hair, good looking."

"I think he sounds perfect for you." Because she did, it would be so cool for Ali to have a 'proper' boyfriend for a change, not just a hook-up. "Has he got a tattoo?" But Ali wasn't biting.

"Lots of them and some piercings. But it's not happening." Her tone made it clear she'd had enough of the subject. "Anyway, this is my local, and I want to keep it that way. You know what they say? You don't shit in your own backyard," she finished crudely and then added, "and that's good advice for you, too," in yet another unsubtle warning about Charlie getting too close to Simon. "Actually, I need to get off now."

Charlie was disappointed to hear that.

"Oh, but I want to hear about what's going on with you at work. How's it going? We never get to chat for long. Made any work chums yet you can hang out with? Have you been to any parties?" She was trying to prolong the conversation but felt her friend's attention slipping away as she spoke.

"I'm fine," said Ali distractedly, "and there is nothing to report because I have zero social life."

"And why's that?"

"Work," she responded sharply, as if Charlie was being a bit dense asking her, "which is both exhausting and endless and very, very challenging."

"In what way?" She wanted to know. Truth be told, she'd never got to the bottom of what her friend did day to day, but she knew it was high-powered stuff.

"Sweet of you to ask, but I'm not going to go into it now. It's quite complicated," Ali said dismissively.

"Oh … OK." Charlie felt a flash of something. Resentment maybe. She might not be a genius like Ali and all her lawyer friends, but she had common sense, and she was a bloody good listener. She shook it off, though, and said in a coaxing voice, "Well, I'm here if you want to talk. And it's—" Ali cut her off again.

"It's fine, Charlie, honestly." Her voice was a little more conciliatory, clearly feeling a bit guilty for shutting her down and trying to wrap up the conversation on a more positive note. "Look, my lover, I must go. Fabulous to catch up. Speak soon. Buyee…"

And she was gone before Charlie had the chance to stop her. She sighed and shook her head, feeling unsatisfied by the way the call ended. Ali seemed …

A wet nose nudged her hand and distracted her. Ted, awake and ready to play, was trying to get her attention. She glanced at her phone. It was nearly time to meet Simon, who, not working for once, had messaged her to see if she would like to go for a walk in Puddlington Woods. Flopsy, the Hobson's crazy Sprocker, needed to blow off steam, as did Ted; the two of them always had a lovely play together. They would take Muffin too, because she hated to be left out and if she got too tired, Simon said he would carry her. He was a bit of a star that way.

Her spirits lifted. What a beautiful afternoon for a walk and a natter! She might not have as much time with Ali as she hoped, but it was brilliant that she and Simon got on so well as friends now. Perhaps she'd ask him if he'd noticed anything wrong with his sister?

MAY 2015

CHAPTER 6

Ali's computer screen glowed. The white page in front of her was the brightest thing in the room. The cursor was flashing, endlessly tempting her to write more words or do more research.

It was midday and, even though she'd been sat at the dining table that doubled as a desk for hours, she hadn't bothered to draw the curtains yet. All she'd done since she got out of bed was make herself a cup of tea, then sit down and start working on the De la Cruz company's latest possible acquisition, and hadn't stopped since. Luckily it was interesting complex work. If it had been a boring job she'd have felt like even more of a loser.

She stood up, groaned and stretched her hands above her head. Then, bum aching and back creaking, she moved stiffly towards her living-room windows and tugged the pull cords – one in each hand. Her apartment was a corner unit and boasted floor-to-ceiling glass on two sides of the room. The dark floor-length curtains that obscured her panoramic view of Bristol glided open and, just like that, the room was filled with a bright light that made her wince and see stars. Tiny dust motes danced before her eyes. Irritated, she turned away from the glare.

She headed back into her bedroom to change out of her pyjamas and put on something suitable for a lunch date with Charlie. Her tummy rumbled in anticipation. She'd booked a table at a well-reviewed bistro in Clifton Village and was going to eat whatever she felt like today, bugger the extra pounds that had crept on because of her mainly sedentary lifestyle.

She considered drawing the curtains in her bedroom but didn't. She did manage to pull up her duvet and make the bed – sort of. Her work clothes were 'hung' on the armchair, the back of the door and the floor; she considered putting them away but didn't, in favour of getting in the shower. The room was too depressing to shed light on.

As she went through the routine of washing, teeth cleaning and dressing appropriately for lunch out in chilly Bristol, rather than sunny Spain, she decided that she missed Madrid almost as much as she missed Antonio. She was different in the UK.

She rummaged around in her wardrobe and found her favourite turquoise silk shirt and was about to pair it with her most flattering but currently a little too tight jeans, then decided in favour of a plain navy blue crew neck cotton jumper and her best navy yoga pants. She looked in the mirror and hardly recognised herself. Her reflection was blurgghhh – dull and boring just like the city she'd found herself in. Cross with herself for being such a misery guts, she poked her tongue out in pique then stomped back out into the living area to make a quick coffee. Perhaps she'd get inspired to put together a decent outfit after more caffeine. What was wrong with her? She was lucky. She'd qualified and landed her dream job, was being paid a lot of money, had an incredible flat – even if it was in Bristol. She was living her best life as her American colleagues liked to say.

After locating a solo, battered Nespresso pod lurking at the back of the drawer, she popped it in the machine and headed to the fridge for the full fat milk she needed to heat up in order to make a coffee of her required quality. She talked out loud to herself.

"A day out in Clifton and a view of the suspension bridge is very pleasant, I'm sure, but give me a walk in the Parque del Buen Retiro and a café con leche in the sunshine, any day." Coffee perked, she waited for her milk to finish frothing and combined the two.

"Should I?" she wondered aloud, looking at the bottle of Mount Gay Rum taking pride of place on the kitchen counter. Charlie had brought it back with her from Zephyr and she was saving it for when they had a night out together. "Would it be terribly naughty to start my Sunday funday with a little rum coffee?" The idea was tempting, she'd like to cut loose today, but she decided against it. They'd probably hit it hard at lunchtime and she didn't want to peak too early as she wanted to take Charlie to the bar and introduce her to Kris later.

Her best attempt at a Spanish-style coffee ready, she sat down on the couch and waited for the drink to become cool enough to enjoy. One of the reasons she felt so at home in the Blind Pig, with its shiny dark wood, low lighting and lemony spicy scent (Kris always had gorgeous candles burning) was because it reminded her of the historic bars she'd loved to frequent in Madrid. Kris could even speak a few words in Spanish, and she'd promised to teach him a bit more as long as he taught her a little Greek.

Ali loved languages and had a gift for learning new ones. She'd taken English, French, Spanish and Latin A-levels at school and received A stars for all of them. Her 'ace language skills', as Charlie always referred to them, were one reason she'd been offered a training contract with Coles, Holt & Wallace, the leading American law firm she joined after she passed her solicitor exams with top marks.

She'd received other attractive offers, but she chose CHW because they had multiple offices and associated firms in countries all over the world. She'd elected to do her final 'seat', corporate law, at their Madrid office and simultaneously took additional business language courses at night and weekends. Ali had even considered taking a conversion course to qualify in Spain, as she loved it there so much. She'd found the herculean workload manageable as her social life had revolved around Antonio, who she'd met a few days after arriving in the city, and who was only available to hang out midweek. Her weekend routine comprised a little exploring and a lot of studying. Her advanced language course paid off, and she was conversationally fluent in Castellano and, if not mistaken for a madrileña, could definitely hold her own when she had a conversation with one.

She curled her legs up under her and attempted to snuggle into the corner of her good-to-look-at but impossible-to-relax-into leather sofa. She slipped and slithered around before giving up the attempt at comfort and sat upright to finish her coffee in a hasty gulp. It was hard to reconcile how much her life had changed since she'd returned to the UK. In Madrid, she'd worked on some demanding projects too, but she'd also had free time to enjoy herself at the weekends and she'd had Antonio during the week as the icing on the cake.

Granted, she was a trainee lawyer at the time, but in Spain, everyone, even the partners, seemed to have a more relaxed attitude to the work-life balance. It was acceptable to take a leisurely lunch, enjoy your weekends and to have a life outside the office. Whereas her English and American colleagues saw it as a badge of honour to work through, sometimes until after dinner, and she inevitably ended up working at the weekend too. She hadn't given herself a full day off for months now. She didn't like to make plans to leave Bristol, either, in case Antonio surprised her with a visit and she wasn't there – like the time she'd promised to pick up Charlie from the airport.

And then there was the fact she hadn't made any friends at work. Most of her contemporaries had qualified in the Bristol office and she was very much the odd one out. Two weeks into the job, she'd overheard a gaggle of her colleagues talking about her, saying that she 'thinks she's something special' because she'd trained in London *and* Madrid and had been brought in to work on the firm's biggest account De la Cruz. Whether it was jealousy or competitiveness, it felt like most everyone viewed her with suspicion, and as they didn't seek her out, she didn't seek them out either. When she wasn't at the office, she either worked from home or hung out with Kris at the Blind Pig. Ali didn't need lots of friends, she just needed a few good ones, but it would be nice to be invited out for a drink occasionally. Currently Antonio, Kris and Charlie – and the few people she'd kept in touch with from university who were now scattered all over the country – were the only ones she cared about.

She disliked her boss, Christopher Falcon, senior partner at the Bristol office of CHW and had a feeling he was the reason her colleagues were less than friendly with her. He too had worked in Madrid for a while and had taken her on to work specifically on the De la Cruz account because of her previous knowledge of the client. That should have created a bond between them, but it hadn't. She found him dismissive, cold and supercilious and was underwhelmed by his interaction with their client even though he was reputed to be an excellent deal maker. He seemed unimpressed by her too – never satisfied, however hard she worked, and had not once offered constructive advice or mentorship. She spent most of her days overwhelmed by what she had to do. Afraid to look as if she couldn't cope, and with no one to ask, she had to figure a lot of stuff out by herself.

She didn't know why Christopher was so tough on her – if it was just his way or because she was the youngest (most recently qualified) lawyer or if it was because she was a single female in a world of married, middle-aged men.

At least, she thought, by working for most of yesterday and getting up early this morning to churn out some more, I've got a bit of a head start on next week's workload, and now I am ready to par-tay. She stood, stretched and smiled. It would be so good to spend time recharging her batteries in Charlie's sunny company.

Sundays used to be fun-days, however much studying she had to do. Back in the day, when she and Charlie shared her student flat in London, a boozy brunch would turn into an all afternoon session in the pub followed by whatever adventure presented itself.

But not since she'd met and fallen in love with Antonio.

Their agreement, when she lived in Madrid, was that she had him during the week. Never at the weekends. At the weekends, he went 'home' to Mallorca to see his kids – leaving her alone. Even though she'd never been inside any of his homes; not the huge pied-à-terre in the Barrio de Salamanca where he stayed during the week when not with her, or the family home on the outskirts of Palma de Mallorca where his kids went to school, or the five-bedroom beach villa in Punta Cana in the Dominican Republic where he went for Christmas, she thought about him in those places so often, she could clearly picture him relaxing and enjoying his leisure time,

She didn't want to dwell on that because it just hurt her. What would help would be to talk to Charlie about him. But she couldn't because she had promised him – like he had promised her – never to tell anyone else about their affair. And so she had this massive secret, and it weighed heavily on her every day. She sighed, taking her coffee cup to the sink, turning on the tap, washing it and placing it on the rack in isolation. Impatient now for her friend to get here and distract her.

She was also worried about Charlie's reaction if she could tell her. She'd been married *and* cheated on. It had been awful for her. What if she disapproved? Charlie's life was so wholesome. Everything was coming up roses for her. Which was great! She wanted the best for her, of course she did, so she was happy her best friend now had a job she loved, a dog she adored and was even dating a hot guy.

"I'm pleased for her," she announced to the room, wanting to believe it. "I really am." And she was, she wasn't that selfish, was she?

The intercom rang and a flower of pure happiness bloomed inside her, Charlie was here and it was time to have some fun! She buzzed her in with a flourish and a minute or so later her friend burst into the apartment, hair flowing, leggy as a runaway colt, bearing a bunch of flowers and a bottle of fizz. She rushed over, leant down and gave Ali a smacker on both cheeks. Her hair, which brushed against Ali's face, carried with her the faintest trace of a man's cologne.

"Mmmmwwww! Mmmmmwww. Hello, daaaahling," she drawled in her best 'Eddie' voice, waggling the bottle in her hand.

"Bolly daaaahling? Maaahhhavellous!" responded Ali in full-on 'Patsy' mode. They both loved *Absolutely Fabulous* and binge or rather booze watched it (as they liked to drink along with the heroines) regularly. They could and did banter for hours in their respective roles – Ali playing Jennifer Saunders' role of Edwina and Charlie Joanna Lumley's role of Patsy. It was an easy way to fake fun too.

"And flowers … you spoil me. Put them in the sink, there's a pet and I'll sort them in a bit. But first things first." She grabbed the bottle out of her friend's hand and made a beeline for the freezer where she liked to keep a couple of champagne flutes chilling.

"Thought you might fancy a little fizz. And as we are celebrating …"

"Celebrating?" Something dawned. "You didn't actually…"

"I did! Well, to be accurate, we did it. And *we* are celebrating my first time with Ryan!"

"You *finally* did it?" Charlie had been on so many lunch dates with the poor guy and all he'd got was a kiss or two for his efforts up to that stage. He must have the patience of a saint. "How was it? Were his balls blue?" Charlie snorted.

"Don't be disgusting. And I'm not answering that. It's weird talking about him as you two work together."

That makes two of us keeping secrets from each other, thought Ali, and said defensively, "It won't make a difference. We don't see that much of each other."

"Really?" Charlie sounded puzzled. "I thought you were work friends. He said he likes you."

Well, he would, thought Ali. *Because he wants to get into your knickers. I bet he thinks I'm a right old battle axe.* "I *do* think he's nice, though," she said reassuringly.

Ryan *was* a nice enough guy, and at least he always attempted to make conversation. Ali found him rather vanilla, not edgy enough for her, but he seemed to suit Charlie.

"It's that I see little of him because he's on another client team, and I kind of keep a bit of a distance from that lot."

"Oh. He said you work hard. And that you don't hang out with them much." She sounded concerned.

She gave a noncommittal "Hmm" in response. She hadn't told Charlie yet that she was persona non grata at the office, and she wasn't about to. It was time to distract her.

"So give me all the deets, then. How was the date? What's his place like and, most importantly, has he got a big one?"

"Ali … you are naughty." Charlie was giving her a stern look, the same one she gave Ted when he was misbehaving, which made her smile.

"Worth a try. Tell me what happened then."

"His flat is nice. Clean, bachelor-like, no pics of ex-girlfriends, didn't set off any alarm bells, but I left my overnight bag in the car anyway – just in case I didn't want to go back there after our date. Then we went for a walk all around the dock area." Charlie smiled dreamily, happy and bashful in equal parts, as she told the tale of their date. "He held my hand, which was rather lovely."

Ali could picture it. Ryan was old school.

"Ahh. Did he present you with a corsage to wear on your date?" she teased.

"Ha, ha. Not quite. But he bought me a rose from one of those people who come into restaurants. And he told me I looked beautiful more than once." Charlie's face had a dopey expression on it as she recounted his flattery. "And he is charming. Good old-fashioned American manners. And well…" she explained further, "he's so positive, Ali. Graham was always snarky. Funny but snarky. Whereas Ryan's super enthusiastic. Everything is *awesome,*" she finished, mimicking an American accent. Their eyes met in mutual understanding, and Ali agreed.

"Those yanks love that word."

"Because it *is awesome.* But seriously, it is incredibly endearing. And he looks gorgeous saying it."

Ali nodded her head in encouragement. The man was a looker for sure. And the date sounded sweet. Ryan seemed almost too good to be true. Too good to be good in bed, to be honest, but maybe she would be proved wrong. Charlie carried on.

"Dinner was absolutely yummy, we both had crab linguine, no worries then about only one of us having garlic! We shared a Tiramisu, and *then* we went back to his place." She looked bashful when she confided, "I thought it might be awkward, him being my first after you-know-who, but it wasn't. Probably because I've got to know him quite well over the weeks and he's such a sweetie, so I didn't feel any pressure to, you know, perform."

"And then?"

Charlie acted out, drawing a curtain across the scene. "He has nice sheets."

Ali raised an eyebrow. "He has nice *sheets*? That's all I get?"

"Yep. No gory details. Wouldn't be fair on him but suffice to say *everything* about the evening was nice."

"Nice?" Ali said, puzzled. Nice wasn't a word she'd ever want to use in the context of sex. Great or good. Hot. Energetic, maybe. Dirty, hopefully. Unsatisfactory, occasionally. Funny, often. Orgasmic, normally. Even a bit painful, sometimes. But *nice*?

"Yes, nice."

"Is nice, good? Or just nice."

"It was nice – good," said Charlie firmly, "and that, madam, is enough."

"That's not fair. How many times did you do it?"

"Oh, Ali!" Charlie rolled her eyes, and said in an exasperated tone, "twice."

"That's good. It's good that it was good enough to do twice." She tried to sound encouraging. "And does Ryan live up to his reputation for being the hunkiest man at the office gym."

"He does. He has a beautiful body. Quite the Greek god."

"So will you do him again?" And she winked, then said faux innocently at Charlie's outraged expression, "I mean, meet up again?"

"Yes. He said, 'he really wants to get to know me better' and 'that I'm the best thing about being in the UK'," she gloated. Then added, "There's a concert in a couple of weeks and we've agreed to go see together, so that's the next date sorted."

"Very good. And when are you taking him to Puddlington?"

"Oh, not yet. I don't think I'm ready for that yet."

Ali couldn't help but notice the speed and certainty of Charlie's response. Perhaps Ryan wasn't all that, after all.

She had topped up her glass during the debrief and realised they'd polished off the champagne in record time. Thirsty for more, she headed towards the fridge and grabbed a bottle of French Chardonnay she'd been saving for today. But Charlie shook her head, refusing the proffered refill.

"Oh no, babe. No more for me. I'm driving."

Ali was confused. "You're driving? But you've been drinking."

"Only one small glass. You drank the rest, you greedy guzzler."

Ali didn't recall doing that. But hey.

Charlie continued, "And Ryan cooked me a big breakfast, so I'm fine to drive."

Ali's heart sank at the news. "But I thought you were staying over and driving back first thing? Aren't we having a Sunday funday?"

Charlie's face took on a stricken expression. "Oh darling. I'm sorry. I can't now. I should have told you earlier. Simon called this morning and I've got to get back to Brown's." She rushed out an explanation. "He needs me to check in on a couple of animals. He can't go himself – some important date with Sandy, and the other two are away. Sorry." Charlie sounded apologetic, but not devastated that she'd had to cancel their plans.

Disappointment knifed through her, but unwilling to appear pathetic or, worse, needy, she said brightly, "It's OK. Don't worry. Another time." And she faked a smile.

Charlie, normally empathetic, but oblivious to the pain she'd just caused, was inching towards the door, still making excuses.

"Yes. Let's do something the day after the concert if that works for you? Or are you planning a trip to Puddlington before that? We never get a good catch up these days, do we? What with your work."

"And yours too now you're working with Dr Doolittle," she joked, attempting to make light of the situation.

"And I was really hoping to go down to your bar and finally meet the lovely Kris."

"Next time," she responded brightly.

"Next time, for sure. Anyway, better get going. Toodle-oo!"

"Toodle-oo to you too, darling," and Ali gave her a short, hard hug before letting her out, closing the door just in time to prevent Charlie from seeing the tears that were welling in her eyes.

She stood with her back against the door and let them fall. Berating herself for being such an idiot. It *was* ridiculous to be so upset over a cancelled lunch plan. She knew that. But she'd been looking forward to it so much and the flat was so quiet. Too quiet. And damn it, she was lonely. She hated admitting it, but she was. Perhaps if she called Charlie now and told her how hurt she was that she'd chosen to help bloody Simon rather than spend time with her, she would turn the car around and come straight back. But her pride wouldn't let her. Anyway, she should just have known. Isn't that what besties did? Know when their friends needed them?

CHAPTER 7

"Oh, isn't he dishy?"

Charlie rolled her eyes. "No one says dishy anymore, Mum."

Helen's periwinkle blue eyes sparkled with happiness and her soft grey hair in its short ponytail quivered gently with excitement as they huddled over Charlie's phone at the kitchen table, scrolling through pictures of her date, with glasses of homemade lemonade in front of them and the dogs lying by their feet.

"I'm glad you had a super time, darling. Ryan sounds like a real gentleman. And he's very easy on the eye." Pouting and making kissing noises to show her appreciation.

It was a standing joke that Helen Pierce liked good-looking young men. She'd adored Graham in the beginning because he was so handsome. She was having a super time oohing and ahhing over the pictures and stopped to examine for a long time the one of Ryan posing for Charlie in front of the restaurant, flashing his engaging, perfectly white American smile. There were a few other people in the picture and their average charms highlighted just how tall, well built and similar to Leonardo de Caprio he was. His open-necked pale blue shirt fitted his torso like a glove, the rolled-up sleeves revealing chestnut brown forearms – he looked handsome and extremely wholesome. Helen zoomed in on the picture to check something.

"Looks like he's got big feet too."

"Mummy!" Charlie laughed. Her mum was very naughty sometimes.

"Just a little joke, darling. When are you bringing him home to meet us?"

"It's early days, Mummy. So not yet. He's very nice, but I'm not ready for anything serious just now."

She really wasn't. Dating was fun, the sex had been good and she wanted to see him again, but she'd rushed into her relationship with Graham and she wanted to take her time with this one – do it at her own pace.

"Just for lunch, or a coffee? We would love to meet him," Helen coaxed. Since Charlie had moved back into the family home following her divorce, they'd been so supportive and, despite trying hard not to show it, worried about her and she knew that seeing her dating meant a lot to them.

So she said gently, "I know you would," then warned her, "but if you don't give it a break, I won't tell you any more." Charlie had a wonderful relationship with her parents, but she'd never talked to them about the intimate details of her romantic life like some children did. That felt icky. There was no need for either of them to know that she had slept with Ryan last night. And again, this morning. The remembrance of which gave her a pleasant trill of satisfaction. Her threat worked as Helen changed the subject.

"And how's our Ali?"

"She's OK. Working too hard, as usual, but you know Super Ali, she thrives on that."

Charlie pushed down a little twinge of guilt. Ali hadn't said she was fine, per se. Ali hadn't said much to be honest. The visit had been quick, and Ali was in full-on interrogation mode, trying to extract all the juicy details about Ryan, but she didn't spill. Normally she would tell Ali *everything* but that would be unfair on him.

"What's she working on?" Helen persisted.

"Oh, I'm not sure. Important lawyer stuff." Her parents had always taken a keen interest in her much cleverer friend's stunning academic record and stellar career rise. "I do ask her about it but she usually brushes me off. Ryan says she's very conscientious, wrapped up in work and she doesn't socialise with the team much."

"That doesn't sound like our second daughter. She loves a drink and a party, usually. Remember the time …" And Helen started reminiscing about some of the scrapes the two of them had got into as teenagers – including a fateful school trip which had led to them both being suspended from fifth form for a week for buying and consuming a potent mix of cider and sherry. They were underage, of course, and Ali's parents had chastised her but as the suspension period coincided with their annual, no-kids-allowed, romantic holiday at the Bear Island Hotel it was a half-hearted attempt. And as Simon, being three years older, had been left in charge, and couldn't be bothered to discipline her, Ali had had a fine old time lolling around the house watching 80s movies and catching up on her reading. Charlie's parents were much tougher on her. Embarrassed that they'd been called into the school and upset that she'd squandered the opportunity to be made a prefect the following year, they put her on house arrest for a week and made her do all the cleaning and gardening chores they could come up with as punishment. Now they looked back and laughed.

"She is taking her job seriously. And maybe she doesn't want to mix business with pleasure? At least she spends quite a lot of time at her friend Kris's bar," she added firmly, but also thinking that Ali's life sounded a little bit, well, boring. Not as exciting as it used to be when they lived together in London or, from what she'd heard, when she was working in Spain.

Helen Pierce's ears perked up at the mention of a potential mate for her second favourite girl.

"Is Kris a *special* friend?"

"No, just a friend, friend. Though he sounds nice, so he should be."

"Oh well, fingers crossed, and as long as she's happy." She stood up and walked towards the kettle. "Do you want another cuppa?"

"Yes, please." Helen filled the kettle, sat back down and said confidingly,

"Charles said to me that they hardly ever hear from her, so they're excited she's coming for his birthday. I hope she has time to visit us, too. I can't remember the last time she sat in our kitchen eating marmite on toast and finishing up all the butter. I miss her."

"I know, me too. I've got so much going on I really haven't seen as much of her as I thought I would."

"Yes, you do. You are doing an excellent job over there. Daddy and I are very proud of you, you know."

"Awww. Thanks Mummy."

"So how were the patients?"

Her mum knew that Charlie had come back to check on a few sickly animals. What she didn't know was that when she got to Brown's, Simon was there doing just that.

"They were fine, but it's a bit annoying, really. Simon was checking on them, which meant I didn't need to come back from Bristol, and I could have had lunch with Ali. And he was in a filthy mood, too. He's so annoying sometimes." Her frustration showed in her tone.

"That's a pity. You two have been getting on so much better. So nice not to have you bickering all the time."

That was the truth. They'd gone through a stage where she could hardly bear to be in the same room as him.

"Well, he was back to his old self today. Annoying *and* grumpy. He didn't apologise that I'd come back early unnecessarily. And he didn't want to hear anything about my weekend. I tried to tell him about how good the restaurant was that Ryan took me to, because he's always going on about being a foodie, but he was rude about it. Said it was a chain. And then I told him about us going to see Coldplay and he just grunted and stomped off to look at the ponies, so I left him to it."

There was a brief pause before Helen said excitedly, "I might know why he was in such a bad mood." Helen's eyes shone with glee. "I have some rather juicy news."

Charlie grinned. Her mum loved nothing more than a bit of gossip.

"Don't keep me in suspense then. Do tell."

Helen dropped her voice to a conspiratorial whisper. "I found out … when I was over at the Hobsons' …"

"Mummy, you can speak up, they can't hear us from the other side of the green you know." She laughed.

"Please act surprised when you find out officially because Simon might not want it broadcast yet."

"Broadcast what?"

"Sandy might be leaving." Helen delivered her big news in an excited, breathy rush.

"What? No way." Charlie was shocked. She would have bet good money on Simon's girlfriend sticking around. She wasn't the type to give up her prey.

"She gave Simon a bit of an ultimatum and it may have backfired."

"What do you mean an ultimatum?"

"I overheard Simon saying that she was angling for a bigger commitment and he said no."

"Overheard? So he didn't tell you himself?" She looked at her mum, who was looking a little flustered and interrogated her. "How did you 'overhear' this, you sneaky thing?"

"I was at the manor, having a cuppa, when Simon popped in for Flopsy to take her for a walk and Penny went out to see why he'd come home early – she'd already told me that the two of them were spending the day at the Boxley Country Club, they had a voucher for one of those couples' massages and—" Helen seemed to be about to describe the full spa experience so Charlie cut her off.

"Yes, Mummy, I know, that's why I came back early." Charlie rolled her eyes. "What happened?" She was dying here!

"Simon said they'd rowed, and Sandy had gone back to the cottage to pack as she was going to spend a few nights in London with some friends and he wanted to go for a walk to give her space and clear his head."

"Oh. Interesting. Did you hear what they rowed about?"

"In the jacuzzi," she said with relish.

"*What*! Not *where*!" She shook her head in frustration.

"Oh. Sandy told him she wanted them to move back to Australia. She's had enough of her job and she quit because she hated it. Which is weird because Penny was always going on about how good at the job she was. She was always going to the races."

"I know! I thought she loved working there, too."

"Simon hasn't said anything about them having troubles?" She shook her head. He hadn't but then she hadn't asked. They chatted about all sorts, but one thing they never talked about was his girlfriend. She just assumed everything was OK between them. Sandy rarely came to Brown's and no one had missed her telling them how to do their jobs better! Ed joked (when

Simon wasn't around) that she was like Lord Voldemort. If you spoke her name out loud, she would appear and try to take over, so they didn't talk about her. Her mum had yet more beans to spill.

"And then I heard Simon say, Sandy had tried to like Puddlington for *his* sake, but it was boring and she wanted her own house, not to live in old cottage in his parents' backyard."

Charlie was outraged! Orchard Cottage was *adorable* and Sandy was privileged to live in it. Her mum read her thoughts.

"I know! Terribly rude of her. So ungrateful. Anyway, at this point Penny starts shouting, saying something like 'bloody cheek of her' and then Simon says 'Mother calm down', and he 'loves the cottage' and he's very grateful to them for letting them live there, that he's committed to Brown's, and he'd given it his best shot with Sandy as she'd made the effort to move here, but if she doesn't like their life here he's not going to stop her leaving." She finished in a rush, spewing out the eavesdropped conversation in one long tumble of information, before taking a deep breath and ending with: "And then he took the dog for a walk, and that was all I heard."

"Sounds like you couldn't help but hear an awful lot, Mummy," said Charlie wryly.

Helen Pierce grinned like a naughty schoolgirl and said without shame, "They were talking loudly – the kitchen window was open and I was at the kitchen table so I couldn't help but overhear. Not my fault."

"And did Penny talk to you about it?"

"When she came back in. She was dying to tell me, I could tell, but at the same time she didn't want to be disloyal to Simon – I'd be the same about you. Bless her, she was trying very hard to be discreet but when I said I'd overheard a little of what was going, well, that was it, she just let it all out, said she'd never taken to her and confessed how glad she was they'd split up."

"Now I understand why Simon was in such a bad mood. His relationship's over. I'm sorry about that." And she was. Breakups were hard, she knew that firsthand. And although she didn't like Sandy, Simon obviously did, and she didn't want him to be hurt.

She sipped her rapidly cooling tea and took a moment to absorb what she'd learnt today and came to the conclusion that life was funny sometimes. Shagger Simon's relationship was on the rocks, Ali the sex siren was going through a dry patch, but she, herself, was having a super time, thanks to the lovely Ryan. She smiled complacently. She loved both the Hobsons to death, but it was quite nice to be one up on them for once.

CHAPTER 8

Ali threw the frozen fish pie back into the freezer in disgust, grabbed her bag and keys then stormed out of the apartment. If she stayed in the flat on her own a minute longer she'd start kicking the walls.

A few minutes later she walked into the cavern-like gloom of the Blind Pig. It was still empty, not many people rushed to spend Sunday in a dive bar while it was sunny outside. Kris was behind the bar, setting up his station and when he saw her he gave her a welcoming grin, which was swiftly replaced with a frown when he looked over her shoulder and noticed that she was on her own.

"Where's your mate? Wasn't she supposed to be taking you out for lunch today."

She heaved herself up onto one of the tall bar stools feeling leaden.

"I got stood up."

"Pity I was looking forward to finally meeting her." He looked perturbed. "I hope she had a good excuse for putting that sad look on your pretty face."

"Thanks for the compliment." She managed a wobbly grin. "The worst. My bloody brother and his dog and pony show."

Without having to tell him what she wanted, Kris grabbed a glass, filled it with ice, and mixed a vodka club soda with a touch of cranberry. It clinked merrily as he handed it to her.

"This will cheer you up."

She took a grateful gulp. "Just what the doctor ordered. Epharsito," she thanked him in Greek.

He looked pleased before a concerned look crossed his face. "I might be out of order here, but is Charlie that good a friend? I mean, you say you and her are so tight, but how come she didn't come to your local yet?" Ali felt the need to defend Charlie.

"We are. Best friends for years. Despite being as different as chalk and cheese."

"How?"

"So many ways! To start off, she's much nicer than me!"

"I doubt it."

"It's true. Charlie is sunny. She's that girl in a Norah Ephron rom com who doesn't know what a great catch she is, but will get the guy in the end. I'm the opinionated, colourful, knows-what's-best for her one who keeps telling her what to do with her life. *She* is the girl next door type. I'm a career girl, a lady boss and I want to travel the world." She was warming to her subject. "Case in point, I always wanted to live in a city, so Charlie followed me to London when I went to university but only because she didn't know what else to do."

Kris raised one perfectly sculpted eyebrow. "To be honest she sounds a bit boring. Didn't she cramp your style?"

Ali laughed. "No!" Charlie was vanilla, but with a tasty streak of salted caramel that added plenty of flavour. "No. She's nice and all that, but she's also great fun and I loved having her there. She was always ready to go drinking when I wasn't studying. She's easy company, very supportive and a great listener – usually. . ." She trailed off, thinking *not so much recently, though*, then pushed that idea away. "She's better at making people like her than I am – which is pretty handy when it comes to getting invited to stuff – but can be annoying when she takes pity on some saddo and I have to be nice to them."

She grinned at Kris to lighten the tone and continued. "We do have a few things in common. Puddlington being one of them. And back in the day, both of us used to be real tomboys, I'm not so much now, obviously, but she's still pretty much one. Although she looks fragile she doesn't mind getting her hands dirty. She's like my brother in that way – not that he's fragile – great big hulking beast." She corrected herself. "That's one thing all three of us have in common is the fact that we all love animals. A lot, and although I wouldn't want to put my hand up a cow's bottom like Simon does, I would like a pet of my own one day."

Kris winced. "The cow's bottom thing was far too much information for a city boy like me, Ali."

"I'm sorry," she said, sounding anything but. "Your punishment and you're making me think about our friendship, which is kind of weird. I take it for granted – it just is what it is, you know." She paused, trying to find something else, something better to describe their bond. "I guess what I love most about Charlie is that she has a wicked sense of humour, and … she thinks I'm hilarious!"

"Who doesn't!"

She acted out a round of applause. "Correct answer!"

"Back to your earlier point, though. I don't think you're giving yourself enough credit. I think *you* would make a fab leading lady with those fiery curls and delicious curves," Kris said flirtatiously.

"You are too kind, sir. It's true. I do have some sweet, sweet curves. But seriously, I don't think I'm what most men want. It has been said that I'm too much to handle. Too sexy. Too greedy for experiences. Too rich a meal. Too much all around." Surprised at herself for expressing out loud what she'd only thought before. She looked at Kris for a reaction. He tutted and looked shocked.

"Not for me. I like you just the way you are."

"Good, because I like me just the way I am."

"Good."

"And, I like you just the way you are, too." Because she did, he was a lovely, kind, funny man and she had grown very fond of him in the hours she had sat on a bar stool, watching him work, admiring the way he interacted with people and anticipated their needs. "You may not have known this before today, but I find lots of people annoying."

"I had noticed that. Remember the guy I had to get rid of?"

They exchanged a warm glance. "Of course. And thank you again. Anyway what I'm trying to explain is that I don't like lots of people, but when I like someone – I really like them. And I really like Charlie and I really like you." She looked up and grinned. "I hope you know what a compliment that is."

"I do. I'm honoured to be a member of such an exclusive club – along with the elusive Charlie and your mystery boyfriend, presumably? Speaking of whom, I hope he appreciates your devotion."

"He does. I'm sure."

Kris looked sceptical. Then changed the subject back to Charlie.

"So if you and Charlie are so different, how did you become friends, then? I love a good origin story and I don't think we're in danger of being interrupted." He looked round the empty bar.

Ali laughed. "We bonded over eighties music, cider and cheese and onion crisps."

"Really?"

She took a big gulp of her drink and settled down to tell the tale. Happy to remind herself of better times. "We met when her family moved to Puddlington. My parents, who I think I've told you, are deeply sociable and who want to know everything about everyone in 'their' village, invited 'the new people' over for drinks. The Pierces, Peter and Helen, who are absolute angels, and who I love to bits now, arrived looking rather overawed. To be fair, the family pile is quite impressive, they wee bearing a bottle of wine and behind them was this tall skinny girl with big brown eyes, a terrible bowl haircut and dodgy jeans, looking like she'd rather be anywhere else." She smiled in recognition, picturing the little family looking nervous in her parents' hallway as clearly as if they were in the Blind Pig with her now. "Mother was in full hostess-with-the-most-est mode. She declared they were adorable and gushed all over them. Father, as always, was the perfect host and told them he had prepared a vat of Pimm's and the four of them immediately set about demolishing it. As no one had thought to make any food to soak it up, they all got pissed as newts in record time." She smiled fondly. "Which, as it turned out over time, is pretty much par for the course with that lot."

"What about you?"

"I was pissed off that my parents were forcing me to entertain some random new girl. I got stuck with her because Simon had popped in, smiled winningly and charmed everyone for just long enough not to be rude then buggered off to play with his mates so Mummy suggested I take Charlie to my room to play so the adults could get to know each other. I couldn't refuse and I didn't know what to do with her so I shoved on my favourite DVD *The Breakfast Club*. You know it?"

"John Hughes! Seminal 80s movie loved by all. But wasn't that ancient even then?"

"It was, but I was a bit of a rebel, I've never liked to conform so I loved all that retro stuff. Anyway, we sat there on my bed, side by side, awkward as anything, neither of us said a word for ages, just watched the film. After half an hour or so, there was still not a squeak out of her so I went downstairs to see what was going on and they were having a fine old time and completely oblivious of us. So, I raided the larder for snacks and I snaffled some cider out of the fridge."

"I thought you were kids when you met. How old were you?"

She shrugged. "We were eleven by then, I think."

Ali was rewarded with a theatrically shocked face.

She grinned. "I know. Far too young to be drinking but I was just trying to piss off the Parentals because they'd stuck me with her." She felt her smile widen. "Anyway, it turned out that the new girl was a lot more fun than she looked because when I offered her the cider, fully expecting her to go running to Mummy and Daddy, she surprised me and took a slug – and that broke the ice. We managed to drink about a mouthful of cider each before admitting it tasted gross and I went downstairs and got the lemonade and we made it into cider shandy which was much more palatable!"

"You were a lush at eleven, Ali. I don't know why that surprises me."

She shrugged in a what-can-I-tell-you way. "That broke the ice because before long we were chatting about the film and turns out that she was this precocious music nerd, loved the theme tune."

She sung a few lines and Kris joined in for a bit then said in a respectful voice:

"Tune!"

"So we talked about music for a bit then conversation turned to school and we discovered that we'd both be starting at the same secondary school at the end of the summer. I found myself telling her I hoped it would be better than my last one because I'd hated it there, because everyone was stupid, and they took the piss out of me for being a ginger and knowing all the answers to everything the teacher asked, which I hadn't told anyone else. Not even my parents or Simon."

"Kids are awful. I used to get called Kris the kebab because I'm Greek. And there was this long-running Costa joke going round – you know 'I like your shirt, did it Costa you much?'".

She shuddered, recalling just how horrible children could be to each other, especially if you didn't conform to their norm. "Agreed – they are brutal. In return Charlie told me she didn't mind moving from their home in Swindon because the area where they used to live had got rough – and her parents didn't like her to go out to play and they'd sent her to a private primary school, and she lost her Wiltshire accent and all of the neighbours thought she was a snob. She told me how happy she was that they could get a dog now they'd moved to Puddlington and that she'd always wanted one.

"When she said that I went downstairs and I rescued our old lab, Tarzan, from the Parentals and using cheese and onion crisps as bait, got him into my room and lying on the bed between us and she loved that. I felt so comfortable with her by then that I confessed that I didn't have many friends either because there were no girls my age in Puddlington, but that occasionally Simon would include me as he had some friends in the village but they were older and sometimes didn't want to play with me. So we shared all this stuff and by the time the grown-ups remembered about us, *The Breakfast Club* was finished. Charlie decided I looked like Molly Ringwald." She pointed to her red curls to help him with the reference. "So she, with her terrible bowl haircut, was Ally Sheedy." She looked at him to make sure he got it.

"I get it."

"And after that we spent the whole summer hanging out, and by the time we started school together that was that, best friends forever."

Kris smiled at her. "Ah bless. Two little misfits finding their soulmates.

And all these years later she's still your besty, a bit like me and my mate Darius. We've been through a lot together."

But was what Kris saying still true? Were they best friends forever anymore? Was keeping Antonio a secret from Charlie taking a toll? As if he could read her mind Kris asked,

"What does Charlie think about your boyfriend?"

All Kris knew was that she was seeing someone who lived abroad.

"Oh, you know, she just wants me to be happy, I guess." She hedged. It wasn't an actual lie.

"And when are you seeing him next?"

"He's promised he'll come for a weekend soon," she said perkily.

"I hope so. It's been a while, right? Let me go see to them a minute." He left to tend to some customers who'd just arrived.

Kris sounded like he didn't believe Antonio would come but she knew her lover would make good on his word this time. They'd spoken, as normal, one evening in the week and after consuming the best part of a bottle of red wine she had the Dutch courage to be honest and tell him how much she missed him and that she was worried they were drifting apart because of the distance. He was so reassuring and caring and said that wasn't the case, it had just been a particularly busy time for him. Then he suggested they had video sex.

As soon as she climaxed, she burst into tears. Whether it was the orgasm that breached her defences, or the fact that they were being intimate in a way that felt close on one hand but distant on another, something cracked inside, and all the pent up loneliness and frustration she'd been feeling came flooding out. She was mortified. She preferred to play it cool with him, he liked independent sassy Ali, and she cringed when she saw alarm flash in his eyes but couldn't help herself sobbing into the screen. He was sweet. He spoke softly in Spanish, which helped to soothe her and eventually, after she'd calmed down and apologised, he said he would make it a priority to make more time for her and they would meet up soon for sure – possibly in London.

She was picturing an elegantly cool five-star hotel room and lots of hot sex when Kris came back and interrupted her reverie, grabbing her hands and holding them tight. Golden-brown, heavily lashed eyes met hers and she couldn't look away.

"Molly Ringwald is one of my favourite leading ladies, you know. And as we're on the subject of films, I'm going to remind you of another one – if your man can't make time for you, it means … '*He's Just Not That Into You*'."

PART TWO

JUNE 2015
ENGLAND

CHAPTER 9

Oh how Charlie loved summer in Puddlington, particularly the long warm evenings in the weeks running up to the summer solstice when it stayed light until after 10pm.

She and Simon had fallen into a bit of routine over the last couple of months. After they left work, if neither of them had other plans, they would meet up to do one of two things: either head up to North Wilts and squeeze in a quick round of golf before the light went, or take their dogs out for a walk.

Nine holes in the evening worked well for Simon as it was hard for him to take a whole day off to play because work was so busy – and she just loved being outdoors in the evenings – it was glorious up on the top of the Wiltshire downs in the 'golden hour'.

They started walking their dogs together after accidentally running into each other so many times that it became a routine. Also, Ted and Flopsy, the Hobsons' hyperactive Sprocker, were in love, so it would be cruel to deprive them of each other's company. The younger pets bounded and raced and panted and played until they were worn out. Grumpy Muffin couldn't keep up and didn't always want to come with them because she was quite the old lady now, but on the days she asked to come out for a walk, they would do a loop of the village green first, then drop Muffin back at home and then head off on a long yomp with the other two.

They had a bunch of diffcrent walks they could choose from, down bridle paths, through woods or along the edges of corn or rapeseed fields. Sometimes they would take their bikes and cycle quite a long section of the Kennet and

Avon canal path, work up a thirst and stop for a pint at a dog-friendly pub by a lock before heading back.

If it was a really nice evening, like today, and they didn't feel like one of their regular routes or playing golf, they'd jump in Simon's Land Rover and drive further afield. Today's walk took them to a pretty village, high up on the Westbury Downs, where they could pass through the bosky cool of an ancient forest of oaks, ash and chestnut trees and then climb up the hill to the ancient White Horse that had been carved out of the chalky ground: a symbol of the county and visible from miles away in every direction. They would scramble up the steep incline, inch across the chalk and sit on the grassy eye of the immense creature, then gaze down on the countryside before them. The different fields of arable crops, hedgerows, riverbeds, copses and forests spread out underneath them like a giant gold and green patchwork quilt.

Today was a day like that. Perfect. Her tummy rumbled.

"That was loud. You hungry, Charlie Girl?"

"Starving. I was on my feet all day looking after those pesky ponies and the Posse was no help as usual." She looked pointedly at her 'boss' in an attempt to remind him that he'd promised to talk to the lazy minxes.

He studiously ignored the implied criticism, and settled himself comfortably, propped up on his elbows, long, strong tanned legs stretched out in front of him, copious golden leg fur glinting in the sunshine. Charlie looked at him surreptitiously from under the cover of her battered baseball cap and swallowed a laugh. His 'farmer's tan' was quite spectacular. She couldn't help herself from noticing the stark contrast between the dark brown of his mid-thigh and the whiter-than-white skin of his upper thigh, which had been revealed when he lay back and his rugby shorts rose up. The tan was profound testament to the amount of time he spent wearing shorts – whatever the weather.

"Shall we go and get a bite, then?"

"In a bit. I don't want to move yet. It's so nice up here."

"It is indeed."

They sat for a while in companionable silence, but Charlie couldn't quite relax. Simon noticing something off about her behaviour raised a questioning eyebrow.

"Sorry, I'm a bit fidgety. I'm feeling guilty, I was supposed to head over to Bristol tonight to see Ryan and maybe try and drag your sister out for dinner with us but …"

"But what?"

"I didn't feel like it."

"Oh. Trouble in paradise? Is Romeo losing his appeal?"

She gave voice to something that had been troubling her for a few weeks: her lack of enthusiasm when it came to going to see her boyfriend. This was the third time she'd cancelled their plans in favour of staying in Puddlington and hanging out with Simon, but she couldn't tell him that.

"No it's not that. I just find I don't want to go into the city. Why do I want to do that when I can be up here?" She gestured around. The view was magical.

"He could come here."

"He could, I suppose …" Charlie sighed, then said in a flat tone.,"I probably should invite him to Puddlington more often." She glanced at Simon to gauge his reaction. His eyes met hers knowingly and a half smile danced on his lips. She felt compelled to defend her position. "Don't get me wrong I really like him …"

"I sense another 'but' coming."

"You're obsessed with butts."

"I … like … big butts and I cannot lie …" Simon sang enthusiastically. Charlie giggled and made a zip-it gesture.

"Well I know I'm safe around you 'cos I do not have a big butt. Worse song ever, by the way."

"It's a classic, Charlie Girl. True you don't have a big butt, you have a small but perfectly formed butt. But enough about butts, let's get back to what's up with you and 'ripped' Ryan."

She shook her head in exasperation.

"Don't call him that." Ali's nickname had stuck, and she was terrified Ryan would overhear them calling him that one day. He was quite sensitive about being respected for his skills as a lawyer rather than his incredible physique.

"He's so much more than a nice body you know. He's a great guy."

"I would hope so, Charlie Girl. I'm sure he is a super chap. But I wouldn't know because you never brought him and his nice body to Brown's to meet us all. Is he scared of me or the animals?" he teased gently.

"Neither."

"The Pony Posse?"

"Well, they are terrifying especially when it comes to young men. But …"

"It's that 'but' again. You're getting boring."

She articulated the thought that had been percolating for a few weeks.

"It's not … right. I think I'm going to finish it." Surprised at herself, she had chosen to share the news with Simon first. She'd piqued Simon's interest.

"Why?"

"I don't … well … he's great, of course … so good to me. So it's not him. It's me."

"Is it because you're still in love with Graham?"

It surprised Charlie to hear her ex's name on Simon's lips. He'd hardly mentioned him before.

"No. Not that, either. I'm over Graham. Took a shockingly short time, to be honest."

Simon didn't respond. She rushed out the next thought, trying to make sense of it herself.

"This thing with Ryan. I feel like if it's not going anywhere, I don't want to waste his time or mine."

"That's very mature of you, Charlie Girl," Simon said, sounding impressed.

Immature, more like, she thought helplessly. Because, as everyone knew, a good man was hard to find. And she'd found one in Ryan. Was she crazy to think about dumping someone so nice? And *why* was she telling Simon this? She should have called Ali! But Ali wasn't answering these days.

"Maybe. But I think I need to do it, before he gets any more attached. And I'm scared. I think I'm really going to hurt his feelings. I've never dumped anyone before," she concluded miserably.

"Really? *I* have," he said showing a complete lack of concern for poor Ryan and making her grimace with his forthrightness.

"Of course, you have." She bloody knew that from first-hand experience. She wondered if he even remembered. "I know, you've loved and left a thousand girls," she joked, shooting a sly glance his way to gauge his reaction, which was to look rather pleased with himself.

It had passed him by that she may be referring to their 'moment' all those years ago at Ali's party. Which meant he'd completely forgotten it or it had meant so little to him he didn't make the connection. Which was a huge relief! She grinned. Something funny had occurred to her – hilarious if you love toilet humour. Which she did. She pointed an accusing finger at him.

"You are always the dump-*er*."

"Don't call me a dumper."

"Big fat stinky dumper," she teased in a singsong voice, trying and failing to hold back a snorting giggle.

Simon didn't seem to find it as funny as she did and said patronisingly, "Your humour is puerile, Ms Pierce."

Charlie relaxed back on her elbows, turned and gave him a wink. Feeling pretty pleased with herself.

"Thanks. It has been said before."

Simon wasn't to be distracted, and turned her attention back to the conversation in hand.

"So how are you going to do it? In person I hope? That would be kindest." He used the word 'kind' but laughed cruelly when he spotted her terrified face and emphatic head shake.

"You're too scared to do that? On the phone then?"

She nodded helplessly. "I guess I'll have to." She could see Simon was enjoying her discomfort far too much.

"Shall I help you? Give you some tips? Ohhh, can I listen in?"

"Don't be horrible. Of course not. I didn't listen to you dumping old Kylie Minogue."

Simon raised his eyebrows archly and said in a fake stern tone, "No need to be bitchy about my charming ex. In the end, it was a mutual decision."

Charlie snorted out a laugh.

"A mutual decision based on the fact she wanted you to go back to

Australia with her and you didn't want to go."

Simon turned to look at her, a wicked glint in his clear grey eyes.

"And how would *you* know what she wanted?" He pretended to ponder, stroking his chin reflectively. "Is it because *your* mother eavesdropped a private conversation between me and *my* mother? And a few days later, when I decide to confide about my painful breakup to Ed, Kitty and *you*, I realised *you* already knew because you can't fib to save your life."

She'd been busted and almost felt bad about it. Almost.

"Sorry, I know it was terrible of Mummy but …"

"It's OK. I forgive you all."

They sat in companionable silence for a moment enjoying the sights, sounds and smells on the empty hill. The air was perfumed with the sharp, green scent of freshly flattened grass. Insects were buzzing and thrumming as they went about their busy way. A few birds were coasting high above them in the hot air currents. And in a distant valley, a rainbow-hued hot air balloon glided over a patchwork of empty fields. A few moments later their peaceful moment was destroyed by the cacophony of two dogs scrabbling over the chalk surface of the horse. They were panting and puffing their way towards the eye, exhausted from their adventures and ready to join their humans. Simon gave them lots of scratchy pats and 'good boys' and 'good girls' in welcome and Charlie poured water from her bottle into the collapsible water bowl so they could have a drink.

The dogs took it in turns to gulp up the water and after making sure they'd had enough to drink, Charlie took a swig of water for herself then offered the last few drops to Simon. Feeling as happy and relaxed in his company as a good friend should, she decided to ask Simon something she'd been curious about for a while.

"Are you over your ex? Do you miss her?" She was lying flat on her back now, eyes narrowed to filter out the still-bright sun, with Ted curled into her side. Her pet baby, exhausted from his adventure, had already succumbed to sleep and she listened fondly to his slow, regular breaths, until Simon eventually answered her.

"No I don't. I don't miss her at all. I don't miss coming home to her after work, or miss going out to dinner with her or trying to find something for us to do together that we both would enjoy. I don't miss watching her and Mum try and fail to get on. Or her coming to Brown's and rubbing everyone up the wrong way. It's a relief, actually." She could sense him looking at her for reassurance, but didn't open her eyes. "Is that terrible? It is terrible, right?"

"Pretty terrible. Are you sure you don't miss anything about her?" she probed.

"Well, maybe just the …" He sounded awkward.

"The sex?" Charlie supplied helpfully, guessing the cause of his embarrassment and marvelling at how far their friendship had come, talking about stuff like this.

"A bit. Which is pretty shallow of me."

"It is. But you're a bloke, so I kind of expect it. That can't have been all it was, though? She must have had some redeeming features. What else did you like about her?"

"She was good looking," he said decisively. "And she smelt great and …" He hesitated a bit before he continued, "And she was so *sure* of what she wanted – which was me. She really wanted me. She made that obvious and I was flattered. That sounds very shallow," he said sheepishly.

She turned her head towards him and opened her eyes to find him looking at her like he wanted her to understand.

She decided to be kind. "You are shallow," she teased, "but it's very powerful having someone want you that way, and, much though I don't want to, I agree she is very attractive. On the outside, at least. Ali and I thought she looked like Kylie Minogue, only better."

He explained how they'd got together at a point where he wasn't enjoying his time in Australia as much as he had done before. The outback had lost its appeal and he'd started finding his work monotonous.

"I missed the British countryside, my mates, and the Parentals, of course."

It seemed he was a bit lonely, which surprised Charlie, she'd never thought Mr Popular himself had ever been anything other than happy 'down under'. She felt like he really wanted her to understand.

"She was very, um, attentive, and us men like that, we like to be made a fuss of…"

She looked at him sideways, assuming he was trying to say she was hot shit in bed without saying it and sounding shallow again. He continued.

"And you probably won't believe this because you didn't really see the best of her here, but she could be a good laugh."

"I can imagine. Not!" Charlie deadpanned.

"Don't forget, we'd only been dating for a few months when I decided to come back to the UK. We were in that first flush. And when she said she'd always wanted to come to England, I thought, well, why not? Let's give it a go. And she came and pretty soon I realised how different we were – but by then I felt responsible, you know."

She wasn't surprised by the last bit. At all.

"I suspected as much because deep down, despite your gruff exterior, you're a bit of a softy, Simon Hobson. Something I have discovered to my detriment, having to deal with the consequences of your lax people management skills – especially where older women are concerned." She couldn't resist getting in another dig about how feeble he was with regard to the SPuRS crew.

Things went quiet for a few minutes before Simon cleared his throat and said with a little catch to his voice,

"So I guess you haven't fallen in love with this American fella if you might be dumping him."

She sighed and sat up, wrapping her arms around her bare calves and hugging them into her chest.

"I *should* love him. He ticks all the boxes; he's successful and he's handsome – a real gentleman – and he treats me like a queen. I *like* him very, very much. But I don't think I will ever fall in love with him."

She turned her head to look directly at Simon, he'd gone silent on her. He was lying flat now, eyes scanning the blue, blue sky, hands crossed behind his head, wearing an enigmatic expression. She would love to know what was going on behind those clear grey eyes. He was very difficult to read sometimes.

She unfurled herself and lowered herself down alongside him – putting her hands behind her head, copying his body language.

"What do you think?"

He sat up suddenly, indicating that he didn't want to discuss Ryan or

Sandy any more by making a joke: "What do I think? That this is a bit of a heavy conversation, mate."

"Yes, it is, mate." She tried not to be offended that he'd moved away from her so abruptly and matched his jokey energy. She knew from experience that Simon didn't like talking about feelings and stuff, and she should be pleased that he'd opened up earlier. Luckily her tummy came to the rescue when a loud grumble erupted from her lower regions.

Simon grinned broadly and said in a fake Cockney accent, "Cor blimey mate, was that you?"

"Yep. It was." Unashamed.

"Not very ladylike. Guess I better get you fed." He leant over her and gently poked her exposed tummy. His messy blonde hair flopping around his face, turned into a scruffy halo by the waning sun. "What do you fancy?"

I fancy you, thought Charlie, unbidden. *I really fancy you.* Being honest with herself for once. *I always have, and I probably always will. But I'm never going to tell you that. Because look at us, look at where we've come. We're mates now – good mates. And I don't want to ruin that.* So instead, she said,

"I fancy fish and chips, mate. Haddock, preferably."

"Ohhhh haddock," he moaned in mock ecstasy, then added with relish, "fish and chips for the lady it shall be. With some lovely mushy peas?"

"Yep, and lashing of tartare sauce."

"Let's go then. Last one to the car's an old kipper."

CHAPTER 10

It was a sunny Saturday afternoon and Ali was heading home to Puddlington. The traffic on the M4 was not too bad, and she was going to sleep in her old bed and stay the night in her family home for the first time since Christmas.

Oddly, she'd spent more time with her parents during the year she lived in Spain than she did now, living an hour away in Bristol. When you flew in from somewhere you felt obliged to stay a few nights. Nowadays, work was always a good excuse to drive back to her flat.

She couldn't avoid tonight's celebration, though, and, to be fair, she didn't want to. She was looking forward to catching up with everyone. Plus, she was in a good mood because Antonio had surprised her with a flying visit during the week – and stayed over at the flat for the night! Too brief, of course, but enough to recharge the old love batteries.

The next morning it had been hard to sit in the CHW conference room and pretend theirs was purely a professional relationship just hours after they'd been lying in her bath together soaping each other's bits. But beggars can't be choosers. Their client, a Spanish billionaire called Sebastián de la Cruz – whose multiple businesses included multiple vineyards in Spain, a champagne house in France, a Bristol-based UK premier league football team and a luxurious worldwide hotel chain – had been insistent that all the team members were there to update him on their upcoming deal; he was purchasing his first UK-based luxury hotel chain to add to his portfolio.

The meeting had gone well, Sebastián had praised her work in front of Antonio and the rest of her team members, and the deal was on track to be signed in a few weeks. Antonio had rushed off after the meeting but messaged later to say what a wonderful time they had together, so she'd been on a high for the rest of the week. She missed him already, but he'd said there was a chance they could meet up again in August which wasn't that far away, and this weekend would be a pleasant distraction.

Today was her father's birthday and to celebrate they were having a special family dinner. It would be just the four of them for the first time in ages. She was looking forward to gossiping with her parents, getting lots of sloppy kisses from the dog and finally being about to tease Simon about how awful his ex was. And then she'd get to hang out with all the Pierces tomorrow over a slap-up lunch with both families at the Lamb.

But when she got home, there was no warm welcome for the prodigal daughter. No Parentals to give her a hug and make her a cuppa, no squeals and yips of doggy excitement to mark her return, which meant, she assumed, that Flopsy was already being taken out for a walk.

Disgruntled and at a loose end, she dropped her bag in her room and called Charlie, but it went straight to voicemail. She didn't bother leaving a message. Checking the time, she realised it was already 5.30pm the Lamb would be open and hopefully still nice and quiet. At least she'd be able to have a bit of chinwag with her friend Sammi.

She was already dressed in her best country casual attire of cut-off jeans and a white linen shirt tied to show off her small waist. She ran a comb through her springy auburn hair, sprayed on some perfume and touched up her bright red lipstick then toddled off, over the village green to the ancient hostelry.

"All right, you old slapper!" hollered Sammi as she walked through the door.

"At least someone's pleased to see me."

Sammi looked puzzled. "What do you mean? Everyone's dead excited you're here for the weekend."

"Oh, it's nothing, just me being silly. There was no one home."

"Your parents are probably out with the dog. That bloody dog gets more walks than anyone I know."

"But the Parentals only take her out if they have to."

"Well absence makes the heart go fonder. They hardly ever get a chance to take her because your brother walks her all the time now."

"Hum," she said, "that's a bit of an about face." But Sammi didn't answer, absorbed as she was in pulling pints at the other end of the bar. Simon hadn't been that keen on Flopsy to start with. She seemed to recall that he'd told the Parentals they should get her into obedience classes as soon as possible and that he wouldn't be caught dead shouting "Come here Flopsy" on the bridle paths of Puddlington. Prior to bringing the crazy Sprocker home, the Hobsons had always had a penchant for black labs, all of whom had been called Tarzan.

Simon's dismay at their poor choice in canine company was exacerbated by the fact that dear sweet Flopsy had an excitable bladder condition. She couldn't help herself from letting out a little wee when she was pleased to see someone. Which was most people. Apart from Sandy. And because she adored Simon despite, or maybe because, he was stern with her, and because Sandy was often by his side when Flopsy got herself going, she had peed on her brother's ex-girlfriend many times.

Smiling, in recollection of Flopsy's past triumphs (in her opinion, anyway), Ali plumped herself down on her favourite barstool and took a deep refreshing draft of the ridiculously good house cider that had materialised in front of her. She was always picky about where she sat, at the Lamb she preferred the dark end of the bar, away from the door and close to where the glasses got washed, a spot where she and Sammi could chat undisturbed when she wasn't serving other customers. Sammi, Charlie and Ali were all great pals; they had bonded when the two friends had tried out for summer jobs at the pub. Sammi had coached, supported and teased them into being good employees and Ali had the fondest memories of the times they'd all worked together.

"So what's new in P town?"

"Nothing much. There's a new B&B opened up down the road, very luxurious, apparently. Attracting posh types from London. We get a lot of them in here at the weekend, which is good. It's a male couple running it."

"Nice. How's that gone down?"

"Surprisingly well. It caused a few raised eyebrows to start with, they have a rainbow flag flying outside, which got people going a bit, but on the whole everyone is being welcoming."

"Good for them! Glad to hear Puddlington is dragging itself into the aughties."

"And, of course, everyone is having a field day talking about your brother's ex. Gloves are off. You shoulda heard the horror stories once everyone realised she'd gone for good."

Ali nodded sagely. "I can't blame them. It's a puzzle to me why he dated her for so long."

"I think your brother's a bit of a soft touch, to be honest." Ali didn't believe that for a second, but didn't say anything. Sammi had always seen the best in him because, of course, he'd worked at the pub too. She always said she loved the whole Hobson family equally. Which was a bit frustrating when Ali needed her to take her side in an argument. "I think he needed *her* to be the one to break it off – as she came all the way from Australia to be with him – or he'd have felt guilty. But he's free now and having the time of his life by the looks of it."

"Don't tell me he's dating already? The sly old dog."

Sammi looked around, checking to make sure no one else could hear her before she carried on. "Not dating. Yet. Just enjoying life. And spending a lot of time with a certain someone, as I'm sure you know."

Ali was puzzled. Charlie would have told her if there was someone new in the mix surely. "Who?"

"Our mutual friend," Sammi said in her best, isn't this a fab bit of gossip voice, topped off with a conspiratorial wink.

Something awful had dawned on her. "You mean Charlie?" Sammi nodded, the excitement in her eyes changing to wariness as she clocked Ali's reaction and realised she didn't know what she was talking about. "No! Surely she wouldn't be so bloody stupid."

Before she got an answer from her, Sammi was called away by a rowdy group of men in shooting outfits, clamouring for pints. By the time the women could resume their conversation, Sammi had evidently done some thinking around the matter. "I probably shouldn't have said anything, so don't get your knickers in a twist before you talk to them, Ali. And don't say it was me either. Because … it may just be me adding two and two and making five. All I know is that they are spending an awful lot of time together."

Ali, soothed somewhat by the cider, decided not to panic. "That's bound to happen, I suppose, as they work together." But she felt a little dart of worry. "Anyway she's only just broken up with her boyfriend, and she'd never cheat. Do you see them together that often, then?" She was surprised Charlie hadn't mentioned any of this to her.

"Yeah. Well, you know about the dog walking. And they play golf quite a lot. I reckon they come in for a drink at least once a week and," looking a bit nervous about the reception her next bit of news would receive, "I overheard them talking about the summer solstice ball? You know the charity event where they always bring in a celebrity host and the DJ that used to play for Princess Di?" Ali nodded. "Kitty and Ed bought tickets and they've invited Simon and Charlie to join them. The two of them were discussing what to wear the other day."

The conversation was making her feel weird. She didn't like the sound of 'the two of them', her best friend and brother, cosying up together again. Simon was and always had been a charming git, and Charlie was just so … trusting and naive and just plain bloody dumb where men were concerned.

It was as if Sammi could read her incendiary thoughts and was determined to lead her away from the impending explosion. She said soothingly,

"Look, she hasn't said anything to me and she knows I know about you know what. So, maybe I'm reading the situation wrong." Then she took her life in her hands and said, "And if I'm *not*, maybe it would be a good thing for both of them? I know he broke her heart back in the day, but they're grown-ups now. And I think they'd make a lovely couple," she finished, a tad defiantly.

Ali shook her head impatiently getting angrier by the second. What did Sammi know?

"No they wouldn't!"

"Mate, you should see them together. They get on so well. It's a bit like watching you two bantering, only more … you know."

Ali snorted. "Over my dead body, Sammi," she said angrily, "don't forget I had to deal with the repercussions last time. He behaved like a complete dick and got away scot-free, as usual, and I paid the price – I had a heartbroken friend on my hands for months, I never want to deal with that again."

CHAPTER 11

"Is it weird that I dream about the ponies when I'm away from them?" Charlie asked Simon as they worked alongside each other, mucking out the stalls where the ponies slept.

"No weirder than the fact I look forward to coming into work to see their funny little faces light up," Simon responded, giving her a self-deprecating grin, then getting back to the job at hand.

He sifted through the straw efficiently, letting it fall through the tines until only manure was balanced on his fork. He then transferred the pooh pellets carefully into the hand cart.

As he forked the muck, Charlie filled up the surrounding troughs with sweet, clean water, picking out any slimy debris and adding it to the muck cart also. Every icky bit they'd harvested would be added to the fertiliser pile, where it would be sold to local gardeners for a small donation towards animal care.

"I wonder what they think about sometimes, if they are just obsessed with grass or they think great deep thoughts about life, the universe and everything," said Charlie

"I sometimes wonder if Bumble loves Bee more, or it's the other way round?" he said, laughing. "Do you think there's something wrong with us?"

She shook her head, and smiled. "Noooo, It's perfectly normal to obsess over those small, spoilt, nippy monsters," all the time thinking there's absolutely nothing wrong with you from where I'm standing. Simon was working a few metres away from her. She peeped at him from under her lashes, admiring the way a shaft of light from the high central window highlighted him from behind, caressing his broad naked shoulders, and making the hairs on his chest and tanned legs gleam like golden wool. His face was dripping, his ratty old baseball cap was stained with sweat, there was straw stuck to his muscular forearms, and all around him dust motes swirled and played in the warm June air. The atmosphere in the little wooden barn was earthy, vegetal and all she wanted to do at that moment was turn the hosepipe on him and join him under the spray in an impromptu shower. He was so bloody gorgeous he made her mouth water.

"Penny for them, Charlie Girl."

Oh God, he'd caught her perving over him. Again. It kept happening. And she kept catching him staring at her! Like yesterday when she'd picked up Ted and buried her face in his furry belly because he was too cute to resist and when she stopped snuffling and blowing tummy raspberries, she'd looked up and caught Simon staring at her with the weirdest look on his face. And last week when he'd told her about the solstice ball and said why didn't they go together, his face was so smooth and young looking, a mix of anxious and hopeful …

"Earth calling Charlie Girl … come in, Charlie Girl."

She needed to change the subject to something safe – something guaranteed to poor cold water on her raging hormones.

"Sorry. In a world of my own. What time did Ali say she was coming?"

"She didn't say but knowing Ali she'll turn up minutes before we sit down to dinner, too late to help." He sighed, his frustration with his sister showing, but then he grinned and said, "Bearing gifts, of course, of the expensive alcoholic kind. She always brings great wine."

"True that. She's so fancy. She really knows her Rioja from her Cabernet Sauvignon these days. She's looking forward to coming home, she said."

"Good. Because she's been pretty crap with Mum and Dad lately." He looked at her, fishing. "Did you know she hardly ever calls them?"

"Well, I'm not seeing much of her, either. It's because she's so busy, Simon," she pointed out in defence of her best friend.

"And that's always her excuse. But I can tell they miss her. Dad loves hearing about her work. Used to be she'd talk to him about what she's up to. Mum doesn't have a clue what she does, of course."

"That's because your mum thinks she's a bit of thicky," Charlie said pragmatically. Penny had confided in her previously. "She told me she'd always struggled to keep up with her clever kids. I commiserated with her. Said I feel the same way." She looked at him and said in response to his raised eyebrows. "Seriously, I feel like that around Ali – and you, too, sometimes."

"Charlie Girl," he said sternly. And gave her a Paddington Bear hard stare – so she stopped what she was doing to listen. "Don't put yourself down. I hate that. Don't ever think you're less than Ali or me because you don't have a degree. You're right, Mother does that, too, and it drives me crazy." She could hear his frustration. "She reads the newspaper cover to cover and is up on current affairs, and knows loads about history and geography. Did you notice she's always on the winning team at the pub quiz?" He then relayed a long list of attributes: "She's very creative, she makes a nice little income out of those antiques she spots, and the line of fabrics she's designed, well, I think she should market them."

Charlie smiled, loving how he was defending his mum. She nodded. It was true. Penny had great taste and a unique country boho style. And she was so clever with her hands. When they were kids, she'd make them all gifts, and she loved coming up with costumes for their many theme parties at the manor. And she'd find all these incredible knick-knacks in car boot sales and charity shops, like the antique sculpture of an odd-looking dog Penny had given her for her 21st birthday – she adored it, even Graham had liked it and said it was probably worth quite a lot.

"That is true. How exciting about the fabric! I didn't know that."

"Well, she's shy about it, but we talked about it the other day."

"Does Ali know?"

"No, of course not, because she'd never think to ask. Too wrapped up in her bloody work."

He placed the fork over the cart, grabbed the handles and indicated they should move out of the barn.

"Hey, let's walk and talk so I'm not too late for the festivities."

She followed him outside, wound the hose back until it sat snugly in its holder, and then caught up with him as he pushed the cart towards the gate a few hundred yards away on the other side of the paddock.

As she came alongside, he slid his eyes over to her and said, "I know I tease you all the time, mate, but everyone at Brown's thinks you're amazing. Brilliant at your job."

She grunted non-committal. She didn't like to assume.

"Do you know what Ed told me the other day?"

"I'm not a mind reader, Simon," she said perkily.

"Well, Ed said the practice had never made as much money as it's making now – and a lot of that is down to you."

"I don't know how. You do all the work." It was nice of him to say, but they all knew that Simon was the one everyone wanted to work with, especially after Ed had his hips done. Ed came in less and less these days and Kitty, well, Kitty was Kitty. She did what she did when she felt like it.

"I may bring in more clients, but you're the one making sure we all get paid – because you have the accounts under control. Imagine, Kitty and Ed used to try to do most of it and it was all lumped in together."

She shuddered. The books *had* been in a terrible state. Sandy had made a start on sorting them out during her brief, unhappy tenure, to be fair, but she hadn't been there long enough to finish the job. Charlie's years working as an office manager at a chartered surveyor's in London had stood her in good stead, and she'd finally got the practice, the charity and the kennels set up in QuickBooks as separate accounts. She'd even got the volunteers doing some of the inputting.

"And he thinks you are ace at cost control because you stop Kitty buying tea, coffee and hideously expensive biscuits for the visitors and volunteers from Waitrose. And you keep stock – apparently the first time that's ever happened. And you pay all the bills and pay the credit card off on time. And now, with my manly support, you have even got the Posse under control …"

She looked at him aghast. What a load of bull. He'd been crap. He'd never once told them off – she had to do it all the time.

"But Simon, you …"

He talked right over her. "Thanks to us …"

She glared at him. He grinned back.

"OK, thanks to *you*, we've got the ladies doing what they are supposed to: running tours, signing up donors, selling the merchandise that's been sitting there for years, recycling all the resources and mostly tuning up when they should."

It was true. She'd made a new schedule and the Posse (mainly) stuck to it.

"And Kitty's Kennels is in profit for the first time *ever*! Not just leaching off the practice. All the boarders are getting bills and paying the right amount because you keep a track of when they come in and what they eat."

His words were making her feel squirmy, uncomfortable, but in a good way. She felt a bit of a fraud getting such fulsome praise for doing a job she adored. She loved it so much she felt bad for taking a salary sometimes.

Simon slowed down to a stop, and said emphatically, "We don't worry about anything when you're around taking care of things. All Ed and I have to do is worry about the animals. And that's, well, that's genius, Charlie."

Her heart bumped and swelled in her chest. She felt her cheeks flame in pride and imagined she must look terrible – a big red-faced mess. She wanted to say thank you for the compliment but felt tongue tied, so instead, said, gruffly,

"As long as we don't skimp on the PG tips, we can suffer own-brand chocolate digestives. As for the rest, well, it's not rocket science."

"It's better than that, Charlie. It's peace of mind."

He looked at her, then stepped closer and reached over the cartload of manure towards her. Then picked up the strand of hair that had fallen across her face and tucked it behind her ear, then, fully absorbed in his work, also peeled a piece of muck off her red face and flicked it to the ground.

"Charlie, I …"

She caught her breath. What was going on here? It felt like Simon was about to … an ear-shattering hee-haw interrupted the moment and they turned away from each other simultaneously to look towards the herd to see which of the little monsters was responsible for such a disproportionately loud noise. And the moment, whatever it was, was gone.

Bumble, as per normal, was the culprit, braying her head off for no apparent reason. Bee looked on adoringly and the rest of the herd chomped away, oblivious to her tantrum. They had moved the electric fence back a few feet earlier that evening and the ponies were grazing the fresh new strip of grass with gusto, she or Simon did this every evening to control how much grass the monsters could reach – otherwise the greedy things would eat far too much and get even fatter than they were.

Simon had picked up the cart and was walking away from her with it. She gave the herd a long look before she caught up with him and they stayed side by side as they walked across the paddock. The ponies painted a colourful picture; some tan and white, some black and white, some solid brown, even an adorable, pinky-grey palomino one, who she called Tinkerbell, the hues of their varied coats complimented by the bright greens of the grass and the darker tones of the hedgerows.

"Every time I look at them and they are behaving themselves and grazing quietly like that, I wonder how a creature that looks that cute could have the capacity for creating so much mischief and mayhem?"

Simon grunted, nodded, rolled his eyes and at the same time said, "Devilish Furbies."

"Nighty night, babies!" Charlie called, waving as Simon locked the paddock behind them and then the two of them walked into the yard to finish up the chores together.

CHAPTER 12

Even though a pleasant breeze was flowing through the room, Ali was hot and bothered. Her conversation at the Lamb had put her in a foul mood and she was ready to have a go at someone, preferably the main culprit Simon.

Dinner was a disaster. Her mum and dad were being annoying, and Simon was behaving like a smug little shit. The food had been predictably terrible. Her mother had always been a crap cook and one of the reasons why Ali had spent so much time at Charlie's house as a teenager because Helen was an excellent one. Even though it was a hot summer's evening, her father had requested a hearty winter dish for their main course, toad in the hole, his favourite meal. Her mum didn't muck it up normally, but today she'd been so busy describing the 'second honeymoon' the two elderly love birds had enjoyed at Saunton Sands the previous weekend that she'd forgotten to turn on the timer, so burnt the Yorkshire pudding and also left huge lumps of cornflour in the almost raw, onion gravy. The men didn't seem to mind. They just slathered loads of mustard on it and scarfed the ugly mess down. The acrid smell of scorched cooking oil lingering in the dining room made her feel sick.

Simon was talking about his bloody practice. Again. And the Parentals were predictably hanging on his every word. She tuned out, only half listening to his 'hilarious' stories about his friend, a young farmer who had a pet sheep called Baa-baa-rah who slept indoors by the Rayburn in his kitchen, and who was best friends with the cat. She couldn't even be bothered to laugh at the antics of the old dears from SPuRS, who had nearly sabotaged a recent interview with BBC Wiltshire about the rescue sanctuary. And literally every other sentence featured a mention of Charlie Girl.

"But Charlie Girl managed to not only get the poo off the camera but also charm the reporter into saying it was probably his fault that Bumble had bit him in the bum. She's amazing."

There was a murmur of ascent and appreciation all around the table and, of course, she joined it, because her friend Charlie *was* amazing. But was he going to wax lyrical about her *all* evening? Had he forgotten that she wouldn't even be working for him if Ali hadn't suggested it!

"Earth calling Ali! You still with us?" Her father was looking at her.

That's such an annoying thing to say, she thought. Simon used that same stupid phrase as well.

She smiled tightly and said, "Where else would I be?"

"How's work going? You've been so busy. Did you get the deal done?" her father asked, keenly interested.

Now all three sets of eyes had turned their attention on her, set to hang on her every word. After feeling side-lined all evening, now she felt under the microscope. Instead of basking in the warmth of their regard, she wanted to say, why do you care?

She curbed her rudeness somehow and reached for the bottle of Rioja, an amazing vintage from one of Sebastián's vineyards. She dispassionately considered explaining this – it was the sort of juicy personal titbit the Parentals would savour and then enjoy relaying to their friends – but she couldn't be bothered to explain the connection. Instead, she drained what remained of the ruby goodness into her glass before answering.

"Yes," she answered. Sounding more like a moody teenager than an international corporate lawyer. Her father's hopeful expression showed he wanted her to expand. She didn't feel like doing so, so she didn't, and in the absence of anything more from her, he said, in slightly strained voice,

"That's my girl. We are very proud of you."

A thought occurred, and it slipped out before she could stop it. "Are you?"

Her parents exchanged puzzled looks. "Of course, we are, silly. So clever, and successful and always so independent," trilled Penny rather nervously.

Charles joined in, in support. "Such a career girl. Never asking us for anything. Not needing a man to help you out."

She glared at her dad. *Who said that anymore?* About needing a man to survive? Penny spotted Charles's boo-boo and jumped in attempting to sooth the situation, but managed to say something even more annoying.

"So different from me, of course, marrying your father when I was nineteen." Then she looked over at Charles and gazed at him adoringly. "Not that I would have changed a thing. The luckiest girl in the world to meet you, my love." And they exchanged a short sloppy kiss on the lips that made Ali feel queasy. They were always so into their PDAs.

Penny rushed on. "So yes, it goes without saying that we are extremely proud of you. Both of you," she corrected, making sure to be fair and include her son in the compliment fest. Then, with the look of someone who had done a good job, she sat back in her chair and beamed at both her children.

Simon, the suck up, beamed right back at the two of them, then reached over and gave Penny's hand a reassuring squeeze.

Ali knew a response was required from her to fully clean up the bad atmosphere but could only manage a tight smile, because when her mum said how proud of Ali she was, it made her sick to her stomach. Sicker than the smell of the rank food. She almost confessed then. She almost blurted out,

"I'm sleeping with my married colleague. He's twenty years older than me and has two teenage kids! If anyone finds out I could lose my job. I've lied to all of you for months. Are you proud of me now?" But she didn't. How could she? The Parentals had been married for thirty years. They'd be disgusted with her. She was disgusted with her.

"Time to celebrate. Let's crack open that expensive port Ali brought," said Simon in his heartiest tone, blithely ignorant of any unpleasant undercurrents, because his life was golden. Soon enough, all eyes and attention were back on him as he grabbed hold of the antique crystal port decanter her mum had found at a car boot sale and where he'd decanted it earlier. He poured generous measures into the matching glasses that were already set on the table in anticipation. Port drinking was a Hobson family tradition and most celebrations ended with a bottle or two being passed around the table.

"Yum. Hold on a sec, I've got some lovely creamy stilton and some tasty cheddar from the farm shop to go with that," said Penny, who pushed herself away from the table and wandered off to the kitchen to collect the cheese board she'd prepared earlier.

The conversation meandered on about life in Puddlington and Ali continued to observe, but not join in. The other three were peas in a pod and she was the odd vegetable out. Charlie was more of a pea than she was. She fitted right in with the rest of them.

Simon saw the Parentals most days as he lived in the guest cottage at the end of their magnificent apple orchard. She noted how they finished each other's sentences and enjoyed multiple in-jokes about Puddlington's cast of characters.

Back in the day, *she* knew what was going on in the village, but now she was out of the loop. She'd never heard of Mrs so-and-so from down the road who'd just been sold a Dalmatian puppy with no spots. But Simon was her vet. She had never met the retired judge and his bohemian, much-younger companion who had downsized from a stately home when he'd bought the beautiful sixteenth century farmhouse on Puddlington village green and turned it into a fancy AirBnB but all three of the Hobsons had gone there for drinks and dinner last week. And despite attending it for years, she had only ever turned up, got trashed and danced to 'Hi ho silver lining' at the village fete, whereas Simon had been asked to be the chairperson for this year's committee. It was less than a year since he'd returned from Australia, but already Simon was a big man in town and she was the outsider, the daughter who lived in the big city and had always put her career first.

She remembered how briefly, after Simon left for university, she'd had her parents to herself. Although she'd missed her brother, it was nice having more of their attention. Of course, they would roll out the red carpet when he came home, usually dragging a bunch of mates with him – proud to show off his family and his home in Puddlington. After uni he went to Australia and the Parentals were devastated but understanding, because it was the best thing for his career. They would fly out to see him for a month or two at a time, staying on a sheep station in the outback, visiting the Great Barrier Reef and touring around different parts of the country with him. He would always take time off to be with them.

Ali, on the other hand, had headed off to London as soon as she could and never looked back. She'd had a happy childhood in Puddlington, especially after Charlie moved to the village and they became besties. She knew she was fortunate. Her parents were good people, they adored her and had given her a great start in life, but she'd never wanted to settle in the countryside. She wasn't like them; she was a city rat and they were country mice. Simon was cut from the same cloth and his return to Puddlington was a dream come true for everyone, it seems. Even Charlie.

"Come on pumpkin, up the wooden hill to Bedfordshire." Her dad, on his feet now, interrupted her introspective meanderings, as he gently helped his wife to her feet, bid his 'two favourite children' a fond good night and steered her out of the dining room, through the kitchen towards the stairs and up to bed.

"Night, Mummy, night, Daddy," Ali said listlessly as she reached for the port and started pouring.

"Whoo. Hold up, there," cautioned Simon as she filled first his, then her glass to the brim. "What's up with you tonight? You on a mission?"

"Just fancy a few drinks."

"I reckon more than a few. Didn't you go to the pub before dinner?"

"So?"

"That's fine. Just saying." He looked a bit hurt by her tone. "No need to be aggressive sis."

She shrugged, unconcerned that her tone had stung. "Guess why I went to the pub?" She looked at him blankly.

"Cause you wanted to see your mate Sammi."

"No. Because when I got home for the first time in ages, there was no one here."

"I was at work." He shrugged. "So what?"

"With Charlie?" He nodded.

"Thought so. I couldn't reach her either. Where were the Parentals?"

He shrugged again. "No idea."

"I know. They were out with the dog. Apparently, they leap at any opportunity to walk her, as they don't get a chance these days because you're always going for a walk with Charlie?"

Simon shrugged, unconcerned. "Flopsy and Ted are in lurveee. It's very cute."

She nodded sagely. "And guess what else I heard?"

Simon's face read somewhere between baffled and don't give a fuck. "Ermmm. I really don't know. That Sammi's been bonking the vicar? That Christmas is coming early. What? You're being weird."

Ali said in a silly, spooky voice, "I heard something strange. Something unbelievable. Apparently you are taking Charlie to the solstice ball. On a date." And she pulled an I-dare-you-to-lie-to-me face. "Is it true?"

"Well," he said evasively, like he'd been caught ducking out of his round. "It's not *exactly* a date. But yes, we were planning to go together."

"Together. Hmmm. Are you picking her up?"

"Duh. Yeah. Makes no sense for us to both drive."

"Humm. Are you taking Ed and Kitty too?"

"No, they will drive sep…" He paused. "What's with the interrogation, Ali? I don't get what the big deal is."

"You don't?" The fact that he was playing dumb, or worse, had no idea what she was getting at, made her even madder. "Shame on you, Simon. All I heard coming out of your mouth this evening is Charlie Girl this and Charlie Girl that."

She'd got his attention now. "*You* have finished with your awful girlfriend. *She* has just dumped her boring boyfriend. The two of you spend every waking minute together inside and outside of work. And *now* you're taking her to a bloody ball, no doubt getting ready to act like some veterinary Prince Charming." And she concluded, with emphasis, "*What* are your *intentions*?"

Simon dumbfounded, scoffed, "What do you mean what are my intentions? It's not the bloody eighteenth century, Ali! Women can vote now and everything." Then he said slowly, sarcasm dripping off every word, "We are mates, and as mates, we are going to the ball to drink and dance and have a bit of fun."

She shook her head no, pulled herself upright in the seat and summoned up her most patronising attitude then said in a tone she exclusively reserved for her annoying brother,

"Oh Simon, simple Simon, silly Simon – are you really so self-centred and obtuse?"

He glared at her. "What the fuck, Ali?"

"Are you sure she thinks the two of you are just 'mates'? Do you think it's strictly platonic for her? … All these long summer walks and dates at the pub?"

"Look Ali, Charlie Girl's gorgeous, we all know that and I'd be luc—"

Bingo! Simon sounds guilty as hell, she thought. *He knows what I'm getting at*. She cut him off.

"Have you forgotten what happened the last time you blurred the lines of your friendship with Charlie? Do you recall the toga party? You in your gladiator skirt? Her in her sheet?" Then she hissed, "Have you forgotten how you broke her teenage heart?" She was laying it on thick, but it felt so good to make another person feel bad about playing with someone's feelings.

"I didn't mean to… "

"You men never *mean* to, but then you do it, anyway."

"Ali, I think you have this wrong. I didn't break her heart."

She grabbed the bottle to pour some more into her still half full glass. She didn't need it. But she wanted it. The look of guilt mixed with denied responsibility on Simon's face reminded her of something. Unbidden, the image of Antonio leaving her flat the last time he'd visited floated into her mind, skirting the issue of when they would meet next. Men were rubbish. They hurt people, well, women, thoughtlessly. Effortlessly.

"Simon. You are an unobservant idiot. You don't notice when someone amazing is there for you. Like most men." She spelled it out for him, not pulling any punches, because Charlie was *her* friend, not *his*.

"How couldn't you have known that Charlie – your stupid bloody, soppy, sweet, kind Charlie Girl – had the biggest teenage crush on you?" She shook her head in disgust at his ignorance. "She thought she was in *love* with you, Simon, and you should never had led her on. But you got her drunk and chatted her up and *fucked* her at that party, and, afterwards when she thought you'd ask her to be your girlfriend, you, you bloody idiot, told her that, you'd had 'tremendous fun'." She put on a silly upper class twit accent to add emphasis, "and not to 'get all serious on him. You utter tool," she ended in disgust.

Simon looked stunned, like she'd truly shocked him. "But I thought, well, we were both so—"

She interrupted him. "Young? Yes, you were. But you were old enough to behave like a man. Not a boy." She was vicious in her righteousness, but she couldn't seem to stop herself despite the look of pain on her brother's face. "Did you know you popped her cherry that night, Simon? Did you know that?" He'd gone a greyish green and was sweating profusely. She didn't think it was possible to make him look worse than he had a few minutes before. But she'd managed it.

She could almost hear the cogs whirling as he processed what she'd told him, almost watch the movie as he scrolled back through his memories of that night, trying to figure it out. When he finally spoke, he said sadly,

"But she didn't tell me. She made out like it was OK."

"Of course she did. She's proud. Women are proud. We don't like you to see how much you hurt us." She was taking all the anger from all the times she'd pretended not to care when Antonio cancelled her at the last minute, or changed their plans to suit his family obligations, and channelled it into her words.

"That's not how I remember it," he said defensively. "She told me I wasn't the first and definitely not the best she'd ever had." A look of hurt crept into his puppy dog eyes. She snorted with delight when she saw and heard his pain and thought, *Congratulations, Charlie. Well done, you for putting my annoying brother in his place with an average rating.*

Simon attempted to bring back some control. "It's all water under the bridge, anyway. It happened a long time ago, and I think if she was that bothered, she'd have said something—"

She cut him off again. "She wouldn't. She would never do that. She was so worried about working with you for just that reason. I had to talk her into it."

"Really?"

"Yes." And she sighed, annoyed and exhausted by the unpleasant conversation in equal measure. She'd always believed her brother was highly intelligent, but tonight might have changed her mind. "I'm not sure you know anything about women, Simon. A lot about animals. Particularly sheep. A hell of a lot about sheep. I'll give you that. But women aren't sheep, mate."

The analogy was a bit of a stretch, but she needed to get her point across before she went upstairs. She was done with this conversation and as tired as a tired thing.

"I'm off to my bed now, Simon. But before I go, I'm going to ask you to think about it again. What exactly are your intentions towards my best friend?"

CHAPTER 13

Charlie checked her reflection in the mirror and was pleased with what she saw: she looked good. Really good. The white off-one-shoulder gown was split up the front to mid-thigh and it skimmed her long slender figure perfectly. She'd shaped her thick brown hair into a loose, glossy plait that fell over her bare shoulder. Her only accessories were large gold hoops in her ears and around her wrist; and she wore a light makeup: a little bronzer and some pale pink gloss. She thought she looked a bit Grecian, but not so much so that it was 'costumey'.

The dress was an expensive one, one of the few items of clothing she had left over from her Graham days. She'd picked it out herself but he'd given it the seal of approval and had paid for it. She'd never worn it before, so it had no embedded bad memories, apart from reminding her a little bit of the toga she had worn to the fated party at the Hobsons' all those years ago.

Getting a ticket to the summer solstice ball was a big deal and she'd thought the dress would be just the thing. She wondered what everyone else would wear. Kitty had briefed her that most of the attendees would be posh: landowners, farmers and horsey types. She imagined she might see a lot of formal silk and taffeta designer ball gowns and worried a little that her dress might be too plain. Ed and Kitty wouldn't say how much the tickets had cost – but she reckoned quite a lot. Anyway, even if everyone else was wearing one, she wasn't a puffy-ball-gown type. One thing she had learnt from Graham, who to give him credit had exquisite taste, was that simple, elegant lines suited her figure best. She'd even donned a pair of delicate white sandals with a three-inch heel, rather than her usual flats. They made her even taller than usual but that wouldn't matter when she danced with Simon because he was so much taller than her. That's *if* they danced. Which was looking less likely now.

She sighed. Had she read the signs wrong again? She'd thought they'd been getting on so well, that maybe… She shook her head in frustration. Had she been imagining it? Or was she delusional? She was so bad at knowing what was going on in men's minds.

She'd hardly seen him, he'd been out on calls, and when he was at Brown's, he always seemed to be heading in the other direction to her. Worse, they hadn't walked the dogs together for days – which wasn't fair to the dogs! After such a long period not seeing his girlfriend, poor Ted was flopping around the house looking as dejected as Charlie was feeling. Trying to pretend everything was normal, she'd sent Simon a message asking if she could take Flopsy out with her, but he'd said no because his parents were on a health kick and wanted to walk her themselves!

It felt so different to last week, especially the evening they'd discussed going to the ball together. Even though nothing was explicitly said about that night being a date, the butterflies in her tummy had led her to believe he saw it as one. She'd been expecting a call all week from him to arrange the details, but it didn't come. And then, this lunchtime, Kitty told her that she and Ed would pick her up as they'd booked a taxi, 'so we can have lots of lovely drinkies'. When she'd asked about Simon, Kitty said he'd drive himself because he had some errands to run and may have to go early if they had any emergency calls!

After that disappointing little update, Charlie's first thought was to call Simon's sister and ask her opinion on her sibling's changeable behaviour, but then she realised she couldn't because Ali didn't know about what had been going on between them. She'd been too scared to tell her about her burgeoning feelings for Simon and her intuition that he might feel the same way. It was because Ali had been warning her off Simon for months now and would tell her off that she'd held off telling her anything until she had something concrete to share. Now Simon appeared to be backpedalling and the one good thing about that was that she didn't have to listen to Ali saying 'told you so'.

She'd thought about calling Marvel. Her American friend knew all about Charlie's history with Simon, (they'd discussed their previous love affairs over long sunny days by the pool in Zephyr) but Marvel had gone AWOL too, not returning her calls or messages. So instead, she called Chix, hoping that he could shed some light on such puzzling male behaviour. Ever since she'd been to see him in February they spoke regularly. She loved him as a friend, and he always sounded pleased to hear from her. Zephyr was five hours behind the UK which meant it was just after eight in the morning in the Caribbean, and he informed her he was at home enjoying his second cup of coffee of the morning on the balcony.

She pictured him, barefoot, Zen-like, cross-legged in his custom-made Adirondack chair with a coffee to hand – contemplating the incredible view from his property. She wished she could jump on a magic carpet right now – just to go see him, have a chat and come back home – she had no desire to be anywhere other than Wiltshire in the summer, however beautiful it was over there. Chix's house had a wrap round porch boasting 180-degree views over the Caribbean Sea, and depending on the weather the water could range from endless turquoise, to deepest aqua all the way through to the truest of blues – especially where the sea met the sky. It was a canvas of colour so glorious that once seen you would never forget it.

During her holiday to Zephyr in February, she and Marvel had hung out at Chix's place a couple of times. It was a beautiful home, tastefully designed to blend the correct amount of comfort with cool, but she secretly felt it was a tad too perfect and it needed a little something to warm it up.

She told Chix everything about the last few months with Simon. About the walks, the jokes and banter and how they kept finding ways to come together. She described the shared glances, the moments where he seemed on the cusp of saying something and the invite to the ball followed by an abrupt cooling down. Her friend listened and cogitated and replied in measured tones and suggested that maybe Simon was into her but that it wasn't the right time, or that something was holding him back, or perhaps he was just 'foolie'. Which made her laugh.

When she asked what he thought could be holding him back he said it was impossible to say because he didn't know the fella, but potentially – unfinished business with his ex, or something personal he had to deal with? He advised her to chill out and wait and see what came next, reminding her that Simon wasn't going anywhere. Pointing out sensibly that a) she worked with the fella, loved her job and wanted to keep it, and b) Puddlington sounded a bit like Zephyr: small. Sometimes it was good to bide your time, as a romantic mistake once made could come back to haunt you for years. She thought about it and said,

"That's what my mate Ali said when I suggested she should go for it with this friend of hers, Kris. We said it much more crudely, though. She said, 'you don't shit in your own backyard.'"

Which made Chix laugh and say he couldn't wait to meet her friend one day.

Chix gave good advice. And she needed to put it into practice. She'd let her imagination run away with her, but she hadn't forgotten how Simon made her feel before, even if she'd forgiven him now. She wasn't an infatuated teenager anymore and she wouldn't let Simon, or any man, however lovely and good with animals they were, derail her again.

She was single (through choice) and ready to mingle. And tonight, she was going to dance, drink and flirt with a handsome stranger.

CHAPTER 14

Ali's phone pinged. It was a message from Charlie. Her normally technophobic friend had finally discovered the joys of messaging in the year 2015, and had sent a picture of her dressed for the ball. The girl looked stunning. *The young farmers would shit themselves*, Ali thought glumly as she texted back a bunch of fire emojis and a short message:

> Enjoy yourself and drink irresponsibly
> Will do :)
> What time's Simon picking you up?
> I'm going with Ed and Kitty now.

She knew already the couple were supposed to be picking her up, but it was good to double check. She'd spoken to Simon earlier, ostensibly to apologise for her 'blathering on', but really to make sure he'd backed off from his silliness with Charlie; she asked him if they were still going together and he'd said no. He'd been rather chilly with her, said he didn't have time to talk because he was on call and had to do some visits before he could join the others at the ball. He finished their call with a bossy reminder to call the Parentals as they were concerned about her; but she was able to tell him she'd already called them earlier and everything was fine and dandy now. Ali texted:

> OK send me loads of pics of the outfits so I can live vicariously through you.
> Kk
> Cop off with a Wurzlemangler

Can't promise that. What are you up to?

She typed 'Nothing as usual' then changed her mind, deleted that response and put instead:

Meeting Kris. We're going out to dinner.

It was Kris's night off and they'd decided to meet up outside the bar for once.

Oh enjoy!
You too!

She pushed down the tiny, eeny weeny twinge of guilt she felt for possibly ruining Charlie's evening – she knew her friend would have preferred it if Simon was picking her up – but she sounded fine!

An hour later, Ali was sitting down to dinner with Kris and his best friends Mario and Darius at the Doukases' family restaurant, Santorini, and she was so glad she'd come. The staff, including Kris's English mum, who controlled the reservation book and his Greek dad who popped out of the kitchen to come and say hi, seemed very interested to meet her. It transpired that Kris had told them all about her, which was flattering.

Dinner was excellent, Santorini served old-school taverna favourites like gigantes plaki, saganaki, moussaka and grilled octopus: dishes that took her straight back to the Greek island holidays she'd enjoyed with Charlie in their teens and twenties. The restaurant even had the type of high-backed wooden chairs she remembered, painted bright blue with hard woven seats that left a pattern imprinted on your bum.

"Shall we have another one?" They'd just finished their second carafe of a delicious white wine from Santorini that Kris's dad imported himself.

The two others said no, they were on their way home. She looked at Kris.

"Not me, I'm driving, not stopping you, though. Or you could just have another glass."

For a moment she thought about ordering a whole carafe, anyway. It was like Kris knew what she was thinking and smiled indulgently. She decided to be sensible and go with the glass.

The couple departed with hugs and air kisses, and she was sad to see them go, knowing the evening was winding down. They'd been fantastic company – witty, educated and progressive – and she realised how much she'd missed talking to people like them. They both lived in Bristol, were a similar age to Kris, who at twenty-seven was three years older than her, Mario was a fundraiser at the Arnolfini and Darius taught; they were just great guys. She hoped they would become friends in time if she stayed in Bristol. She hadn't had such a nice, relaxing evening *forever* and it was all down to Kris.

"I really enjoyed myself this evening. Thank you."

"My pleasure, beautiful."

The restaurant was empty apart from them, but the staff were still busy, tidying up after a busy evening and setting a table for themselves to enjoy their own, well-deserved dinner.

"Can I ask you something, Ali?"

"Sure."

"Why do you drink so much?"

"I drink too much?" she said in mock outrage.

"I don't think you're an alcoholic. Don't worry about that. But do you ever think you might use alcohol too much?"

"Like how?" She was trying not to take offence because she'd had such an enjoyable time and didn't want to spoil it.

"Seems like it's your go-to when you're stressed at work, or that mysterious boyfriend of yours lets you down, or even like last weekend when you came back early from your dad's birthday celebrations."

Last weekend had been a disaster. Embarrassed by her behaviour but not ready to own it, she'd used work as an excuse and gone home instead of having the looked-forward-to lunch with the Pierces as planned. Ignoring the disappointed looks on her parents' faces, she'd slithered out after breakfast, bolted back to Bristol, worked all day and then spent the evening in the bar getting plastered.

Her distress must have shown on her face. Kris said sweetly,

"Hey you, don't be sad. You know I love the fact you're at the Blind Pig so much you have your own bar stool. Your company makes all those long nights and annoying customers bearable. But seeing you out tonight – you shone. In a way you don't there." Her eyes filled up at the compliment. Kris said the nicest things. "You looked so beautiful when you were entertaining us all with your stories, I couldn't take my eyes of you. The guys are obsessed with you too, Darius texted me, raving."

"I had a great time."

"I thought so, too, but then I could tell you wanted to order another bottle of wine."

It wasn't that she *needed* it. She'd wanted more wine so the evening wouldn't end. But she didn't say that.

"I kind of want to say 'fuck off, Kris. I can drink what I like so don't judge me'." She smiled wryly to soften the message. "But my tummy is full as a bull with the best dinner I've had for months. And as I'm in a great mood, and as I crashed your night out, I'll let you off."

"You didn't crash, you were invited." Kris seemed happy to let it drop, but she felt like she needed to explain more.

"I've always loved getting drunk, you know. It's my high of choice. Charlie and I, well, we got into drinking from an early age – and our parents bonded over booze – I think I told you that story." Kris nodded. "My parents would say, 'have a glass of wine with dinner' or 'try this gin and tonic so you don't feel like we've denied you something and you turn into an alcoholic.' Bless them!"

Kris said, "I can see the sense, in that most Europeans offer their kids wine from an early age, and they don't seem to binge drink like us Brits."

She laughed. "Clearly it didn't work on me because now they're all like 'where did we go wrong' which is rather hypocritical because the whole family drinks too much! Did I tell you Charlie and I got suspended from school when we were fifteen? For getting drunk on the school trip!"

"No. Sounds naughty."

"It was hilarious. Our parents were furious but it was worth it because Charlie and I got this kind of cult status at school. We'd never been as cool before and suddenly we were the wild ones. Maybe that's why I love it so much."

"Because it made you seem cool and you pissed off your parents?"

"Yes. It meant I didn't get to be a prefect like Simon. Well, he was head boy, of course."

"Simon's your brother, right?"

"Yep, my perfect older brother. The vet? Well, he's not perfect but he's pretty close to it. He's actually a really good bloke. Everyone likes him…" she trailed off, wondering if Simon would like Kris.

"You get on well?"

"Yes. Normally. But I'm pissed off with him now."

"Why?"

"I've told you about Charlie?"

"Once or twice," Kris said dryly.

"Oh, of course. Well anyway, last weekend I found out the two of them had been, well, they maybe like each other." It sounded childish when she put it that way.

"And that's a problem?"

"Too bloody right. It's a disaster."

"Why? Because you want Charlie for yourself?"

"Don't be silly. Because it's a stupid idea, she's going to get hurt," she said crossly, resorting to teenager tactics to stop having to answer questions she didn't have the answers too.

Kris held up both hands in surrender, familiar enough with her now to know when to press and when to stop. Wanting to change the subject, she started asking detailed questions about something he had raised earlier in the evening: his plans to open a cocktail bar and restaurant one day. It had a name already, Nu Greek and it would reimagine traditional Greek food to create a modern, elevated, stylish restaurant that would appeal to Bristol's upper echelons.

She thought it sounded fabulous, and suggested that she may be able to introduce him to an investor if required. An hour flew by. She consumed two more glasses of wine as they batted ideas around and in that time everyone else left, leaving Kris to lock up and insist on driving her home even though it was out of his way.

Pleasantly buzzed from her evening out and ensconced comfortably in the speeding car, she found herself looking at her friend in a new way. Acting with a will of its own, her hand slid over onto Kris's thigh.

"Stop that, Ali." Kris laughed.

"Why?" she said sulkily.

"You know why. I'm just going to put that naughty little hand of yours back where it can't cause any trouble."

"My self-esteem is low and you're making me feel even worse because you don't fancy me," she wailed.

"I do fancy you. You're gorgeous. But you know you're not my type, darling."

"You don't like redheads!"

"I love redheads. I just need my redheads to be men."

CHAPTER 15

Charlie had been chugging champagne at the cocktail reception and was 'having a ball' – a turn of phrase she thought was quite, quite funny considering where she was, so she kept saying it. Her giddiness and good humour was infectious and, as they sat to eat, the rest of the table joked and laughed along with her.

As promised, the solstice ball had turned out to be a very glamorous affair indeed. After passing through the imposing carved stone arch that delineated the beginning of the impressive Georgian country house, they drove for what seemed like miles. Traversing through acres of immaculately maintained grounds that boasted a championship golf course, arboretum, sculpture park and even a decorative lake complete with boats and fairytale grotto. Kitty pointed out the sites as they went. As they approached the house, Charlie gasped in pleasure. It was magical. The fountain and the whole of the front of the house had been floodlit in pink and there was an enormous bow strung across the impressive entrance – the décor indicating that all proceeds from that night were in aid of breast cancer research.

The house was famous for having one of the best collections of equestrian paintings in the world: some of the best works of art by masters like Stubbs and Reynolds to be found outside a major gallery. The mainly horsey crowd were in art heaven. There was a silent auction table and Charlie spent some time perusing the offerings and tried to imagine having enough money to bid for a private box at Ascot racecourse, dinner cooked by Gordon Ramsey, an animal portrait by David Shephard or an all-expenses trip for four to watch the Monte Carlo Grand Prix, travelling by private jet. Hundreds of thousands of pounds would be bid that evening, and Charlie thought how much Graham would love to be there, and how he would have worked himself into a frenzy trying to network.

Ed and Kitty were hosting a table of eight that consisted of the two of them, her and Simon, and two other couples who were their old school friends. Her hosts were so hard working and unassuming that Charlie never thought about how posh they were. But they were. The three older men had met at the famous Marlborough College in Wiltshire and Kitty and her two girlfriends had gone to Cheltenham Ladies, just over the border in Gloucestershire. She'd really enjoyed hearing their stories; how they'd partied together as youngsters, then headed off to various universities but had always kept in touch. Despite having had other boyfriends and girlfriends, they finally paired up to make three couples.

She loved their history. As always with old friends, the conversation was relaxed and easy, while the others, seeing her as part of Ed and Kitty's extended family, made a real effort to make her welcome – which was a good job because Simon had not.

When he'd arrived, she'd smiled and stood up from the table to give him a welcome kiss. But instead of responding with a move towards her proffered cheek, he'd just gawped at her. Gaping like a goldfish, eyes darting over her, checking her out from top to bottom. He muttered something under his breath which sounded suspiciously like 'for fuck's sake give me strength' and then, just about remembering his manners, moved away and started to greet his table mates. She sat back down watching him closely until Kitty caught her staring, so she stopped.

She was finding it hard not to look, though. Because Simon had scrubbed up really well. He looked good in his work attire of shorts or jeans and a polo shirt with the practice logo on it but tonight he'd transformed himself into Wiltshire's answer to James Bond. And the older women at the table clearly thought so too, as they were all touchy-feely and fluttery around him. She knew that he'd hired the black tuxedo, but it fitted like it had been made for him, drawing attention to his broad shoulders and long legs; the black cummerbund hugged his waist and disguised the little bit of belly he'd been cultivating recently. The sparkling white dress shirt, open at the neck, framed his strong brown throat and tanned face with its smattering of laugher lines around his grey eyes. The only thing that looked familiar was his dirty blonde hair which was as tousled as usual. He'd obviously forgotten to comb it.

That was typical Simon, she thought, so unaware of his spectacular good looks that he'd didn't even glance in the mirror before he left the house. She settled down to eat her starter.

After a delicious dinner of salmon, prime fillet with new potatoes followed by raspberry millefeuille, the DJ changed the mood of the music and the dancefloor began to fill up. Charlie who loved her music and dancing – and was pretty darn good at it even if she did say so herself –was swaying in her seat and inching to shake a leg but was not holding out much hope of it. The oldies were too busy drinking port and gossiping and she wasn't going to ask Simon.

She was delighted when a tall, dark handsome guy in his late thirties or early forties came over and after greeting Jack and Liz (the couple that lived just outside of Marlborough and who loved racing) asked to be introduced to the rest of table then asked her to dance. As she took his hand and headed to the dancefloor he told her she looked stunning, which was nice.

His name was Davide, and Liz had said was a horse trainer, 'a very good one', during her brief introduction. He was tall and elegant, quite a lot slimmer than Simon. He too looked immaculate in his tuxedo which he'd accessorised with a white cummerbund. He had deep brown eyes which seemed to smoulder when he looked at her. As he pulled her into his arms to dance to 'Dr Beat' by The Miami Sound Machine, an oldie but goody, she could smell his woody cologne even though he was holding her at a respectful distance. He had one hand on her waist, the other in a classic partner dance stance, and within seconds she could tell he had a great sense of rhythm.

"I hope this doesn't sound creepy but I've been watching you since you arrived. I couldn't tear my eyes away from you," Davide spoke softly into her ear when the music brought them closer together.

"It does sound a bit creepy." To be honest, she wasn't keen on it when men were so 'full on' with her. She preferred her men a little less smooth – especially post Graham. But she softened her words with a smile, and said, wanting to make him comfortable, "But I'm sure you're not one because a creep doesn't normally admit to being a creep."

He laughed and twirled her away from him.

"Touché." As the music changed to another song with a slower beat, he continued, "Well I knew I had an 'in' with you because Jack and Elizabeth Major are sitting on your table. But I wanted to make sure I wasn't stepping on anyone's toes first."

He must have been trying to figure out if she and Simon were a couple. Should have been pretty obvious from their body language they weren't.

"I can promise you that you have no toes to avoid – if you were referring to Simon. He's just my boss," she said sharply, then grinned up at him. "Just make sure you don't step on mine because these sandals are leaving them vulnerable."

He laughed, playing along with her. "Beautiful Charlie, I do not plan to step on your toes, I plan to sweep you off your feet," and he proceeded to tip her backwards into a professionally executed dip, that had her breathless then giggling as he pulled her back up.

She was enjoying herself. A lot. Davide was a great dancer, and fun too. They danced, laughed and chatted their way through a few songs before he asked very solicitously if she was thirsty or tired. She admitted to being parched and they decided to go back to her table and grab a drink. The others greeted them both warmly, complimenting them on their dancing skills. Simon had disappeared so Davide slipped into his seat, leant back and draped his arm on the back on Charlie's chair. The conversation bubbled and flowed as the others at the table bombarded him with questions about his work. She quickly found out that he was a highly successful horse trainer based in Lamborn and that he knew Jack and Liz quite well as they had recently taken their horses to him to train. She listened on, impressed as he talked about his business which was quite the enterprise. She learnt that he ran not only one but two yards and was one of the biggest employers in the racing village – with two vets on call. And one of his horses had placed second in the Gold

Cup at Ascot last week and he'd trained a stream of winners and high-placing horses this season.

He *was* a little arrogant, but given his success, good looks and easy charm, that was hardly surprising, and Charlie felt the tiny flicker of attraction she'd experienced on the dancefloor re-ignite when he grinned wickedly at Liz and told Jack to be on his guard because one of his head lads had a bad reputation with the ladies. She was smiling at Davide's gentle teasing of the older woman when she heard someone close by clear their throat roughly in a way that clearly meant 'get out of my seat'; she looked up to see Simon sending daggers at her and then shooting the same daggers at Davide. Her dance partner however was not a man to be cowed, even by a six-foot two, built like a heavyweight, grumpy vet; he took his own good time to rise from the table and pull back the chair, offering it to Simon with a theatrical flourish. The action made Simon's mouth tighten and his grey eyes dull to a shade as bleak and cold as the North Sea in January.

"Thanks for the use of your chair, Simon, nice to finally put a face to the name. I've heard a lot about you," Davide said as he extended his hand to meet Simon's. Superficially polite but with a knowing look in his eyes that Charlie couldn't read. By now the frosty interaction between the two men had attracted the attention of the rest of the table guests, particularly Ed and Kitty who were watching anxiously. Charlie felt an ill wind blowing.

"Davide," Simon briefly acknowledged him. "I've heard some things about you, too."

The two men were staring intently at each other. Hands locked together for longer than necessary, as if no one wanted to be the first to break his grip. She'd never seen the normally affable Simon react like this in polite company and raised an eyebrow at an enrapt Kitty, to see if she could shed any light, but Kitty just shook her head and mouthed 'later' and went back to the show.

After what seemed like a very long time, Davide was the first to break the grip, and Charlie, looking at him fresh, thought that maybe he didn't look quite as suave and sophisticated as he had earlier. But he quickly recovered and said snidely,

"How's Sandy getting on back in Australia?"

Ahh, thought Charlie, intrigued as always by the possibility of news about Simon's ex.

"Fine I believe," said Simon tightly.

"Glad to hear that. She was a good girl, very helpful, very helpful indeed." Davide responded with the same knowing look. "She put in a lot of overtime, I hear." When Simon didn't answer he carried on, "My best mate, Ben Trailor…" (Simon remained unresponsive to the name of the trainer Sandy had worked for in Lamborn.) "was surprised she left before Ascot. She really seemed to relish the riding."

Charlie heard a quick gasp from the other side of the table. Liz had put her hand on Kitty's arm and both women were looking stunned.

"I guess the job wasn't everything it was cracked up to be," Simon said eventually.

Davide grinned. "Or was it *more* than she was expecting?" Then he looked down at Charlie and, seemingly satisfied to have got the last word, grabbed her by the hand and dragged her up and away from the table, before she could protest. "Come on then, dancing queen, second round?"

Intrigued by the exchange and always happy to dance, she went with Davide, but cast a glance back to see what the others were doing. Simon had pulled up a chair close to Kitty who was talking fast into his ear. She'd love to know what she was saying but she'd get it out of her later – whatever was going on?

Seconds later they hit the dancefloor and as soon as her body started moving to the famous Abba song, she relaxed and started having fun again. She danced for a bit but curiosity got the better of her, so she leant in and asked,

"What was that all about?"

"Just that Sandy worked for one of my friends, another trainer called Ben." She made a 'so what' gesture with her face and hands. "And I used to see her out racing."

He wasn't exactly spilling the beans.

"And…" she encouraged.

"And around his stables. Now, pretty lady, why don't you stop asking so many bloody questions and dance with me?"

His tone brooked no argument, and she felt the full force of the arrogance that had been simmering under the surface. Whatever little part of her that had warmed to him turned to ash.

He may be handsome but there was something ugly about him, she decided. She'd find the right time, make her excuses and leave the dancefloor as soon as polite.

Just then the music changed, this time the DJ was playing one of her favourite anthems 'Give Me Everything' by Pitbull and Neo. Easily distracted by the banging tune, she started singing along, at the same time putting as much space between her and Davide as possible, wanting to stay on the dancefloor but not stand so close to him. The distance gave her the chance to observe him better. She watched as Davide's gaze raked up and down her body, boldly, his look appraising and lustful. The charming man from earlier had gone and now handsome, chisel jawed Davide reminded her of a horny raptor with glittering slitted eyes and rather pointy teeth. She guessed he was showing his true colours.

The music swung him towards her and, grabbing the opportunity, he moved to pull her close, the idea of which she found repulsive. She took a large step back and found her escape blocked by a solid column of human flesh. Before she could step away, strong, rough hands slid down her arms and, encircling her wrists gently, guided her backwards and, when there was space, turned her round.

She knew immediately, from the big, square hands and the familiar smell of Dove deodorant combined with a tiny whiff of Vetiver aftershave, who had grabbed her. She looked up to see Simon eyeing her ruefully. She looked pointedly at her encased wrists and he released her from the gentle hold, then said,

"I don't want to cramp your style, Charlie Girl."

She raised an eyebrow.

"But that Davide's a tosser even if he's good with horses." Then he finished under his breath, "And you deserve much better."

She was just about to give him a mouthful about how she could decide for herself and why was he behaving like a caveman by dragging her away from the dancefloor, when she saw his face contort; the side of his lip curled in an angry snarl. She followed his gaze over her shoulder and saw what he saw: Davide staring openly at her arse and nudging the guy standing next to him on the dancefloor, a tallish, stocky man with flashy good looks and a too-tight white tuxedo, to check her out too. When her erstwhile dance partner clocked her looking at him looking at her, he shrugged unapologetically, made the universal hand signal for 'call me' popularised by wankers all over the world and fist bumped his friend. Then the two of them turned on their heels and left. Charlie was disappointed to see how many smiles and admiring glances they garnered as they glad-handed their way towards the other side of the dancefloor.

Another one bites the dust, she thought, then sighed and said, "Yes, I think I have to agree with you, for once."

"Glad to assist," chirped Simon, looking rather pleased with himself, as he swayed along to the music. His face broke into his first genuine smile of the evening as the music hit its stride and he shouted, 'Grab somebody sexy' and put his hands out in a supplicating way, bent over and wiggled his bum in time to the music, tempting her to join in. "Come on, let's dance."

She sighed. The man turned as hot and cold as someone with the flu. But he looked so silly she couldn't help herself from responding to his invitation. And she, like the DJ who kept playing him, just adored Pitbull. The two of them started dancing around like maniacs, jumping and singing. Without doubt the tallest and uncool-est dancers on the floor. Charlie giggled as Simon launched himself into an ambitious spin and nearly fell flat on his face but caught himself just in time. Then the DJ segued into another huge dance anthem, and she found herself waving her arms in the air, like she just didn't care, shouting the lyrics with a silly grin on her face. The song ended and Simon, faking exhaustion, bent over and held his sides and panted out,

"Blimey Charlie Girl, that was knackering."

She put her hand out to pull him up and off the dancefloor, grinning as she said,

"Come on you lightweight, time for a glass of champers for me and nice refreshing Henry for you."

"I'd rather have a pint; I've drunk so much orange juice and lemonade tonight I might turn into a boiled sweet." He grumbled at the reminder he was driving, then let himself be led. Two steps later, Charlie heard the DJ announce something she couldn't hear and then the lights dipped, and the music changed tempo. The song the DJ had chosen to kick off the slow dance session, was one of Charlie's absolute, all-time retro favourites: the Phyliss Nelson classic, 'Move Closer'. She paused, unsure if she should bolt for the table or. . ., then felt Simon's hand twitch in hers. He pulled her to face him, executed a sweeping bow quite professionally, and said,

"Can I have the pleasure of this dance, milady?"

She looked up to his dear, familiar face and saw that it was wearing a smile that was equal parts hopeful, rueful and sad. Despite his hot and cold behaviour with her, Charlie found she was helpless to resist, powerless under the spell of her favourite song in the most beautiful setting and a man she had tried so hard not to want but still did. The silky, sexy-as-hell ballad flooded her senses. She didn't say yes but she didn't say no, and taking that as her assent, Simon pulled her in close. She curled willingly into him. Naturally her head found the perfect spot to rest on his chest. Instinctively her arms wrapped around his waist as if they did it every day. His chin was buried in her hair, she could feel his breath ruffling it and the little stubble he had on his jaw lightly chafing against it. He'd placed an arm around her waist and the other across her shoulder before pulling her in so she felt his strength and breath along the length of her. She turned her face further into him, and her senses were flooded with his scent; a warm, clean, manly smell; soap, deo, a little cologne and a lot of Simon. She could breathe him in all night.

The ballroom lights had dimmed to the deepest rose colour and the dancefloor chatter faded away so that all she could hear was the perfect song and the steady beat of his heart in his tuxedo-clad chest.

CHAPTER 16

Ali called Kris the following morning and grovelled out an apology for her inappropriate, half-hearted attempt at seduction, and thanked him for being such a trouper about it.

"Can we still be friends? I really hope so."

"Don't worry, I still love you, despite you disrespecting my boundaries."

She let out a giggle, relieved to hear it. "I can't believe we finally go out, and I have the best night I've had in ages and then I nearly ruin it."

"Don't worry. I'm flattered I'm butch enough for you," Kris said kindly, making her feel a whole lot better.

"I don't usually hit on my gay friends, but I've always loved a challenge," she joked back. "As it appears that you have forgiven me, can I take you out for breakfast to make up for it?"

Kris said that as long as Ali didn't try to get off with him again, he would be delighted to, which made her laugh a lot, and they agreed to meet at Wapping Warf, at a well-known bakery called Nice Buns for a quick sugar fix.

She wanted to know what had happened at the ball last night but she'd had no news from Puddlington. She'd messaged Charlie for an update as soon as she woke up, but the message remained unanswered. She hoped she'd had a good time and not moped over her brother. The guilt crept in again and she shook it off ruthlessly. She'd done nothing wrong. She'd just told Simon to shit or get off the pot. And left it up to him. But if she knew her brother, he'd get off the pot, otherwise he'd have to put himself out there, tell her what he wanted, and he wasn't used to that. He had a more passive approach – she snorted in disgust – all his other girlfriends had spotted him and moved in for the kill, like lionesses chasing after a tasty antelope.

Yes, Ali congratulated herself, it was much better for Charlie to start over with someone new. And she would try to be a better friend, make up for being a bit distant recently. Think of something fun they could do together or plan a night away somewhere.

The colourful, multi-purpose container village was bustling with attractive millennials enjoying the weak, British sunshine in search of a coffee, food or gift fix. Looking around, taking in the vibrant scene, she decided she quite liked Bristol today and felt a trill of hope for the first time in months. Everything was going to be OK. Charlie was safe from Simon, and she had a breakfast date with a friend.

After they settled down to enjoy flat whites (the closest she'd found to a café con leche in the UK) and, according to Kris, the best cinnamon rolls in Bristol, Kris started pumping her for information about her love life.

"Since we are now intimately connected, don't you think it's time you tell me what's going on with this guy of yours? I mean if you're coming on to me, there must be something wrong."

She guffawed. He was right. She loved the fact that he felt comfortable enough to tease her about the faux pas last night already.

"You're just so hot I couldn't help myself," she teased back, then said in a more serious tone, "I think that's why I did it. I'm very frustrated at the moment."

"Who is he? You're so secretive about him. Or is it her?"

"He's a he, but I can't really talk about him. I promised," she said, willing him to understand.

"Is it something to do with work? You lawyers have rules about that sort of stuff, I guess."

She looked at her coffee, and said nothing, trying to convey with her body language that he should change the subject. It was normal for friends to ask about each other's love lives and keeping this secret was a burden she was finding increasingly harder to bear. It was one reason why she'd found it so hard to be around people these days. She felt the urge to cry. How pathetic. Kris noticed the incipient signs of tears and reached over to pat her hand.

"Its OK. No pressure, Ali. I guess you'll tell me when you can." Then he said in a teasing tone, kindly changing the subject, "Anyway, I always prefer to talk about myself when I'm with a beautiful woman. It's the most heterosexual thing about me." She looked up and laughed. Kris was a trip. "Did I tell you about the time Darius and I went to Mykonos and met a diva?" She shook her head. "No? Well, It was just before he met Mario and settled down." He sighed. "It was an amazing trip, we met this big group of gorgeous Italian boys and girls at the nude beach and hung out with them all week."

She raised her eyebrow at him. "Nude beach. How naughty."

"Nudity is tame in comparison to some of the things that go on there. Beach bonks, hand jobs on lilos, pool parties – you wouldn't believe your eyes and the sunset sessions…"

Ali's eyes widened in shocked pleasure. She was seeing a different, more risqué side of Kris and she loved it.

"Mykonos sounds like a lot of fun." She thought she and Charlie should go. Then she remembered Antonio and how much he would hate it if she did that – he got so jealous – it was food for thought.

"It is. And straight girls like you have the best time there."

"Really?"

"Because lots of gorgeous guys working in the resorts and bars aren't gay – so you can have your pick really." He put his clasped hands up to his heart in a gesture of pride. "Love my big fat Greek heritage! Anyway, not to be distracted, Darius and I are at this fabulous club. We'd been told it was owned by Ambrosia – you know her?"

"*The* Ambrosia? The original diva!"

"Yes! And it was rumoured that on the rare occasion she was in the mood to do it, she would make a guest appearance, so there we are…"

For the next forty minutes Kris entertained her with stories about the good times he'd had on the magical Cycladic island. Totally engrossed in the five-star gossip, Ali didn't think about Antonio or Charlie or the pile of work that had been growing steadily every hour she hadn't been working on it.

As soon as Kris left for work though, she felt her spirits sink. She checked her phone to see if anyone had messaged or called her and when she saw no one had been in contact, she had to stop herself from jumping up and following him to the Blind Pig. Even though she was desperate for company, she was determined she would not spend all day indoors drinking vodka and tapping on her laptop.

The Arnolfini Gallery was only a short walk away and, as Mario had mentioned the current exhibition was interesting, she decided to go take a look. The Arnolfini was packed with earnest looking people commenting eruditely on the artwork, which consisted mainly of photos of piles of stones placed in long lines in the countryside surrounding Bristol. She tried to find something to like in the exhibition but concluded that contemporary art was not her thing. Far too conceptual.

She analysed her feelings about the art she'd seen and liked at the Prado and decided she liked art to be recognisable: either a moment in history, or a landscape, or a person who she could imagine talking to. She left the gallery at a loose end as to what to do next. She wasn't hungry or thirsty yet, so she sat on one of the benches that lined the waterfront, got out her phone and even though she knew she shouldn't, messaged Antonio in the code they had agreed for out-of-work communications.

> Sorry to interrupt your weekend but the Pelirroja client has some contractual issues and wants you to attend a meeting in Bristol next week. Do you have any availability? Just wanted to bring this to your attention ASAP.

She watched the two black ticks by the side of the WhatsApp message turn blue. He'd read it. She held her breath hopefully when she saw the word 'typing…' appear – then disappear. The word 'typing…' didn't reappear, but she still waited. Nothing came. A few minutes later she stood up and trudged back to her apartment, opened an expensive bottle of Rioja and then worked until the early hours, uninterrupted by calls or messages from anyone.

CHAPTER 17

The morning after the summer solstice ball, Charlie woke to find two messages waiting for her. One from Ali asking about the ball, which felt she couldn't do justice to in a text so would call her about instead. The other, more intriguing one was from Simon.

>We need to talk. I'll grab Flopsy and come for you at 10.00

What does he want to talk about? she wondered. *Our dance?* It almost felt like it hadn't happened. Looking back the whole evening had taken on a dream-like quality. The beautiful venue, the freely flowing champagne, meeting Davide, dancing with him and enjoying it until he became someone awful, Simon's rescue and then their brief but incredibly sweet moment together on the dancefloor before Kitty interrupted them and Simon rushed off to a farm on the Wiltshire downs to try to save the life of a prize cow who'd suffered through a breech birth. Not the most romantic end of night scenarios but par for the course for her.

"What does 'We need to talk' mean, Teddy Bear?" she whispered in his whiskery ear; he didn't offer up any words of wisdom, but he was the best listener. Her fur baby had snuck into bed last night although he wasn't supposed to; she had let him sleep the night with her, wanting the easy comfort. She'd spooned his solid little body murmuring sweet nothings before she fell into a fitful sleep from which she woke in a panic, from a horrid, horrid dream. Nightmare, more like, in which Ali, dressed in a Britney Spears-style school uniform, of all things, was hanging out with a bunch of mean girls in what looked like the *Twilight* movie school canteen. Ali was making her feel bad about joining the group and being sarcastic every time she said something. Then Simon appeared, wearing a black outfit that looked like a cross between a toga and a superman costume, looking handsome but cruel, and started telling her, over and over again that 'it was just a bit of fun, Charlie Girl' meanwhile Ali and all the mean girls were laughing at her. It was awful. She'd needed to have a big glass of water and listen to some music before she could go back to sleep.

She shuddered recalling it and shook her head trying to shake the memory away, then slowly got out of bed and started dragging some clothes on, all the time thinking about what she had overheard on the drive home.

The doorbell rang and she made her way down the stairs carefully, negotiating Ted who was charging down to the bottom then hurtling back up again, on repeat, unable to contain his excitement. She reached for his lead, sighed and paused, reluctant to open the door and face Simon yet. Angered by her delay, Ted started making little growly yips to speed her along.

She didn't know which Simon she was going to find waiting for her. "One minute he's hot, the next he's not," she said under her breath, then opened the door and stepped out into the morning sun.

*

Simon hadn't said a word to her yet. The only soundtrack to their walk was the beat of their feet swishing through the long grass the covered the bridle way, punctuated by the pants and puffs of two over excited dogs diving in and out of the hedges and frolicking under the giant oak trees that lined the route to the old iron bridge.

Simon was giving off a weird energy, like he was scared or nervous of her. He'd look over occasionally and grimace, as if he was about to tell her off about something – then not say anything. It was disconcerting. Fed up from being pulled out of the house before breakfast she was determined not to be the one to break the silence. He was the one who'd been behaving weirdly for the last week.

The atmosphere between them was so different from the last time they'd walked this route. Back then they chatted companionably about all sorts of things – moving from one topic to another effortlessly: the Radio Wiltshire debacle, the Alpacas that had taken up residence at a nearby farm and agreeing that the South American beasts just didn't look right in their Wilshire surroundings, their plans to play golf that evening.

The dogs raced further away from them as they got closer to the village's trickle of a river and the simple iron footbridge that spanned it. Bashing tunnels through the grass with their sturdy bodies as it got longer and longer closer to water, they caught up with them a few minutes later. Only then, as they stood on the top of the bridge, looking down at the dogs dashing in and out of the stream, did Simon deign to speak – clearing his throat he said in a strained voice,

"Charlie Girl, I have something to ask you."

"About bloody time! You were the one who said you wanted to talk and then proceeded to ignore me." She was fed up with him and was damned if she'd pull any punches.

He started pacing back and forth across the bridge like he was agitated. She leant back against the railing, crossed her ankles and her arms, and observed his jerky movements with interest, even though she was impatient for him to get to the point of this little adventure. In contrast to last night's elegant appearance, today he was scruffily dressed in his casual summer attire. He was wearing battered Blundstones and short red Aussie Rules football shorts replete with bleach spots, which hugged his buttocks tighter than his ex-girlfriend, and showed lots of tanned, muscular thigh. She could see that fascinating little band of white winking in the sunshine as he paced. His shorts, the 'red devils' as he affectionately referred to them, were shorter than the average shorts. His top half was covered with a tight, black, ribbed-cotton vest, which clung to his v-shaped torso and allowed a peek of curling dark blonde chest hair. He was repeatedly running his hands through his hair, causing it to curl wildly.

It was so frustrating that he looked just as good in this ugly get-up as he did in a tuxedo. And, as usual, he was completely oblivious to his appearance, which considering the effect it was having on her pulse, would likely set many other maidens' hearts beating wildly. She hated how much she still fancied him, and how much others did too. *He'd be the winning bachelor in one of those farmer-wants-a-wife reality TV shows in that get-up*, she thought glumly.

Unable to stand the silence anymore, she cleared her throat and was just about to say something snarky about wearing a hole in the ground, when he stopped, glared at her, put his hand up in warning and said sternly,

"Please don't interrupt."

"I didn't say anything. But go on, then."

"Thing is, I had a bit of an 'aha' moment last week and I've been trying to figure out the best way to tell you, actually, ask you something."

"I'm listening." Matching his serious tone. Intrigued despite her annoyance with him – presumably he was about to shed light on his erratic behaviour.

"We've been spending a lot of time together, working, of course, and outside of work too, and, well, I've noticed that, well, that despite us being together all the time you don't get on my nerves. Like Sandy did. And even though I have to tell you what to do with the horses…"

She nearly swallowed her tongue in amusement and said, "Tell *me* what to do? You're delusional. It's the other way round, matey—"

"Shussh, Charlie Girl, let me finish." Then he muttered under his breath, "Even if my sister won't like it."

He was weirding her out. Charlie's body tensed like a rabbit that sensed it had been spotted by a dog. She could tell Simon was about to say something unwelcome. There was a longish pause as he scratched his head and looked at her awkwardly, before he cleared his throat and spoke.

"The thing is, I know that back in the day, when we had that thing and, well, we… well, you know?"

She'd been right. She had no desire to hear this. She felt her stomach lurch. Of course she bloody knew. She hadn't forgotten just because they never talked about it. A wave of tingly embarrassment overwhelmed her, the expression of which must have alarmed him as it showed on her face.

"Which, don't get me wrong, I remember fondly. Really fondly."

Fondly? she thought, even more mortified. Fondly! You think of your aunt or a deceased pet fondly. Unaware of his awful choice of words, he pushed on, using the same matter-of-fact tone of voice he might use to update Ed on a tricky patient.

"I know now that it meant a lot more to *you* than you let on at the time." His head moved to one side, smiling at her encouragingly like he wanted to reassure her it was safe to confirm what he'd just said.

She turned away from him, and picked up a twig then threw it into the stream below for the dogs to retrieve so he couldn't see her face and read her mortification. *Why was he suddenly bringing that up? And how on earth did he know how she'd felt when he rejected her?* She'd thought she'd successfully hidden her feelings back then. That's how she'd been able work alongside him like an equal, not some sad sack, heartsick ex who was still yearning for him.

Not getting a reaction from her, he expanded on his theme, making her feel even worse.

"Which was hardly surprising, I mean, I was a bit of a catch, being a bit older, at university, while you were still at school. It's perfectly normal that you had a little crush on me…"

She turned back to face him to find him smiling at her in what she imagined he thought was an affectionate and teasing way. She felt an almost overpowering desire to slap the smugness off his handsome face. How could he joke about something so important to her! Patronising git!

He cleared his throat before he continued, looking at her seriously and putting on a rather silly faux-official voice to match his expression, "What I'm trying to say is that I look at you quite differently now and, despite you working for me and being my little sister's best friend, I think…"

"What's this about Simon? Get to the point." She rolled her eyes at him, pretending boredom, trying to hide the fact that she just wanted this humiliating conversation over and done with. She flashed a look at his face which was flushed with some emotion she couldn't read, he smiled weakly at her before she looked away again.

"We have fun together, you're brilliant with the animals – despite your lack of training. And unlike Sandy, you understand that I need to work all hours and come home covered in shit," he joked weakly. Something was beginning to dawn on her, it appeared that Simon, in a very clumsy way was proposing something. "And you're also a pretty decent golfer and next season I thought I'd get you a season ticket, too, so we could watch Bristol together."

Words delivered, he bent down and ruffled the dogs' fur before looking up at her hopefully. Her hardened heart melted for a moment at the look in his soft grey eyes, then, as the reality of his words hit home, turned to set concrete. This weird proclamation of his – where he'd told her he liked her despite the fact she was just a secretary and his sister's annoying little friend – was him getting round to asking her out, and he thought, because he was such a superior being and she'd adored him for so long she'd just say yes!

"Simon, I'm going to stop you there," *before you embarrass us any more*, she thought, but he wouldn't be stopped.

He stepped towards her as if he was going to take her in his arms for a clinch. She stepped back abruptly – keeping a good distance between them. He laughed, assuming she was teasing him, and moved towards her again and she stepped away again in an awkward dance. She didn't want him to get close enough to touch her. He didn't seem to care about her reluctance, and laughed self-depreciatingly.

"This isn't easy, you know. Talking to you about this. Which is weird because I normally find it easy to talk to you," and then, said in a rush, "so I think it's time to take it up a notch. Instead of us just being mates, I think we should add some 'benefits'. What do you think, Charlie Girl?" He looked at her expectantly with a shy smile playing around his gorgeous lips.

"You want us to be mates with benefits?" she asked, needing him to clarify the outrageous thing he'd said. Apparently Simon bloody Hobson thought he was such a bloody catch he didn't need to ask her to be his girlfriend to get her into bed.

"Yes," he said decisively, seemingly oblivious of how crass and insulting his suggestion had been, then he beamed at her. "We both have an itch that needs to be scratched. I don't want anyone else to scratch mine and I don't want you scratching anyone else's. Especially not that creep Davide."

She watched him in stunned disbelief. "You're asking me to be your scratcher?"

He nodded happily, looking more relaxed now he'd had his say – completely oblivious to how badly their conversation had gone in her eyes. "It makes sense. I mean, I catch you looking at me."

"You what?" Arrogant bugger. Only occasionally! When he had his shirt off. Or was being cute with a kitten. "More like *you* look at me. All the time," she snapped. She couldn't believe the cheek of him.

He was enjoying himself now, pleased to have made his pitch and ready to seal the deal, imagining he was on the home stretch straight into her knickers. He stepped towards her again, seemingly intent on kissing her, but she pulled away from him again. Still smiling, but less confidently now, he said,

"Charlie Girl, don't be shy now. We know each other too well." She wasn't so sure about that. Something seemed to occur to him. "By the way, you looked great last night. All those Lamborn arseholes fancied you in that dress." She noticed that his light eyes had turned dark and stormy as he growled out, "What's important is that *I* fancy you when you're mucking out the horses and taking the dogs for a walk. I even fancy you when you wear those scabby old cutoffs and your rescue dog tee-shirt. Which, by the way I suggest you chuck. Those holey armpits – not a good look."

"You have the cheek to criticise my wardrobe when you're wearing those ridiculous shorts?" she scoffed.

"What's wrong with them? I love my red devils." He looked completely puzzled.

"They're rank, and I noticed you only started wearing them after Sandy left, so I guess she thought they were rank, too."

A look of frustration flitted across his face, he didn't look quite as cocky now. "Look I don't want to discuss her now. I want to talk about us." Undeterred by her lack of response he carried on, "I think we should take it slow. We don't need to tell anyone just yet, don't want to upset the applecart at Brown's and it's probably best we don't mention it to Ali or our parents yet, until… what? What's wrong?"

"Are you asking me out?" she asked in a wondering way.

He looked at her like she was from another planet. "Yes. Of course. Didn't I make my intentions clear?"

"Yes. I suppose you did," she answered as her insides curled in disappointment. Simon had made her an offer she could never accept. He'd finally asked her out and admitted he wanted to be with her, but only if they kept it quiet.

Charlie knew if she said yes to Simon now, all she'd ever be to him was a friend with benefits. A mate he dated, an obliging female sidekick who'd let him watch endless rugby, make his cuppa how he liked it and share in the mucking out. He hadn't said one thing about how she made *him* feel. What made *her* special. What he loved about *her*. His only plan for their future together appeared to be the purchase of a joint season ticket.

She bent down to scratch the dogs' heads, needing to think, buying herself time, aware he had gone quiet on her and would be wondering what she was up to. She'd short changed herself before. She'd married Graham for all the wrong reasons, biggest of which was lack of faith in herself. But she'd grown some lady balls since then.

Loving and being excellent at her job had boosted her self-confidence. Dating a man like Ryan had shown her how important it was to be courted sweetly and honestly. She'd experienced first hand how nurturing it was to be treated like the most precious thing in the world, even if it was by a man who would never make her feel the way she did about Simon. And it was because of just how much she felt for him that she could never, ever settle for the jokey, half-arsed sexual arrangement Simon was suggesting.

CHAPTER 18

It was three days before Charlie called her about the solstice ball. She blamed the hangover from hell on the Sunday followed by two brutally busy days at Brown's.

Ali, who had been in a work fog herself, still hadn't received a response from Antonio. She was trying hard not to be upset that the two people she loved to hear from most couldn't find a moment to contact her. Even though she was peeved with Charlie, she perked up when she saw she was calling, closed her document, logged her hours, shut down the computer and flopped onto the sofa to give her friend her full attention as she gushed about the summer solstice ball.

"So in summary, I've waited three days to hear it was a fairytale setting, you drank oodles of champagne, enjoyed your time with the oldies, danced with a hottie from Lamborn who turned out to be a prick, danced some more until sober Simon had to rush off to save a cow and a good time was had by all?"

Charlie snorted. "Yes. But the most interesting thing about that night was Simon's run in with the Lamborn hottie and what I discovered about Sandy on the way home."

"Oh. Now we're getting somewhere. Do tell."

"I sat in the front seat on our way back to Puddlington so Kitty and Ed could snuggle in the back and I was exhausted from all the dancing so I zoned out for a bit, but when I came to, those two were chattering away about Simon." She sounded a bit guilty. "I'm not sure they knew I could hear them.

I think they were trying to be discreet, but you know how that goes, Kitty has a voice like a posh fog horn when she's tipsy."

"Very much so."

"They were discussing the moment when Davide came to our table. He asked how Sandy was and made some comment about her getting 'lots of overtime' at the stables in a very suggestive way. There had been this sort of strained hush around the table, then he asked me to dance and I sort of forgot about it. Of course, Ed being Ed had noticed none of this, but Kitty, ever on the lookout for gossip, had picked up on it and, as her friend Elizabeth is part of that Lamborn set, asked her what was going on. "Turns out Davide is best friends with Ben Trailor, Sandy's ex-boss, and his comments to Simon were an unsubtle dig about a scandal that had titillated the racing fraternity for a few months. According to local gossip, Sandy and Ben had a hot and heavy affair. She'd been spotted emerging from the stables with straw in her hair and him on her heel, on more than one occasion."

Ali, gasped in excitement. "Oh. Juicy scandal! Love it." And with phone tucked under her chin, she walked to the kitchen, reached into the fridge and found herself a nice cold Estrella. She needed refreshment before she heard any more. "I *knew* she was a bad 'un. Go on, then."

"Because the two of them were making the beast with two backs, Sandy had wangled trips to attend all the most prestigious race meets – a real treat that, as the newest practice secretary she would not normally be invited and that made her very unpopular with everyone at work, although I remember Simon talking about her going to the races and he didn't seem to mind at all."

"Grateful to be rid of her, I expect."

"Anyway, the reason Jack and Elizabeth, who were not part of the core racing community or big gossips, had only just heard the rumours."

"And how did they find out?"

"Apparently Davide's jockey, the one who usually rides Jack and Elizabeth's horses, is a gregarious Irish chap called Jack who loves to gossip. And over drinks he regaled them with tales of a sex-mad secretary from Australia, who thought she was hot shit but wasn't, and who had rubbed everyone's noses the wrong way by having an affair with her boss."

That makes two of us, thought Ali, feeling both guilt and shame that she had something in common with the awful antipodean. It wouldn't stop her from gossiping about her with Charlie though. She took a swig of beer to settle her stomach and said,

"Very bold of her. Didn't she realise the racing community is tiny and Simon might find out?"

"I don't think she cared because I think she'd set her sights on him."

"I think you might be right," Ali said, "I remember that she went on and on about what a big deal working with Ben was last Christmas day. Then she'd rushed off the following morning to go to a Boxing Day meet. Leaving Simon at home. Not that anyone minded. We played Trivial Pursuit with Baileys shots. I won, of course."

"I remember, you came to the pub that night for our annual Boxing Day drinks already shredded."

"Funny she never mentioned old Benny boy had just got divorced."

"Funny that. Anyway, according to the Jack fellow, Sandy was not the only one bonking Ben, I told you I saw him, right?"

"Remind me."

"He was the one that was hanging out with Davide, looking creepy."

"Ok yes. The arse watcher."

"Well, apparently, he's a randy thing, having lots of affairs with a steady stream of owners, riders and stable girls, who are all hoping to be the next Mrs Trailor and Sandy didn't stand a chance. So when she pushed for more than the occasional roll in the hay, he gave her the push," Charlie said with relish, sounding spiteful for once.

"And she said she'd left of her own choice."

"Of course. And then went and put pressure on Simon to marry her, and the rest, as we know, is history."

"He's well out of it."

"He is." Charlie's voice broke for a second. "He told me he was happy they split up, and that he's ready to move on. But it's bound to hurt his pride." Ali could hear the slightly wistful tone in her friend's voice but was damned if she'd pursue any line of questioning on Simon's romantic aspirations.

For a moment, she felt sorry for her brother. It was awful being cheated on. She felt cheated on. It wasn't logical – she was the other woman, but she felt like Antonio was cheating on her when he went to Mallorca. Her heart hardened against Simon when she thought how he must have been lusting after Charlie while he was still with Sandy. The two of them were as bad as each other.

She and Charlie talked for another half an hour, mostly digging into the minutiae of the duplicitous Sandy's bad behaviour – united over a common enemy. When she hung up, after making plans to meet up in two weeks' time, Ali felt happy that their conversation felt normal and things between them were back on track.

Antonio had asked her to remain quiet, so she would, and she hadn't told her about Kris, either. But then Charlie hadn't asked *her* how her Saturday night had turned out. They didn't have to share everything, she reasoned, to remain friends.

PART THREE

Azul Verdadero

SEPTEMBER 2015
MALLORCA, SPAIN

CHAPTER 19

Charlie looked across the iridescent swimming pool at the gin palaces moored in the marina, and then turned her gaze towards Palma's magnificent cathedral. What a sight! It was so exciting that Ali had got a massive bonus and decided to treat them both to a two-week holiday in Mallorca to celebrate. She welcomed the relaxation and the distraction and the chance to spend quality time with her friend.

The fateful summer solstice ball was months ago. She and Simon had muddled along since his embarrassing proposal on the iron bridge, which she'd turned down as kindly as she could. He was a bit awkward around her but always behaved professionally. She missed their easy intimacy, but it helped that they'd all been incredibly busy, so she didn't see that much of him. The veterinary practice was booming, and Simon was out on calls all the time which meant that Ed was doing most of the clinic work. She'd been doing all their secretarial and office work, as well as managing a rollercoaster of comings and goings at the other enterprises. She was more than ready for a break.

Kitty's Kennels had been packed to bursting with guests all summer long. SPuRS was attracting record numbers of visitors because Gloria was Facebook mad and had set up a page for the sanctuary which had gone viral. Bumble and Bee were social media celebrities and the volunteers had sold every bit of small pony merchandise they had in stock to the besotted visitors and had to order more. Charlie had fielded so many enquiries from people wanting tours she'd had to put a booking system in place. Luckily some of the village kids, home from uni for the holiday, who love walking dogs and grooming the ponies and could occasionally be persuaded to muck out for a pittance, were helping out. But even though she had extra hands, she dropped into bed exhausted most nights.

Things had just begun to slow down when Chix paid a flying visit to Puddlington. It had been a spur-of-the-moment decision on her Caribbean friend's part and a nice distraction for her. The limited time she'd been able to spend with him (because Simon said they were still too busy for her to take a day off) had been fun. Chix had loved the village and staying at the Lamb. Because she had to work, she took him in to Brown's where he charmed everyone *apart* from Simon who was out on call all day when he didn't strictly need to be, giving the distinct impression he had gone out of his way to avoid meeting Chix.

And then, shortly after Chix left, she found out that Simon had gone to Australia! It was a tremendous shock as he'd failed to mention it to anyone other than Ed. Poor old Ed, who had to cover Simon's work with the help of a locum, had offered up an unconvincing story about a last-minute invitation to go on a cricket tour with some of his Aussie mates. She didn't believe a word of it. She was convinced it had something to do with Sandy, and she felt ever more grateful she hadn't entertained his half-hearted offer.

She inhaled deeply and exhaled slowly a few times, willing thoughts of Simon's annoying behaviour to disperse and disappear. She was on holiday! She would be wholly present here in Mallorca! She would enjoy every relaxing moment in these beautiful surroundings! She would not allow herself to be distracted by thoughts about bloody Simon and whatever stupidness he was getting up to.

She took a gulp of her *caña*, a delicious icy draft beer that tasted so much better than its British equivalent – a half of lager – and said a mantra in her mind: *Simon is a man-child emotionally, but I respect him professionally.* She'd resolved to continue working with him; maintaining a polite professional friendship should be possible. But no sooner thought, her traitorous mind was hoping he'd landed back in the UK safely – Flight Tracker was a terrible temptation – he'd be home now and she wondered if he'd checked to see if the animals were all well.

A cloud passed over the sun and suddenly the rich blue of the Mediterranean Sea darkened to a deep greyish navy and she felt a chill creep over her sun-warmed skin. It was late afternoon, and as the sun dropped, the shade advanced, creeping over the sunbeds that ringed the tempting infinity pool. Inching its way towards her gorgeously freckled, green bikinied, redheaded, yet nicely tanned, best friend. Ali was sound asleep, making gentle snorts and adorable little whimpering noises.

She loved her, she really did, but something had changed between them, and their relationship was showing more cracks and tears than her dad's favourite leather armchair. They'd made an effort to talk more this summer and had bonded over the Sandy gossip and Chix's visit. But then they'd ended up having an argument on the evening she'd taken Chix to Bristol. Ali had been in top form and the three of them had been enjoying a wonderful time, until Ali got a text from work and ran off to do something or other urgent. Charlie, disappointed in her and too tipsy not to speak up, had told her not to go, but Ali, who was wasted, wouldn't be reasoned with and snapped her head off in front of Chix, which had been embarrassing.

Angry with her, and unwilling to be the one to reach out, meant they hadn't spoken for a few days – until Ali called and apologised for spoiling their evening. She blamed work and offered to make it up to her by treating her to a holiday. True to her word, Ali had booked and paid for the swanky hotel they were staying at in Palma de Mallorca. All Charlie had been expected to do was get the time off work and buy her own plane ticket; and then when they got to the airport, Ali upgraded them both, anyway! The hotel was lush, much posher than where they'd normally stay, but as it was the first proper holiday poor Ali had allowed herself in two years, she said she wanted to push the boat out. When she'd expressed concern about the price, Ali had shrugged and said that she'd got a 'humongous bonus' recently and she could afford it.

Charlie looked at her slumbering friend. She'd drunk tonnes of champers in the first-class lounge, while carrying on answering emails from work. When they got to the hotel, she stopped working for a bit but started guzzling white wine. After their long lunch at the poolside restaurant, she promptly conked out – leaving Charlie alone with her thoughts and a banging Balearic-inspired play list.

What was clear to her was that Ali was exhausted and overworked; but there was something else wrong, too, that she couldn't figure out. Ali was drinking more than normal which was to be expected on the first day of their holiday, but her drinking seemed to be making her hyper rather than mellowing her out. Charlie had hardly touched a drop of the second bottle they ordered at lunchtime, wanting to pace herself for this evening, but Ali had finished it off without a problem, calling her a wimp.

There was something different about her, something not quite right, and Charlie was determined to get to the bottom of it this evening – by hook or by crook.

CHAPTER 20

Something incredibly irritating, a fly or a mosquito was bothering her, dragging her out of a lovely deep sleep. Ali moaned and flapped at it only to find a human hand touching her instead of the anticipated insect. Charlie was tickling her side tummy, the roll of fat that squished up and out the side of her too-small-but-who-cared-anyway bikini bottoms.

Ali winced in pain. Her neck hurt because she'd slept with it twisted to one side. Hot and disorientated she slowly raised up onto her forearms, trying to ease the cricks out.

"I feel like shit." She really did. Her mouth was dry, and her head was pounding, and she needed a drink badly. The bottle of mineral water on the table between them was empty, so she grabbed what remained of Charlie's water and gulped that down, then glared blearily at her friend, further annoyed by the highly amused expression on her face. She growled at her, but Charlie was not to be intimidated and said chirpily,

"You've got towel imprints on your face."

"Thanks."

"And your hair is all flat and sticking to your head on one side."

"Kind of you to tell me. I'm a goddess then." And she slumped her head back down, avoiding looking at her. Charlie wasn't to be put off.

"Don't be grumpy. You're always a goddess. In my eyes, anyway."

"Hmmm," Ali harrumphed into the towel, irritated by the compliment. Even with her face buried, she knew her friend was looking at her with affection. She could almost feel it burning into the back of her curly hair. Ali didn't deserve it. Having Charlie on her side used to give her peace of mind. But these days it just made her feel guilty, and she hated feeling guilty, so she'd rather feel annoyed.

She sighed. She should have fessed up about Antonio before she'd dragged her along for this holiday – but she hadn't. Anyway, she reasoned, Charlie still hadn't said anything about her romantic dalliance with Simon. This trip was the perfect example of how little deceptions had wormed their way in between them: Charlie thought Ali was treating her to a lovely holiday so they could bond, but she had another bird to kill – if she could find him.

Charlie was muttering something about not being able to hold it any longer. Ali struggled to sit up as her friend uncurled her long slender form effortlessly off the sun bed to go to the loo. She scanned the now almost empty pool deck for the young woman who'd been looking after them. Catching her eye and encouraging her over, she ordered a couple of *cañas* and one of the delicious coca Mallorquina flatbreads they'd had at lunchtime – a snack to tide them over before dinner. She enjoyed any opportunity to flex her Spanish language muscle, and chatted with the girl for a while in Castellano before she headed off to get their stuff.

The sun was now low enough on the horizon to burn her retinas, so she closed her eyes and tried to figure out her plan of attack for this evening. She'd called Antonio's office on a work excuse earlier and found out that, as anticipated, he was on a plane to Mallorca as she spoke. One of her old colleagues filled her in on the latest office gossip, then, when she casually asked about everyone's plans, went on to say that the lucky bastard was taking another week off and would be out of contact as he was on his boat making the most of the late summer weather. 'Another week off' rankled, particularly as he'd repeatedly told her he was too busy to meet up with her for any extended amount of time this summer.

Ali looked over the pool and out at sea, idly checking out the masts of the yachts in front of her, wondering which one was his. She'd selected this hotel, which was owned by her client Sebastián de la Cruz, because she knew it overlooked the marina where Antonio kept his sailing yacht, *Azul Verdadero*.

Ali really, really liked Sebastián, he was a true gentleman, a pleasure to work with and, for a man who had been born into immeasurable wealth, was surprisingly down to earth and grateful for her work, even though she was a junior member of the team. As soon as she'd told him she was thinking of visiting Palma with her friend, he had offered to comp her stay, but she couldn't accept that. She felt like she had to book one of the best rooms at the hotel, so he couldn't 'accidentally' upgrade her. Because that was the sort of thing he'd do. She could afford it as she'd spent so much time on her job she'd hardly touched her generous salary or her recent bonus.

"So, my lover, what are you smiling about?"

"Just a work thing. I was actually thinking about my client."

"Sebastián, the one that owns this place?" Charlie was back and looking at her expectantly over the top of her beer.

She nodded.

"Are you sure he isn't a possible…?"

"No! He's a client!" she said firmly, brooking no argument.

"Alright. But he sounds lovely. Did you get any reccos from him? Have you decided where we're going tonight?"

She nodded. He had indeed recommended a veritable plethora of wonderful places to eat. Including the Michelin-starred restaurant in their own hotel. She was grateful for his wisdom, but tonight she was going to eschew his selection in favour of a restaurant he'd probably describe as 'average' at best and a tourist trap at worst.

"Yep, he did, and we're going to one on the marina that looks good," she said confidently as she wasn't exactly lying, because he *had* given her a list. She just wasn't going to take Charlie to any of the restaurants on it. At least not tonight. I will not feel guilty, she reasoned with herself. The place she'd selected would be fun! It had a DJ from ten and a wonderful view of boats on anchor. "I thought we could head down to the Paseo Maritimo…"

"Oh, I love it when you speak Spanish," Charlie squeaked, overly enthusiastic at Ali's easy pronunciation of the name. Ali couldn't help but grin.

"Down girl! Well, let's finish up here, then, get tarted up and have a wander round the marina before we eat," then added, mischievously, "*he hecho una reserva para dos a las diez.*"

Charlie looked puzzled. "What does that mean?"

"I've booked a table for two at ten."

Charlies eyebrows shot up.

"Ten?"

"I know – a bit late for you, my country cousin, but that was the earliest they would take a dinner reservation. Viva España!"

CHAPTER 21

So far, their 'amazing' girlfriend getaway had failed to live up to Charlie's expectations. The evening had started OK. They'd finished up at the pool and retired to their amazing suite (they had a room and bathroom apiece as well as a communal lounge-dining area and a huge balcony, too), where Ali shrugged off her sluggish behaviour and ransacked the complementary mini bar, quipping that it'd be better described as a 'maxi bar' as it featured full-sized bottles of every premium spirit and enticing mixer known to mankind, as well as 'real' champagne.

She'd freshened up quickly, changed into her favourite crisp, white cotton, belted shirt dress with gold accessories and dancing flats and was waiting for Ali on the balcony – rehydrating with a glass of sparkling water and enjoying the lavender-scented evening air – when her friend finally emerged from her room.

She let out a small gasp of pleasure at her appearance. Ali had taken a lot of time to get ready, but she was worth the wait because she looked stunning! She was wearing a turquoise jersey sheath dress with a deep v-neck that clung to her curvy figure and really accentuated her most notable features – a tiny waist and large high bottom. The turquoise set off her curly red hair and lightly tanned skin to perfection and Charlie wolf whistled in appreciation.

"Wowser."

Ali's grey eyes, the exact same colour as Simon's, glittered. Her expression was almost triumphant, like she'd just beaten the opposition to a gold medal.

"I guess I look good, then?" she'd said with confidence that was bordering on arrogance.

Charlie let her off. She'd always admired her friend's self-assurance, and was pleased to see it alive and well, and making an appearance.

"You look more than good, my lover. You look amazing. Have I seen that dress before? It really suits you. And that necklace, it's fabulous."

Around Ali's neck was a short silver chain, with several fine cords dropping from it. On the end of each of the different length cords were teardrop-shaped gems in myriad shades of pearl, turquoise, blue and green. The beautiful collar gleamed and glistened like the sea. Ali smiled, almost like she was holding on to a secret.

"Probably not. It's one of my Madrid outfits. I haven't had the chance to wear it this year." She was still preening, looking at herself and fluffing up her hair in her reflection in the window. "No one dresses up in the UK," she grumbled.

Seeing an opportunity to talk about Ali's life in Bristol, she pounced on it. "Hearing you say that reminds me. I wanted to ask you if you're happy you made the move back to the UK? Sometimes you seem a bit…" Ali turned away. Charlie persisted, speaking to her back now "well. . . not your normal sparkling self. I know you're working hard, but is that all it is?"

But Ali didn't answer, instead she gestured towards the door with her head, showing she wanted them to leave, and said with a touch of impatience,

"We can talk about that over dinner."

Charlie sighed. Ali was being evasive, but she would pick her time and get to the bottom of this later. She stood up like the good girl she was and said,

"Let's get going then. I want to explore a bit."

After leaving the hotel, they crossed the road and made their way to the huge marina that was visible from their suite. Charlie bit down her disappointment that Ali didn't want to join the throngs walking along the big, paved walkway that hugged the bay of Palma. She had noticed them from their balcony, talking as they walked, stopping to chat or eat an ice cream, exercising dogs and pushing their babies. Curious as to why there were so many people out and about she asked Ali if something special was happening that night to draw such a crowd, but Ali explained that a slow walk or stroll for the purpose of socialising, which took place in the evening was an integral part of Spanish life and had a name, it was called the *paseo*.

Charlie thought it sounded like the Spanish equivalent of the Caribbean pastime of liming – and wished they could have 'paseo-ed' all the way to the cathedral and back as they still had an hour or so before dinner, but Ali was on a mission to get into the marina and find their restaurant. They found Agua Bebe and discovered that everyone was busy getting the place set up for dinner. Ali went to the bar and ordered two Aperol spritzes to take away, assuming that Charlie would want one too. She didn't want it, but took it anyway. Bevvied up, they started exploring the huge marina, walking up and down the different pontoons, checking out the boats.

Charlie had never realised her friend had such an interest in sailing. She had heard that the Hobsons had purchased a RIB a few years ago, and they kept it at their holiday cottage in Dorset. But she hadn't realised Ali loved boats too, so she pointed out that if Ali had joined her for the trip to Zephyr, she would have spent plenty of time out on the water, but Ali didn't respond.

It was fun looking at all the different types of vessels moored up – there were all sorts there, from power boats to huge mega yachts and the graceful sailing ships that Ali seemed the most interested in. There was tonnes of people watching to be had too: people hanging out on their boats, drinking and eating, listening to music or playing card games. Some had little barbeques set up on deck, some had music pumping and full-fledged parties going on. It was clearly a cool place to hang out in the evening.

The two of them attracted plenty of attention as they walked the pontoons, and they turned down a number of offers to 'jump on board', always from groups of guys who seemed to think they'd come looking for them. Ali dealt with the offers politely but firmly, in her (to Charlie's ears, anyway) fluent Spanish. Eventually, after walking to the end of another long pontoon and spending a few minutes checking out a sleek navy blue sailboat with a gleaming wooden deck and shiny gold fittings that Ali seemed to particularly like, they wandered back to their restaurant and sat down for dinner.

Ali immediately ordered a bottle of champagne. Charlie had gulped when she'd looked at the wine menu before Ali took it off her. The cheapest bottle (and Ali hadn't ordered that) was over 200 euros! Her shock must have shown because Ali immediately reassured her,

"Don't panic! I'll pay. I'm in the mood for fizz."

She wasn't about to argue. Charlie had money in the bank, a lump sum from the divorce settlement, but that was earmarked as a deposit for when she found the right cottage. She lived day to day on what she made at Brown's – her and Ali's wages were polls apart. A glance at the menu had confirmed that dinner for two at the eye-wateringly expensive restaurant would set her back the best part of a week's wages. The difference in their disposable income was another way in which she and Ali had grown apart.

She left it to Ali to order for them as she was the foodie: a seafood rice dish, some grilled prawns and a salad. The champagne arrived, followed by some country bread and a tomatoey paste to smear on it. Charlie, who thought ten was far too late for dinner and was starving, grabbed a piece, chewed hungrily and with a little bit of something in her tummy to offset the booze, settled down to enjoy her night.

They chatted for a while about how nice their surroundings were and how pleasant it was to be dining under the stars. Ali seemed relaxed, and she was just about to ask her about her job again, when her friend's peculiar body language stopped her in her tracks. Ali was sitting bolt upright and had the focused predatory look of a cat who'd spotted a mouse. Charlie watched fascinated as Ali's eyes became unblinking, razor-focused beams and she swivelled her head back over her shoulder like an automaton. Charlie stared at the back of Ali's head of curly red hair for a few heartbeats, waiting curiously until she eventually turned back to face her dining companion.

"Ali? Are you alright? You look like you've seen a…"

She didn't know how to describe what she'd witnessed but if she said 'you look like you spotted something you want to devour' she would sound super-weird, so she finished lamely, "ghost".

"I'm fine," Ali croaked, then bolted the rest of the champagne in her glass, and reached blindly into the ice bucket for a refill. "Thought I recognised someone," she corrected herself, "actually pretty sure I did see someone, I mean, some people from the Madrid office."

Charlie looked over her friend's shoulder to see if she could see the people she was talking about, but couldn't figure it out because there were a number of different groups walking on the pontoon heading in the direction she'd been looking.

She was intrigued. She'd never met anyone from Ali's time in Madrid. On her one and only weekend visit, the two of them hung out alone.

"Why don't you go check and see? See if they want to come and have a drink with us? I don't mind. It would be nice for you to see someone from the office, right?"

Ali nodded. Then gave her an odd, twisted smile, before she jumped up and hurried off, saying she'd be back in a sec.

Charlie pondered her friend's expression and didn't like the conclusion she came to. It was an expression she knew all too well. The same guilty face that Charlie's ex-husband Graham had used to pull when he was hiding something from her. It was crystal clear to her now that Ali had a secret, and that was the reason they were here in Mallorca. Her gut was telling her it was to do with the mysterious client who owned the hotel. But why would she hide that?

She tipped the last of the water into her glass and tried to make sense of what was going on. And thought, not for the first time, that it was unlike Ali to be without a man for any amount of time. And she'd been remarkably quiet on that front. Charlie tried to think back over their recent interactions and drew a blank. The only man she ever mentioned was Kris, who was definitely not a love interest. It struck her that she didn't know that much about Ali's life anymore. But, she thought guiltily, even with a high degree of crappy friend-ness, she wouldn't have missed something as huge as Ali being in a relationship. Or could she?

CHAPTER 22

Ali caught up with Antonio just as he and his friends were about to board his yacht. She could tell from his expression that he was both shocked and not particularly happy to see her. He pulled himself together quickly, though.

"Ali? I wasn't expecting to see you here."

"What a nice surprise to see you, too," she'd said sweetly. "I was having dinner with a friend at a restaurant on the marina when I saw you walk past … such a coincidence … I just *had* to follow you and come say hi."

She was pleasant and charming and maintained her distance, offering up her cheek for two chaste kisses. He made all the right noises – complimenting her on her choice of Palma as a holiday destination and even introduced her to the group, who by then had made their way on board. He'd called to them in English, saying she was his "esteemed colleague", one of the best young lawyers he'd ever had the privilege to work with.

He told them to go on without him and to make themselves comfortable, using a version of Spanish she knew to be Mallorquí, the dialect of the island, and Ali watched them move to the stern of the boat and help themselves to drinks.

"What are you doing here, Ali?" Antonio said harshly in English, as soon as they were out of earshot. Then, in a disconcerting change of pace, he looked her up and down like she was a juicy piece of rib-eye and said in a husky voice, "You look good enough to eat, *mi amour*."

She smiled triumphantly. He was so predictable. She'd deliberately worn his favourite dress, paired with the only gift he'd ever given her: the necklace he'd bought at the beginning of their affair. Her physical presence was still like catnip to him.

"I needed to see you," she said directly, looking up at him amorously from under her lashes, then she rather spoilt the effect by hiccupping once, very loudly, the champagne and the relief of finding him catching up with her. He was staring at her with an expression she chose to interpret as excitement rather than panic. Of course, he'd be blindsided by the fact she'd come to Mallorca to find him, but as soon as he got over the shock, he'd also be flattered she'd made the effort. Men loved being chased.

"I understand, I feel the same way, and want to take you in my arms right now, *mi amour*, but…" He shrugged. "It's impossible." Then added, in the most heartfelt of voices, eyes pleading with her to understand, "Please, darling, I wish I could, but I can't risk everything just to be with you, however sweet the reward."

"But Antonio. I came all the way here. Surely you could slip away for a little…"

His face tightened in frustration. "No Ali. It's out of the question. It's family time, and you should know that. You should *not* have come."

His words hurt. Just a few small words, but they were as pointed and disproportionately painful as a bee sting. She stared at him; he looked different tonight, wearing an old polo shirt and long shorts with deck shoes, but he smelled the same, the spicy citrusy cologne that she always associated with him. She was hyperaware of her surroundings; the warm, salty air, the sway of the pontoon under her feet, the jingles, creaks and knocks of all the boats on anchor, the groups of friends and lovers walking by, the jokes and conversations going on around her – telling her she was an outsider, she was not welcome and she shouldn't be here.

Antonio was looking at her curiously, trying to gauge her next move. She wondered if he could tell she was having an out-of-body experience, that she felt like she was standing to one side of their little piece of theatre, watching the action unfold rather than playing the lead role. Needing to connect with him somehow, wanting to prove what they had was real, she reached out to touch his hand. He moved it away.

"Ali, don't be stupid."

This wasn't how things were supposed to go. She felt overwhelmed. "You think I'm stupid? Do you want to end it, Antonio? You can end it. Just tell me. Don't keep me hanging on. It's cruel."

"*Mi amour* … don't, don't be like that," he said in a kinder tone, but he still didn't move towards her, and kept darting quick looks back towards the boat, checking to make sure his friends were not watching.

"Why not? Can't you see how hard this is for me? I love you and I've missed you so much that I had to see you, but you hate it that I'm here."

He shook his head in denial, but she knew he was lying.

"I adore you, my darling, you know that. But this is not the right time or place. You agreed to the contract. You know what this thing between us is. What it must be."

She shrugged and said crossly, "Yes. For you to have your cake *and* eat it."

He was getting more and more fidgety. "Lower your voice, *mi amour*. My friends are getting curious."

She ignored him, her voice getting louder and louder with each word she spat at him.

"But you don't even want to eat my cake that often these days. Why? Do you have another bakery you prefer?"

He hated it when she was bitchy or used sarcasm; she saw a tide of something dark and unpleasant rise in his hooded eyes and it spilled out into his voice.

"Shut up, Ali," he ground the words out, "don't be childish and don't raise your voice at me. Go back to your hotel, reflect on this conversation, and your impulsive and immature decision to come here uninvited. Consider the consequences and when you've had time to think through your actions, we'll talk."

He was dismissing her. Sometimes she found it a turn on to be bossed around by him, and he probably thought she would follow his instructions. But the tone he'd just taken with her was reprehensible.

"No. I want to talk now." She gave voice to the questions that tormented her: "Why *are* we still doing this, Antonio? Why keep me hanging? We hardly meet up, we rarely have sex. I can count on one hand the times we've made love since I left Madrid."

Antonio was unused to being disobeyed, and she could tell her refusal to leave was infuriating him. His body was swollen tight with tension and he was struggling to control the volume of his voice. An intrigued passerby turned to look at them, sensing a couple's argument which enraged him even more.

He hissed at her, "We are attracting attention. You need to leave. Go back to your restaurant and eat something, but no more wine, Ali. You've had too much already."

"We still need to talk Antonio," she insisted, stubbornly. She'd be buggered if he'd run her off now.

"And I said not now," enunciating each word slowly, "I have to go back to my friends before they think something's up." He moved infinitesimally closer to her and said in a coaxing voice, as ordering her around was not working, "*Mi amour*, please go back to your hotel, sleep it off and I guarantee that tomorrow you'll wake up and regret this." Then, when she shook her head 'no', unconvinced by his change of tactics, he added meanly, "It's very unattractive seeing you like this."

"Unattractive?" The dig really hit home. "You found me plenty attractive in the past. When you couldn't get enough of your little *pelliroja*." She laughed mirthlessly, then gestured around her at the people on the pontoon. "You think I'm causing a scene – but this isn't a scene. No one is listening. Your friends are quite happy drinking your booze up there. They can't hear us. But I *could* make my voice louder, a lot louder, and make it clear we are more than work colleagues. Now that would be a real scene."

His previous coldness was nothing compared to the ice in his eyes at present.

"Don't you *dare* threaten me, Ali." He spat out, "That would be an incredibly stupid thing to do."

She'd regretted her words as soon as she'd uttered them. She'd made a mistake. He was right. She shouldn't have come. Or she should have warned him she was coming. She'd gone too far – her instincts seemed to be way off these days. Her eyes searched his face. He looked like a different person to the man she loved. He'd aged. How come she'd never noticed before that he had deep lines etched across his forehead and down the side of his nose? Or that when he was angry, his mouth formed into such a thin straight line that his lips almost disappeared. The face she adored was a stone mask – carved to portray disgust and wariness. This wasn't her Antonio. Her arrogantly confident lover. This man was scared, but trying his hardest not to show it.

A wave of desolation and hopelessness struck her. How could he believe she would expose them? If he thought that, then he didn't know her at all. He should know how loyal she was. They'd set the rules of their engagement jointly, total secrecy, absolute discretion, and she had upheld that because she loved him. For fuck's sake, she hadn't even told Charlie!

She needed him to understand. "I'd never do that to you, Antonio, never, I know what havoc it would cause – for both of us. I'm sorry. I am, truly. It was an empty threat. I wish I could take it back. Honestly."

She wanted to reach out, touch him, reassure him, but she knew she couldn't. Instead she hoped her words would be enough to calm him down; and it appeared they were. Forcing a tight smile, he responded in a neutral voice.

"It's OK, Ali, we all say things we don't mean in the heat of the moment. I know you would never do that to me." Then finished woodenly.,"You are still my special girl, I promise."

Ali watched as Antonio took a deep breath and exhaled for five counts. She guessed from his more relaxed expression that he'd made up his mind up about something. He looked over his shoulder to check on his friends. They were still drinking beers but were casting ever more frequent and curious looks in their direction. He smiled at them reassuringly, and gave them the thumbs up, showing that he was nearly done with her.

"My guests are getting restless and I need to join them. Why don't you come back tomorrow around one thirty if you can get away, and we'll have lunch and talk? Just the two of us."

CHAPTER 23

Ali had been gone for ages. The rice had cooled and congealed, the champagne was done and there was still no sign of her best friend. Unwilling to believe she'd been dumped and worried in case something had happened to her, she texted:

Where R U?

and a few seconds later got a curt response:

Back at hotel. Pay the bill I'll sort it out with you later.

Charlie shook her head in disbelief. She had been dumped! No sorry. No explanation. Pay the bloody bill! Good job she had a credit card on her. Hopefully with enough credit to pay the massive *cuenta*.

Her waiter took her card and she waited for his return anxiously. Seriously worried that it would be declined, and she'd have to add humiliation to the roll call of negative emotions she was experiencing on this horrible holiday. Thankfully the card worked, and she scurried back to the hotel, upset with Ali but hoping she would get to the bottom or her increasingly bizarre behaviour.

She found her exactly where she expected her to be: propping up the bar. She spotted her turquoise dress first – the colour jarring with the neutral tones of the hotel's tasteful décor. Her friend was, no surprise there either, chatting to the bartender with a drink in front of her.

Charlie approached warily. Her anger at being stood up now tempered by frustration and concern. Surely the girl had had enough to drink by now?

She'd been at it all day; the only time she'd taken a break was when she fell asleep by the pool. When Ali finally noticed her presence, alerted by the barman, who looked over her shoulder to offer Charlie a drink, she smiled crookedly, and tapped the bar stool next to her, indicating she should sit down.

"No thanks, Ali, I've had enough for one day. Maybe you have too?" she said crisply.

Ali made light of her tone. "Don't be such a spoilsport. Have a drink with me."

"Are you going to tell me why you left me at the restaurant?"

"Oh yeah. Sorry about that. Something came up."

She wasn't about to be brushed off again. "What?"

"Stuff."

"Stuff? Care to elaborate?" Charlie was struggling to hold it together.

"Nope. Not now," Ali said stubbornly. Not giving an inch.

Charlie had never seen her like this. Well, she'd seen it but had never been on the receiving end.

"I don't believe this shit." She couldn't hold it any longer. She didn't want to make a scene at the bar, so she kept her voice to an angry whisper, but this was unreal. "What's going on with you?"

Ali looked at her blankly, the alcohol and some powerful repressed emotion making her eyes red and squinty, then shrugged her shoulders and attempted a nonchalant response.

"Nothing. Chillax, babe, and get with the programme." Waving her martini glass around so much, she spilled half of it. "Have a drink. We're on holiday and girls just wanna have fun."

Charlie could feel her anger rising again and tried to keep it down. She wanted to grab Ali and shake some sense into her. She was being awful – weird and cold and selfish. But there must be a reason for it. Something awful must have happened when she went off to meet her Madrid colleagues. She bit back her frustration and tried persuasion.

"Why don't you come back to our lovely room with me? We could have a drink from the mega bar?" in a coaxing voice.

But Ali out and out refused, and told the barman that she was being abducted by a goodie two shoes who wanted to cramp her style.

Charlie had had enough. She left Ali at the bar, where, she reasoned, she was safe and couldn't get into too much trouble, and went back to their room. Though why, she thought, she should care if Ali was alright after the way she'd behaved was a fucking mystery.

She didn't sleep at all well that night, despite the incredible beds. Worried despite herself, she left her door open and heard Ali stumbling in at around 3a.m. Even though she'd left some lights on in the lounge area to help her find her way, she could hear her banging into things and muttering swear words as she made her way to her bedroom. A few moments later she'd heard her flop onto the bed and a few minutes after that, the rhythmic sound of snoring. She crept out of bed and peeped into her room to check she wasn't in danger of choking on her own vomit. Ali had passed out, fully clothed. She hadn't even taken her shoes off. Her bag was open on the bed, her phone peeking out of it. There was an empty cocktail glass dangling out of her hand; the remnants of the drink had spilled onto the pristine cream comforter. Charlie shook her head sadly. The girl was a hot mess.

The next morning, Charlie got up and checked on Ali, who was still breathing, but out for the count, and hadn't, as far as she could tell, moved at all, apart from to fling one arm over her eyes in defence. There would be no point in trying to wake her, so she went to breakfast on her own and then went on to the pool where she worked on her tan and swam off some of her frustration. She was going to have to have a serious talk with Ali about her behaviour.

Charlie was a coward when it came to confrontation and was not looking forward to that conversation, so the morning passed quite pleasantly. When Ali finally surfaced she approached Charlie wearing a defiant expression and with a bloody Mary in hand; there was no fulsome apology for her behaviour or any griping about her hangover. She was dressed to impress again, in a stiff white summer dress, tailored to perfection, gold sandals and some large tortoiseshell sunglasses, which made her eyes unreadable. Her lips were painted bright red to match her drink and her body language read unrepentant and ready for action.

You have to hand it to the woman, Charlie thought and said dryly, "You have the constitution of an ox Alison Hobson. Not sure how you can face a drink or look that good after the skinful you had yesterday."

Ali shrugged. "Hair of the dog. Sorry about leaving you with that bill by the way. How much was it? I'll transfer the money to you asap."

That wasn't the apology she wanted. "It's not the money, Ali. And you should know that. It's the fact you ran off on me. And I have no idea why. Where did you go?" She couldn't stop herself from sounding hurt.

But Ali blithely avoided answering her and instead muttered something about meeting a colleague for lunch and left her without a backwards glance. Flabbergasted, Charlie watched her exit, gawping like a goldfish out of water, as the woman formerly known as her best friend left without a expressing a modicum of concern for what Charlie was going to do for the rest of her day.

The bloody cheek of her. What on earth was going on? Needing to vent to someone, she realised there was only one person who knew Ali and she could talk to freely without feeling disloyal. So she reached for her phone and dialled Chix – not caring the call was going to cost her a fortune in roaming charges.

"Chix?" Her friend answered the phone eventually, but she could hear a soft giggle and a slight kerfuffle in the background.

"Chix, have you got company?"

"I have." He sounded pleased with himself.

"Well then, let me call you back another time. It's just I…"

"It's fine," he said patiently. "She's making us some coffee."

"She? She's making coffee, is she? That sounds very domestic. Who is this person you are allowing to use your sainted coffee machine?" She knew how important his daily coffee ritual was.

"It's new. Well, kinda. I'll fill you in sometime. What's up? You sound worried."

"It's Ali."

He chuckled. "What is it with you and that family? First you complain about the brother, now it's the sister. Don't know which one of the two of them gets to you the most." Then, sounding concerned, "What about her? I like that girl. She's got spice."

"She's got too much bloody spice, if you ask me. Oh Chix, we're on holiday in Spain and it's all gone wrong," she blurted out, then tried to explain. "She's acting weird. To be honest, she's been behaving oddly for months. She got so drunk last night she ran off and left me at the dinner table. On my own. In a foreign country! Girl code states you never do that."

"She hits the juice hard."

"You noticed?"

"Hard not to."

"What do you mean?"

He chuckled. "Remember that night in Bristol we had? She was out of control."

"When she left us to rush off to do some work?"

"Work? Is that what she told you?"

"She said she had to do some work, and I told her off, and we…"

"You got into a fight."

"Not a fight, a disagreement. We don't fight." Which was true. They never fought. Until recently. "We've been OK since then." But as she said it she realised that they hadn't been, really. She tried to remember the course of events that night in Bristol but her recollection was hazy, "I think she said she was going to work to meet a colleague … who was over from Spain for the night…" She trailed off as something obvious hit her. And then Chix chimed in, making it even clearer.

"What 'work' did you think she was doing, Charlie? What important legal work would she be doing at 9 o'clock with a pitcher of margaritas and a bunch of shots inside her?"

"Well, I don't…"

He chuckled. "You really are an innocent, my friend, that was a booty call, Charlie, I thought you realised that. I thought that was why you were so mad at her."

"No. I was angry because I thought it was work taking advantage of her – she works all the time."

"You didn't suspect she's got something going on with someone she works with?"

"No. Because she'd tell me if she did. Because we tell each other everything." Or, she thought, we used to.

"Do you really? Most people have a few secrets, you know."

She tried to rationalise it rather than think her bestie had chosen not to tell her she had a boyfriend at work, which seemed to be what the evidence was pointing to.

"She wouldn't jeopardise her career like that … I mean she can't do that … she told me a few weeks ago about how some folk got caught having an affair and they lost their jobs over it."

Chix didn't press his point, but she knew he had one. The logical explanation was that Ali was up to something with a colleague, presumably the one she'd gone to meet for lunch and she didn't trust Charlie enough to tell her.

Hurt and flustered, she thanked Chix and hung up, completely forgetting to ask him about the mysterious lady she'd heard in the background.

CHAPTER 24

When Ali got to the marina she discovered an empty slip where *Azul Verdadero* should have been. Antonio had done a runner. His ship had sailed without her and she couldn't face the idea of going back to the hotel where she would have to deal with Charlie's hurt and confusion over the way the evening ended last night. Instead, she scuttled back to the same overpriced tourist trap restaurant she had failed to enjoy dinner in last night to digest what she had learnt and obsess over the fact that her lover had tricked her.

According to the chatty senior who popped his head from the cabin of the boat anchored in the next slip, a flirtatious little fellow who had been happy to share what he knew, the 'big shot lawyer from Madrid' and his amigos had sailed off into the early morning sunshine, to meet up with their respective wives and girlfriends and 'party a little' in a place called Puerto Andratx.

The old guy was either a stalker or had too little else going on in his life because he seemed very well acquainted with their plans. He informed her the group was going to explore the south-western tip of Mallorca – maybe even take a trip up to Deia after that. She felt numb as she listened to him explain what a wonderful part of the island that was, not touristy at all, and now free for the local sailors to enjoy, as most of the visiting sailors who hired boats for the summer had gone.

On reaching Aqua Bebe, she did the one thing she knew would help make sense of it all and ordered a drink. Then, fuelled by fury, she tried to call Antonio. Of course he didn't pick up, so she sent a text. She didn't mince her words.

> DON'T WORRY – I GET THE MESSAGE – YOU FUCKING COWARD! I HOPE YOU AND YOUR AMIGOS DROWN. GILIPOLLAS!

In the meantime, she logged on to her personal email, sending a longer message this time, biting back tears as she typed.

> Antonio, you THINK you're the big man but you're just a little boy. Why are you such a coward? You should have met with me. Not run away. Just be a REAL man about it and tell me you don't want this anymore. Don't just ghost me like a fucking teenager. I want to hear those words from you in person. I deserve that you asshole.

Sending the missive didn't make her feel any better, nor any less rejected or frustrated. Neither did she feel any less guilty for being the shittiest friend in the world. But alcohol did. By the time Charlie tracked her down, she'd finished her bloody Mary and had made headway into a rather good vodka tonic, unable to face anymore tomato juice.

Charlie pulled a pious face when she spotted the drink, sighed deeply, and said, "Look I'm not judging, Ali, but you're drinking an awful lot."

That holier than thou shit made her see red, and she responded scathingly, "But you are, Charlie, you're judging me a lot." And she treated her to a withering look to add emphasis. She'd always found attack was the best form of defence.

Charlie's face crumpled with hurt, and Ali assumed she would retreat wounded. But rather than back down, Charlie held her ground and stared back at her, big dark brown eyes awash with pain, until Ali had to look away. She fixed her attention on the empty glass in front of her and willed Charlie to leave her alone, but she didn't budge.

"Why didn't you tell me you were in a relationship with someone from work?" Charlie demanded out of the blue. Taken aback, she said angrily,

"Who told you?"

"You don't deny it, then."

She shrugged. "Who told you?"

"You just confirmed it, but I worked it out myself. With a little help from Chix."

"Chix? What's he got to do with it?" It pissed her off Charlie had been talking about her with her 'new' friends.

"I called him," she said defensively but firmly, not giving an inch. "Because you disappeared, and I was concerned. I told him you were acting oddly. He pointed out you'd gone to meet 'someone from the Madrid office' that night in Bristol and he'd assumed it was a booty call. I thought he'd got it wrong. I said it was actual work because that was what you told me – but then I'm too trusting. It's easy to pull the wool over my eyes, but not someone like Chix. He saw straight through the situation. Said I was too bloody innocent." And she laughed in an unfunny, self-depreciating way.

Ali attempted to defend herself. "Look, Charlie, it's complicated—" then she stopped, aghast, as her friend started sobbing her eyes out.

"What are you crying about?"

"Because you said 'it's complicated!' – that's what Graham said when I asked him if he was having an affair. You're just like him. I can't believe you've been lying to me about something so important."

CHAPTER 25

Ali had finally spilt the beans. Turned out that her friend had been having the love affair of her life with her boss at the Madrid office, a married-with-two-kids man called Antonio Garcia Fernández, It had been going on for nearly two years. Charlie was in shock.

Over the course of the afternoon, room service club sandwiches and two large bottles of water, Ali talked about how she'd met Antonio through a dating app when she'd first moved to Madrid. She had been staying in a hotel for two weeks before she started work, part vacation and part getting acclimatised while looking for somewhere to live for her six month 'seat'. Ali, being Ali, went looking for company online. She described the intense sexual attraction that had blazed between them the first time, how they'd met for another two sessions before he disappeared off the app. She hadn't expected ever to see him again, but she did, a few days later, holding court in a conference room at her new office. It had been an even bigger shock when she found out he was one of the founding partners of the firm, so not only a colleague but also her boss. When he'd reached out to her via the app again, she'd intended to ignore him but instead, she met up with him again.

"Why didn't you end it there if you knew it could get you into so much trouble?"

"I was addicted, so was he."

"Addicted to what?"

"Sex to start with, then it grew into something more."

Charlie could have done without hearing the intimate details of their relationship. How Antonio had pushed every one of her buttons and pleasured every inch of her body with his. How he'd made her feel like the sexiest woman alive. But Ali seemed compelled to explain, willing her to understand she'd been powerless against the force of such primeval attraction.

"But didn't he have even more to lose than you?"

"Yes, and I think that was part of it. He likes danger. I liked it too – to start with, it was exciting and illicit. And I got a big kick out of him choosing me over good sense. Or maybe he just thought he could get away with it because he's who he is, whichever way, he was the one who said we should keep meeting – as long as I stuck to the rules. And," she added sulkily, looking as pissed off as a Persian cat caught in a downpour, "I was on my own in a new town. I was lonely, and I thought I could handle it. For six months."

Charlie could see some sense in that. It had been a time of change for both of them and she'd missed Ali tonnes when she'd left London, she suspected that was why she'd got too serious with Graham too soon; he'd filled the void.

"And then I fucked up and fell in love with him. He was exactly what I wanted, a powerful, sexy, successful man – the full package."

"But he was someone else's package, Ali," Charlie said firmly, trying not to sound as disappointed in her friend as she felt. She remembered something Ali had spewed out earlier. "What did you mean when you said you had to stick to *his* rules, that sounds…" she searched for a word she rarely used but which seemed appropriate, "sadistic? I don't like the sound of that at all."

"They were _our_ rules" Ali said, defensively, making it sound like she was involved in the decision-making process, but Charlie didn't believe her. Her read was that the guy was controlling as hell. An opinion that didn't change after she heard a synopsis of said rules, which were all stacked in Antonio's favour.

"And that was enough for you?" It outraged her that the man had treated Ali like a call girl and she didn't seem to mind.

"Yes," she said defiantly, ignoring Charlie's censure, "we were happy together, it suited me. You know I like to focus on work – and work was good. I was studying too, perfecting my Spanish. The city was amazing, and I got to see plenty of him during the week, until…"

"Until?"

"This time last year, around the time I qualified. Did you know it was his idea that I move to Bristol?"

"No," Charlie said, exasperated, "how could I? I didn't even know he existed until today." But Ali seemed unaware of her frustration and carried on in a dreamy voice.

"He set it up because the Bristol office was working on a big deal for De la Cruz and he thought it would be the perfect place for me."

"Oh," she said, thinking it sounded a lot more like he was trying to get rid of her.

"He's like a mentor to me, too. *He* was as concerned as *I* was about my career – there's so much competition in my field – I would have liked to have stayed on in Madrid, really, but that would've meant doing a conversion course to qualify in Spanish law, which would have slowed things down a bit, and I've always been fast track material," she said with a little smirk of pride.

"So that's why you came back to the West Country? I *had* wondered – you'd never wanted to live here before."

During their conversation, Ali kept her phone in her hand obsessively checking to see if Antonio had responded to any of her messages. When she started scrolling frantically Charlie figured he had.

"What is it?" she asked, assuming it was bad news, as Ali looked winded, like she'd been punched in the stomach.

"Shit! Shit, shit, shit, shit, shit!"

Rage propelled Ali out of the chair and towards the in-suite bar as effectively as a wave pushes a surfer to shore. Within seconds, she was pouring herself a huge vodka tonic with shaking hands. Once made, she stood staring into space, alternating taking a deep swig of her drink and making an animalistic growling noise.

"Ali. What's happened?"

"I'm too fucking angry to tell you. Arrgghhh," she screamed. Then did it again. "Arrrghhhh".

"What?"

"Check my fucking email. Check it. You'll see."

Deeply concerned, she picked up Ali's phone and started reading the official-looking email. It was long and full of legalese. She didn't understand much of it but what even her uneducated brain could figure out was that it implied that Ali Hobson might be in breach of her employment contract for entering into an unprofessional interaction with a client. It sounded scary.

"I don't know what it means, Ali? What are they saying you've done?"

"They are using the fact that I'm on holiday here, which, incidentally is something only Antonio would know because I told him last night which hotel we are staying in, to show that I'm in breach of contract by accepting favours from a client."

"Why?"

"I suspect it's a mechanism to give me the push. Or start the process. Stupid men should get their facts straight before they do that."

"But they can't do that, can they?"

"I don't think so. But I'm not sure. It would be a tough call because I think Sebastián would have a few words to say about it – he really likes me and they wouldn't want to lose him as a client."

"That's good then, right?" she said, trying to be reassuring. Ali was pacing the room as she talked.

"Well, not really, because I'm still a very junior player. Fingers crossed it's a bluff on their part. That this is just Antonio firing shots, being an arse, paying me back for surprising him. I guess I really pissed him off if he's getting someone else to do his dirty work." She took a massive slurp out of her drink, said 'fucking coward' and promptly burst into tears.

CHAPTER 26

By the time they'd made it to the beautiful port of Andratx it was after eight and Charlie was beginning to regret her decision to accompany her friend on what was in all likelihood a wild goose chase. Ali's energy levels had flat-lined again. After whirling around their hotel room in a frenzy organising the trip, she had collapsed when they got into the taxi and spent most of the journey slumped against the door with a sourly morose expression on her pretty face.

Back in Palma, she'd said she had a plan and Charlie wanted to know more so she could initiate damage control. Ali had based their hasty departure to an unknown destination on hearsay. A guy she'd met at the marina had told her that the loathsome Antonio had headed to Andratx to party and Ali, incensed by the email she'd received, and fuelled by yet more vodka, was determined to find him. It sounded like a terrible idea to Charlie, but she hadn't been able to convince her otherwise and so had come along in the hope of moderating her erratic behaviour.

As they entered the pretty harbour, she could see the town was much bigger than she'd expected. The bay was packed with hundreds of boats moored up as far as the eye could see. Finding Antonio's boat would be like looking for a needle in a haystack. Her patience with Ali had now all but been used up. She was tired; it was late; they'd left a perfectly lovely hotel room to stay god knows where to waste even more time on a guy who was obviously not worth it. When did Ali get stupid?

She asked the taxi driver if he could recommend somewhere to stay. It was apparent that Ali, who was scanning the harbour for her prey, was not leaving

Andratx until she hunted Antonio down. He took them to the Hotel Brismar, a small, simple-looking hostelry situated on the main road overlooking the port. Luckily, they had a twin room available. Ali perked up enough to hand over her credit card and get them checked in. Afterwards, as Charlie turned wearily towards the stairs to head to their room, Ali tapped her on the back and stopped her.

"I'm going to check out the yacht club. Take my bag up, please."

"Ali, really? Not tonight. It's too late."

Ali shrugged her off. "I didn't ask you to come."

Appalled by her attitude and exhausted by Ali's histrionics, Charlie just wanted to get to the room, lie down and chill out, yet, annoyingly she was still worried about what Ali would do if she found Antonio. She made one last attempt to stop her.

"Stay here. Sleep on things – you're not in any state to deal with him now."

Ali had always hated being told what to do by anyone, and Charlie's suggestion only hardened her resolve to go out on the hunt. She flounced over to the lobby mirror, checked her appearance, and tossed her curls impatiently. All she needed to do to complete the stroppy, grounded-teenager effect was to stamp her foot.

"I'm going, and there's nothing you can say that will change my mind."

She was fed up to the back teeth with her and snapped back, "Please yourself, Ali. You always do," then turned sharply and headed upstairs without a backwards glance.

Once in the room, which was perfectly serviceable but a depressing comedown after their glorious suite in Palma, she found herself unable to relax. She was battling too many conflicting emotions; on one hand, she felt angry and hurt about how Ali had lied to her for so long. On the other, she couldn't help but be concerned and feel responsible as her friend was clearly vulnerable after being taken advantage of. Ali's behaviour had been so irrational, erratic and extreme that she couldn't help but worry she was on the verge of some sort of breakdown. She didn't know what to do, but she *did* know she didn't want to deal with this by herself anymore. She wanted to share the load with someone who knew and loved Ali as much as she did. She picked up her phone, scrolled and hit call.

"To what do I owe this booty call, Charlie Girl?" Simon answered after four rings even though it was past midnight in the UK. Despite his jokey words his voice was tinged with concern. "Is everything OK? I thought you two were in Mallorca?"

As soon as she heard Simon's voice, she couldn't help herself from blurting out, "No, it's not OK. Ali's in trouble." She really didn't want to rat her out to her brother. She was going to get earache for being a snitch, but it was better than calling Charles and Penny.

Simon immediately started firing questions at her, assuming she was calling about a medical emergency. She quickly reassured him they hadn't been in a car crash or admitted to a hospital with Spanish tummy. When he calmed down enough to listen, she outlined the shenanigans of the last few days. Simon listened quietly until she finished, then blurted out,

"I *knew* something was wrong. She acted up at Dad's birthday and I should have said something then, but I didn't want anyone to worry, and now I wish I bloody had. Even though she's so bloody annoying sometimes." He sighed deeply and carried on, confessing his sins. "I've been so wrapped up in my own drama that I didn't pay Ali enough attention." Charlie's ear's pricked up at the drama comment, dying to know more, she couldn't help it, and was just about to ask what he meant when she realised it wasn't a good time to ask – this call was about Ali. So, she just kept mum until Simon asked anxiously, "So where is she now? What's she doing? We can't let her confront this guy in front of his family, Charlie. That would be a disaster."

"I know," she said glumly. She felt guilty because she'd enabled Ali. She'd followed her to Andratx rather than making her stay in Palma. It was instinctive for her to be Robin to Ali's Batman even when the plan was a bad one. "We shouldn't have come on this wild goose chase but when she got the email, she just turned into a crazy lady – throwing on clothes and ordering taxis and I just…"

"It's OK, Charlie Girl. We both know my sister's a force of nature. You didn't stand a chance."

She paused, let out a sigh and spoke. "I think I know where she is, she muttered something about going to check out some yacht club," then added in a pitiful voice, "I know I shouldn't have let her go on her own, but I was just so tired, and honestly, Simon, I'm fed up with all her drama."

"I don't blame you, but could you…?"

She knew what he was going to ask her. "Yes, I can go find her." She sighed deeply. "Let me text her. Hopefully she will answer."

"Only go if it's safe."

Charlie smiled to herself; it was nice to hear the concern in his voice. She was happy to alleviate his fears.

"If you could see where I'm sat you wouldn't worry." She was on a tiny balcony enjoying a five-star view of the pretty port. Puerto Andratx, an exclusive tourism destination for a certain 'set' was pleasantly busy that evening. Well-dressed people meandered along the well-lit promenade, visiting the bars and restaurants that lined the bay. She laughed lightly. "This place is pretty darn gorgeous, the Puddlington of Mallorca by the looks of it." *And it's quite romantic*, she thought unbidden, as she watched couple after couple pass by, holding hands.

The two of them discussed 'Ali strategy' for a few more minutes and, feeling better able to cope after getting Simon's support, she ended the call, located the club on Google Maps, sent Ali a text to say she was on her way to meet her, then set off to find Simon's annoying sister.

CHAPTER 27

The following morning Ali woke up late. She was a bit groggy but filled with energy at the same time, because her sleuthing had paid off and she had a plan! Her visit to the yacht club had led to two important discoveries: firstly, Antonio was not only a member of the hallowed spot (a whole wing of the building was dedicated to his family), and secondly, he had a table booked for lunch later today.

    Charlie, who she'd entered into a truce with last night after being followed to the club where she was enjoying a drink and chatting up the barman for information, was flitting around their room offering to go get some 'coffee con letches' and a cheese toastie for their breakfast. Ali murmured thanks, then headed to the bathroom. She stood under the shower, enjoying the sting of the cold water on her skin, as she planned her next move and concluded that she didn't want to hear her friend's concerns or listen to her kindly intended advice today. Charlie had been looking at her like she was a wounded bird, which was all wrong! She felt strong and filled with purpose and she didn't want to waste that energy talking – she wanted to take action! However, she couldn't confront Antonio wearing day-old clothes and soiled knickers. Hindsight is a wonderful thing and she should have anticipated an overnight stay in Andratx and packed accordingly rather than leave everything except her makeup bag and laptop in Palma. Luckily, she'd spotted some cute boutiques yesterday. Going shopping for a stunning new outfit to wear into battle was just the thing to keep her occupied until lunch.

    She dried herself briskly, cleaned her teeth, applied some red lipstick and deo and stalked naked out of the room, feeling amazing! Super Ali was back! Yes, she might have made better decisions – about Antonio, and her job, and Kris, and even the Charlie and Simon situation – but they were *her* decisions and she stood by them. Telling Charlie about Antonio and fielding her questions designed to make Ali think that Antonio had only used her for sex had made her uncomfortable and even question what they had. But she *had* loved him, and *he'd* loved *her*. She was sure of it, even if the events of the last few days had changed the way she felt about him. He should acknowledge that love! He couldn't just ghost her out of his life.

"The gloves are off, Antonio," she said out loud as she yanked on yesterday's jeans and top, grabbed her bag and rushed to get of the room before Charlie came back. If she was quick, she could slip out the back of the hotel without being spotted. She was sick of being mistreated and ignored. She was on a mission to expose Antonio to his wife, his friends and his entire community. She'd wipe that smug married look off his face and she didn't need Charlie putting a spanner in her works.

She chuckled as she raced down the stairs and out the back of the restaurant, just in the nick of time, pretending not to hear Charlie's surprised voice shouting out about where she was going. She haired along the road, took a left and then a right and then a left again and found herself in the old part of the town. The boutique she'd been aiming for wasn't open yet, nor the shoe shop beside it, but the sign said they would open by eleven, which still gave her plenty of time to get an outfit and get back to the room to tart herself up. She went into the café next door to get the café con leche she'd missed out on, and asked them to add in a shot of rum for luck. Everyone knew rum coffee gave you wings!

A couple of hours later, Ali and her four enormous shopping bags lurched up the corridor and struggled through the bedroom door. Relieved that Charlie wasn't there to ask her where she'd been or what she was up to, she began pulling her new clothes out of the bags. She'd gone full shopaholic and bought tonnes of stuff: a trouser suit, a jumpsuit and three dresses. All the clothes in the store were by one designer, a Spanish man who specialised in resort wear. He favoured strong block colours – red, peacock blue, cerise, tangerine and a couple of fresh greens – and all his designs had similar style elements like oversized buttons, exposed zips and lace detailing. She loved the clothes – they were expensive and striking – and the shop assistant had been very encouraging, making her try on so many things that she'd got quite overwhelmed and didn't know what she liked best, so ended up buying too much. Then she'd gone next door to get some shoes, but by that time the clock was ticking, and she'd just grabbed a few pairs without trying them on, so she really hoped they'd fit.

She eyed the rainbow of clothing laid out on her single bed in the austere little room and experienced a twinge of doubt. Were the outfits too dressy for lunch at the yacht club? She dismissed the thought as being unhelpful. The most important thing was that she would look amazing.

She decided it was between the cerise jumpsuit or the tangerine skater dress. The two most casual outfits. She grabbed the dress and yanked it over her head, forgetting to undo the zip. There was a creaking sound as the tangerine lace that made up the side panels of the corset-style top split away from the seams, leaving her side tummy gaping out. She looked at herself in the mirror and realised that in the daylight, as opposed to the cocktail hour lighting of the boutique, the colour looked awful on her, contrasting unpleasantly with her auburn hair and making her skin look pasty. She whipped it up over her head and threw it in the room's tiny wastepaper bin, shouting "good riddance to bad rubbish", then picked up the jumpsuit and crooned to it, "pretty in pink – you were my favourite, anyway."

She scampered into the tiny bathroom, showered for the second time that day, spritzed herself with his favourite perfume, Aura by Loewe, and made up her face in an instant. She had a brilliant beauty routine; she congratulated herself, one she could do in her sleep. She'd run out of time when she was shopping and hadn't found an underwear shop, so she'd have to go commando. She carefully unzipped the jumpsuit and eased it on. It was made of a thinnish, stretch jersey material which looked shinier in the room than it did in the shop. Although it was one of the plainer items in the boutique, it still featured some of the designer's signature touches, including a heavy black and gold zip that ran down the front of the suit, cerise lace motifs on the edges of the pockets, as well as triangles of lace sweeping from inside her elbow up to her armpit, spanning across to the elasticated sinch waist. Looking at herself in the mirror as she lifted one arm and then the next, she realised that the inserts were actually batwings. She'd missed that design detail somehow.

Interesting, she thought, as she flapped her arms up and down, *that rum coffee really has given me wings!*

Even with the batwings, she thought she looked freaking hot. True, the colour was a bit full on for a casual lunch, but she was feeling feisty and, like Molly Ringwald, she'd always believed that redheads looked pretty in pink. The one-piece style was elongating, and the elasticated waist was wide enough and tight enough to nip in her waist. In fact, raising her (bat) wings, made her waist look even smaller, she thought with some satisfaction as she raised her arms up and posed in front of the mirror. She turned round and checked the back view over her shoulder. The jumpsuit was a little tight on her bum, but as she didn't have knickers on at least there were no panty lines. It was a bit short in the body and the seam was threatening to go right up 'in there' but she could deal with that because the overall effect was good. She decided against wearing any of the new shoes, instead slipped on her comfy black pumps, put her phone, a card and some cash in one of the lace bedecked pockets and made her way downstairs. She had half an hour to get to the club, which was only 10 minutes' walk away so she may as well have one for the road – having worked up quite the thirst getting ready.

She walked into the bar, ordered a vodka and orange (the vitamin C made it a health drink) and preened a little when the elderly bar man give a double take at her appearance, and said, "*muy* sexy".

The zippered neck is quite low she thought, as she leant against the bar and surveyed the room. She tensed when she spotted the back of Charlie's head and shoulders. She was sitting in one of the bar's banquettes, chatting to someone, most likely a man, because he was taller and wider than her, but she couldn't see what he looked like because the sun was streaming in from the marina.

Curious, but not wanting to be seen, Ali crept forward and hid herself behind one of the opaque glass screens that separated the banquettes. She could hear Charlie clearly. The guy was talking back to her in English. Her heart stopped. She knew that voice.

It was bloody Simon. What on earth was he here for? She crept closer, trying to hear what they were saying, and discovered they were talking about her!

"Is it possible that she's back in the room? Or will she head straight to the yacht club?"

"To be honest, I have no idea. I've been waiting down here, drinking coffee, hoping she'd come back and then you called and surprised me."

"Sorry, a flight came up, and I didn't have time to let you know until I landed – and then I didn't have any service for a bit."

"It's OK. I'm just glad you're here. Lord knows how she'll react when she sees you, though. She's in a very peculiar mood."

"Yes, you said. Any update?"

"This morning we didn't really speak and then she disappeared without a word. But last night she was quite chatty. All giggly and over excited about her 'plan'. She's obsessed with that bloody man. I think she'll hang out over there 'til she finds him."

"My stalker sister," said Simon wonderingly. "I never would have thought that of our independent Ali."

"Don't call her that, Simon. It's not fair. He's really done a number on her."

"Sorry, I didn't mean that. I'm worried too. I just can't believe Ali's gone all bunny boiler."

"It's his fault she's like that, Simon, you should've heard what she was saying about him. She adored him and I'm sure he took advantage of her. He was her boss in Spain, you know. Do you want to see a picture of him? I found one on the company website."

Ali watched as Charlie handed her phone over to Simon who studied the screen carefully.

"He looks like a right tosser."

"Agree. Arrogant was the word that came to mind."

"What was he thinking, diddling one of his juniors? That's a serious no-no. He could get in big trouble for that."

"I was thinking about it and I think that's why she got offered the job in Bristol. To get her out of his hair. Get her away."

Ali was getting more and more furious with every word she overheard. How dare they? She got the job on her own bloody merit.

"But he carried on seeing her?"

"Just enough to keep her on side, passively waiting for scraps from him."

"And that's why she's been so odd for the last few months, I assume?"

"You know, she hates to be wrong about anything, and he's taken her for a ride. I think she didn't want to admit that – and had kept it under control – because of work she was too busy to really confront him about it but now she's here in Spain, asking for something from him…"

"And she's not worth it anymore. He's scared his mates or the missus will put two and two together, so he's avoiding her…"

"And she's seeing his true colours…"

"It's tragic how badly us chaps behave when we feel cornered…"

"And he's going to want to reassert his power like the macho arsehole he is…"

"Yep, and my sister likes to be in control, so she's feeling embarrassed he's rejected her…"

"And hurt as well that she got it so wrong and wasted all that time on him like a fool…"

"She *will* want to hurt him back…"

"I'm so worried she will do something that will hurt her too…"

"It's a real concern, with the way she's drinking and the erratic behaviour, I think you're right to be worried."

Ali listened on, horrified. *Fool? Erratic? Desperate! How fucking dare they say those things about her?* And she hated the way the two of them finished each other's bloody sentences, in perfect bloody harmony. She couldn't believe their cod psychology. She wasn't erratic! She was in control! She was Super Ali … a warrior woman … seeking justice! A frustrated growl escaped her.

"Ali? Are you OK?"

Simon was looming over her. She'd scooted back into her seat, finished her drink with a defiant slurp through her straw and stood up, trying to look nonchalant.

"Hi, Simon. What are *you* doing here?"

"I've come to see you, silly," he said gently. *He* was looking at her with concern, too. God, that pissed her off. She wasn't a bloody invalid. She was fed up with people giving her concerned looks, first Kris, then Charlie, and now her brother.

"What are you wearing, Ali?" Simon asked. She shrugged, it was none of his business. "You look like … well, words fail, to be honest,"

"Oh, Ali." Charlie had stood up and joined Simon; the two of them stood side by side, like a married couple united as they dealt with their problem child – the one who'd got caught shoplifting. Her body flushed with anger. They thought she was stupid. And she wasn't stupid. She was the cleverest girl in the room. And she knew what was best for herself.

CHAPTER 28

Ali stormed off and Charlie watched her go – the hideous pink outfit making her easy to spot as she galloped down the promenade towards the yacht club. Charlie looked at Simon, his face was contorted into the weirdest expression and she realised he was trying and failing to hold something in.

"What is she…" he gasped, laughs racking his entire body.

"Wearing? I know," she said, unable to stop the hiccupping giggles that were threatening to explode out of her. She felt terrible, but she couldn't hold them in any longer. Now Simon was crying with laugher, too. Neither of them able to say anything for a few minutes as they gave into hysterics. Charlie leant over and grabbed his hand and squeezed it, trying to communicate without words how brilliant it was to have him here with her, witnessing Ali's weird behaviour. He squeezed her hand back in support.

"Na na na na – na na na na. Na na na na – na na na na, Batman!" he sang-gasped a few seconds later and set her off again.

When she could, she said, "I've never seen her wear anything like that before."

"Where do you even get a pink jumpsuit with wings? It was like a cos play outfit on steroids."

"Honestly, I didn't know where to look. And neither will Antonio if he gets a glimpse of her in that."

The thought of Ali confronting her former lover in front of his wife – the scion of Puerto Andratx, one of the most powerful lawyers in Spain, a man who could kill her career dead in a heartbeat if he wanted to – snapped them out of their jokey mood.

Simon turned to her, and said urgently, "Come on, let's go, I've got a car – we can beat her there."

They ran outside and jumped into the rental car he'd driven from the airport and set off towards the yacht club at full speed. In the distance, they could see Ali, gleaming pinkly in the sun as she hurried along the promenade with her head down.

Charlie felt a huge lump in her throat and tears threatened to overwhelm her as they drove past her suffering friend. Despite the determination of her stride, Ali emanated hurt. It made Charlie want to both hug her and slap some sense into her in equal parts.

"How's this happened, Simon? What's wrong with her?"

"I think she may be having a breakdown."

"We've got to stop her. He's not a nice man. If she humiliates him in front of his family, he's going to crucify her."

They reached the club before Ali, but the guard wouldn't let them park as they weren't members. Charlie could see Ali approaching the club on the other side of the wall, heading towards the entrance, so she jumped out of the car and left Simon to go to park. Rushing inside, she looked around the busy dining room. No pink anywhere. There was only a handful of guests eating, and none of them looked like the picture of Antonio, which was a relief. Most of the room was taken up by a long table, for twenty plus guests she would estimate, set in the middle of the dining room, a primo spot with views over the marina.

She asked the bartender, a different one from last night, where the toilets were, and he pointed down the corridor. She pushed the door to the ladies open hard and almost fell, colliding into an attractive dark-haired woman who was leaning against the vanity, watching a beautiful teenager with the same glossy straight black hair apply lip gloss.

"I'm so sorry."

"No problem," the lady said in accented English, and smiled like she meant it. She said something to her daughter in what she assumed was Spanish and which Charlie figured meant "hurry up", as the teenager stopped titivating herself and joined her mother by the door. The two of them exited right towards the dining room, holding hands as they went.

"Ali?" Charlie said softly. There was no answer. "I know you're in there." The sun was streaming through the window, illuminating the room and leaving Ali nowhere to hide; Charlie could see a gleam of hot pink where Ali's outfit reflected onto the shiny white floor tiles of the bathroom.

"Go away," Ali said in a miserable little voice.

"Please come out. I know you're mad at us."

"You two are ganging up on me," Ali snapped childishly.

"Simon and I are just…"

"Simon and I," she said in a nasty snarky voice, "You just couldn't resist the opportunity to call your knight in shining armour."

"I called him last night, yes. I needed to talk to someone, because I was worried about you. But I didn't ask him to come to Mallorca. Honestly."

"You expect me to believe he just showed up?"

"Yes. It was a surprise for me, too," she reasoned through the door.

"Yeah, but a good one right? You two get to hang out and gang up on me."

"No, silly." She couldn't help but laugh a little. Ali sounded like she did when they were young. On the rare occasion Charlie had sided with Simon over her, Ali would always pout. But Ali wasn't laughing on the other side of the door. She was sobbing. Making a lot of noise. Charlie went and locked the main door into the bathroom from the corridor to stop anyone else coming in and overhearing her. She would feign being an ignorant British tourist if anyone tried to get in.

"Why are you here, Ali?"

"To make him shit a brick in front of his friends and family. He's having lunch in there in a minute. I was going to go up to his table and…"

"Ali, please don't do anything stupid."

"You think it's a stupid idea? Of course you do. Because YOU. BOTH. THINK. I'VE LOST IT." She raged from the other side of the toilet door.

"I don't think you've lost it," she soothed. Of course she *did*, but she didn't want to set her off again.

"You know I heard you talking about me? Simon said I was a bunny boiler," she wailed pathetically. Ali was vacillating between anger and self-pity.

"I'm sorry you heard that. And I fully support you, wanting to make Antonio suffer for what he's done to you, but this is—"

"And you're supposed to be my friend and you think I'm a bunny boiler, too." Ali sniffed pathetically.

"A very cute one," she chanced as a little joke. There was a loud nose blow and some snuffling in response, but at least she'd stopped crying. "Look. I get it. You want to go out there and give that asshole what he deserves, but you should—"

"Think about what it would to my career?" she said in a small, defeated voice.

"Yes."

"And what it would do to his wife and kids…" And with that, the sobs started again. "I could pretend they don't exist as I've never met them. But I'm sure I said hello to his wife and daughter just now. I locked myself in the toilet and stayed there because I couldn't stand to look at them. They were talking about their lunch and…" each word now punctuated by a fresh sob, "the … little … girl … guessed … what … her … Papi … would … choose … for … lunch."

"I saw them too. The girl was sweet, and the mum seemed nice. She was polite to me when I nearly knocked her over."

"Just make me feel worse, why don't you?" she howled, "I don't want to be a marriage wrecker. A revenge-filled bitter, twisted old spinster for the rest of my life."

Ali's words made Charlie smile. She sounded more like herself, which meant that reasonable Ali was in the building! Charlie said affectionately,

"You'd be *my* bitter, twisted old spinster, though. Anyway, there's got to be a better way to get back at him than by bringing yourself down to his level. You're the cleverest person I know. If you can't figure out a cool way to get your revenge, no one could."

"I *am* clever," Ali conceded.

Charlie laughed. "There's my girl. You know I love you so much, you're my best friend, the best friend anyone could have and I just don't want—"

"To argue with me? Me neither, my lover. Especially over a stupid man." Ali opened the door, tears streaming down her face, bat winged arms stretched wide. "Can I have a hug, please?"

"Only if you promise to put that bat costume in the bin the moment we get back to the hotel."

CHAPTER 29

After she'd given Ali the longest hug in the whole world and made her promise she wouldn't leave the bathroom until she came back for her, Charlie went in search of Simon.

She found him at the bar in the exact same spot Ali had been sitting yesterday, chatting to the barman, nursing a small beer. She couldn't help but smile at the sight of him and thought once again how similar the brother and sister were. Not physically, because Simon was a tall, heavyset man and Ali was petite – curvy but petite. They were similar in essence.

The siblings had the same eyes, an unusual clear grey which could shift closer to the blue of their mum's or green of their dad's depending on their moods. Simon had ruddy, tanned skin with a few crinkles and laughter lines around his eyes from all the time he spent outdoors – usually without sunscreen, however much she and Kitty nagged him. Ali who spent most of her time indoors at the office had skin that was freshly pink and white, adorned with cute freckles, and her eyes were always ringed by glamorous eye makeup.

Their hair was different colours, Ali's was a vibrant auburn and his was a dirty blonde with just the tiniest gleam of ginger in its depths, but it curled off their foreheads in a similar way. What made it clear that they were related was more subjective – their body language, the way they held themselves, the expectation of being welcomed wherever they went – a way of being that made them so similar and equally lovable to her. Their confidence had been instilled in them by dint of an excellent education and from growing up in a beautiful home with adoring wealthy parents. A way of being which, Charlie realised, with a deep pang of regret, Ali had been faking for some time. But she was going to fix that, with Simon's help.

She filled him in on Ali's whereabouts and Simon sighed in relief when she said Ali was behaving normally again, had promised not to do anything rash, and was waiting in the bathroom for her instructions.

"Do you trust her to stay there?" said Simon.

"I do. Where is el Prick?"

"He's over there, looking like a complete tosser." He turned and flicked his eyes toward Ali's nemesis. Antonio was at the head of the table, acting like the king of all he could survey – ordering things and bossing the bread server around. She noticed that the good-looking woman from the bathroom sat to his right, and the sweet girl was at the end of the table with a bunch of other teenagers.

She studied him surreptitiously. He was in good shape for his age and handsome in a tough way. He had powerful, meaty forearms and a well-developed chest like a bull. He looked like he would win a street fight as easily as a court case.

And, she thought, *if I replace the light blue polo shirt with a black hoodie, give him a neck tattoo and put him on a motorbike rather than a sailing yacht, or behind a deck, he'd look just like one of Ali's typical one-night stands.* She shook her head in disbelief, her girl loved a bad boy, but this one had brains and influence too – a potent combination – she was understanding a little more why her friend had fallen for him.

The waiter appeared to be recapping everyone's orders, and that gave her an idea.

"Ask for a table for three. It needs to be that one over there," she said pointing to the empty table at the opposite end. "I'm going for Ali."

Simon gasped. "You're not bringing her here?"

"Trust me. I know what I'm doing." Feeling confident that she had come up with a great plan.

"I know you do, Charlie."

Basking in Simon's faith in her, she walked the length of the room –

sensing, rather than seeing, Antonio check her out as she walked past the big table. Even though it hurt her heart to do so, she looked up, met his eye and smiled. He gave her an arrogant wink back, which made her want to throw up in her mouth.

Back in the ladies' room, which was actually more like a nice dressing room with toilets, she found Ali sitting in front of a mirror, tidying up her makeup. She could not do much to hide her tear ravaged eyes, but Charlie wanted her to wear her sunglasses, anyway. She explained her plan. And Ali, the trouper that she was, said she was up for it.

After squeezing her hand for courage, Charlie left her in the bathroom and made her way back along the corridor then walked across the dining area to join Simon. Charlie sat down opposite him, leaving one chair free for Ali. A minute later, perfectly on schedule, Ali sashayed slowly across the room, swaying her hips subtly, head high, rocking her pink jumpsuit like she was Beyonce. She kept her eyes locked on Charlie's and didn't glance towards the people at the other tables in the restaurant – many of whom were watching her entrance with unconcealed interest. As she reached her destination, Simon leapt up and solicitously pulled her close for a hug and a kiss, then held out her chair which she slid into with grace, her back firmly presented to Antonio.

"Can he see me?"

"Yes. Perfectly." The waiter rushed over and handed them the menu and wine list and they all pretended to look at it.

Then Ali stage whispered, "Did he notice me?"

Charlie, who was trying not to glance at Antonio for too long, lest he caught her checking him out, was trying to hold back a grin at the shellshocked look on his face.

Simon, who sat directly opposite his sister, had the best view of him. He could watch Antonio's face easily over Ali's shoulder.

"He saw you, alright. His face went white when he realised it was you. Then he took a gulp of water and I thought he would choke. He couldn't believe his eyes. He kept looking at your arse, and then up at your hair. He definitely recognised your arse. He's transfixed."

"I knew this jumpsuit was a good choice."

Charlie and Simon exchanged glances, but neither said anything.

"What's he doing now?"

"Staring at the back of your head and looking sick. Oh – now they've put a big old fish down in front of him. Ohh – he looks like he's going to throw up," Simon continued with his running commentary.

"Has anyone noticed he's acting funny?"

"There *is* another guy looking this way. I think maybe he's spotted something."

"Maybe it's one of his buddies from the boat. He might recognise me."

"OK, so the friend's got up. He's walking over to el Prick. And now he's whispering in his ear."

Charlie gasped. "Ohh!"

"What?" hissed Ali.

"I wish, oh, I wish I could video this."

"What? You two are really annoying! This is torture."

"Oh, just his face. Classic."

Simon seemed to be enjoying himself as much as he did when he was watching rugby.

"Classic play on your behalf, girls. That piece of shit is petrified. So el Prick has brushed his mate off. He's shaking his head, making out like the guy's got it wrong. He really doesn't want any of them to notice you."

Charlie took over the commentary. "I think his wife's noticed something. She's looking concerned, asking him something. Oh, now he's reassuring her. Oh, but if looks could kill. He's got to get those daggers under control or he'll give himself away."

Then Simon had an idea. "Stand up, sis, then just pause there for a moment like you're getting ready to go somewhere, that's good, now pat us both on the shoulders reassuringly, now, I'm going to look up at you adoringly and say something loudly, Charlie you check his face, tell us what he's doing". Simon delivered his words: "Are you sure you want to do that, Alison?"

Charlie was trying not to laugh out loud. "He looks like he's gonna shit himself, to be honest."

"That's because he's worried you're coming to his table now."

The waiter was heading towards them with a bottle of wine, some bread and a puzzled look on his face.

"Can I sit down now?"

"Yes."

"Can I have a drink?"

"No," said Simon

"Just one," said Charlie concurrently.

"Go on, Simon, you can't expect me to go through this experience cold turkey." Ali pouted.

Simon harrumphed, acknowledging the sense in that. "OK, but just one. I'm keeping an eye on you."

Lunch passed by in a blur. Charlie was proud of her friend. Ali, true to her word, managed to stick to her one glass of wine and drank most of the mineral water like a good girl and steadfastly kept her back to Antonio.

Simon and Charlie continued to watch the lunch group over her shoulder, commenting on his actions and reporting that his stony, tight-jawed face remained a picture of annoyance for the whole lunch. Not long after their own meal was served, Charlie reported that he'd sent away his fish, barely touched, which made Ali beam. He was greedy and normally consumed his food with relish.

A few minutes later, Simon reported, "I think we've successfully run him off. He's asked for the bill and everyone's looking pissed off. I think his wife's telling him he's a party pooper. She's put her hand on his arm and he just shook it off like she was a fly, and oh, the mates are standing up and booing him, I guess they're not ready to finish lunch after…" he checked his watch, "a full forty-five minutes."

Ali snorted. "He spends at least two or three hours over a meal."

"Oh, watch out, he might be heading this way."

Ali's face, which had relaxed a little over lunch, tightened. Charlie could see fear in her eyes and pain in the hard line of her jaw.

"It's OK, Ali, stay strong, talk to me, face this way so he can't see your face," Charlie urged.

"Tra la la la la la la la la, Charlie?" Ali sung nonsense in a breathy way, then leant in towards Charlie, like she was discussing the most salacious gossip. "What's he doing now?"

"Fascinating, darling. Simply fascinating." Charlie's voice rang out, then she added, sotto voce, "Simon, what *is* he doing?"

"He's shooting looks at her back, and he looks really angry. He's shaking his head now, he can't believe Ali hasn't turned round. Oh now he's given up glaring at you and he's making signs for his family to get up from the table." Simon maintained his football commentary style monologue, alternating glances between the girls and Antonio so it wasn't obvious he was talking about him. "Now, the wife and kids are saying their goodbyes and he's standing there glaring at them, oh, he's left them. He's stormed out the door like a boy band fan having a hissy fit. He thinks it's all over, and it is…"

"Ali, he's gone. And they've followed him," said Charlie softly a few seconds later and grabbed her friend's hand under the table to give it a reassuring squeeze. "You did it!" Her simple plan had worked, Charlie congratulated herself. She'd read somewhere that there was nothing that narcissistic bullies hated more than not getting a reaction from the people they tormented. Ali pointedly ignoring Antonio, in his place, his hometown, where he'd been petrified she would confront him but hadn't, would have messed with his head big time.

Antonio may have ruined her friend's life for the last few months, but she'd ruined his lunch at least. It was a minor victory but a necessary one for Ali's self-esteem.

The crew of three, relaxed now that "the git had gone", enjoyed the rest of their delicious lunch of grilled fish and salad. Ali, free to listen and able to translate what the remaining guests had to say, entertained them with her own running commentary. She could get the gist of most of what was being discussed. She grinned as she told them what his 'best friends' were saying about him: that he'd left without paying his share of the bill and how he'd ordered the most expensive thing on the menu, as always, but then left half of it. They then went on to talk about his lack of sailing skills – how if they didn't help him he wouldn't even be sitting there, as the boat was too big for him and he needed them to sail it.

As they were leaving, Charlie watched Ali cast her gaze over at the table, checking out the rest of Antonio's party for the first time. She scanned the faces until she settled on the guy that Simon had watched get up and talk to Antonio. She pushed her sunglasses down her nose, met his gaze of recognition and, confident he knew exactly who she was, smiled and turned away.

CHAPTER 30

Ali could hear the happy music of Charlie's giggles and Simon's snorts harmonising from two stories up. They were downstairs in the Brismar Hotel bar enjoying the delights of Andratx together and she was upstairs alone. The low buzz of their conversation, the comings and goings of the busy bar and the ripe smell of spilt wine and cigarette smoke combined and drifted up and through her open window.

They had decided to stay on in Andratx for one more night. Then tomorrow morning, Charlie and Ali would go back to Palma and resuscitate their critically ill holiday and Simon would get on a flight back to the UK to rescue Ed from his backlog of patients. Ali imagined the other two were having a fine old time, celebrating today's offensive, congratulating themselves on humiliating Antonio. They may be proud as punch to have gone out to battle for her, without considering that because she'd loved him it had been a pyrrhic victory for her and now she felt as low as a toad's belly.

She pulled the sheets over her head trying to block the ambient noise out. Her mind was racing, looping endlessly, trying to figure out what she should have understood months ago: the ramifications of having an affair with one of the most powerful lawyers in her firm.

Practicality was now her priority. Her passion for Antonio, the naive infatuation which she believed was love, had made her behave like a madwoman. Her passion for him hadn't completely burnt itself out – you can't just flip a switch and stop caring about someone – but his behaviour had doused it in cold water and it was down to the dying embers.

She threw the sheet off her in frustration. She'd trusted him and convinced herself they were partners, like an idiot! She could see what she'd stubbornly refused to see before: their relationship wasn't equal and never had been; the power rested in his hands.

She'd adored him for being successful, intelligent and worldly. He was the only man she'd ever put on a pedestal. She thought he loved her, but no, he'd wanted her because she was young, foreign, biddable, willing to fit into his schedule and provided the sexual services of a weekday geisha.

By turning up in Mallorca and intruding on his 'real life', she'd challenged the status quo and got introduced to the real Antonio: a selfish, entitled cowardly prick, a man who may possibly take his revenge on her humiliation of him by ruining her career.

She was scared silly by the prospect of what might happen next. Anxiety rather than Spanish tummy twisted her insides at the mere idea of having to deal with Antonio on the De la Cruz account. And what would her Bristol office boss, the awful Christopher Falcon, do next? Would he try to sack her? He was the one who'd sent her the threatening email, so he probably already knew about her affair. Why did she let it get this far?

When she'd discovered who Antonio was on the first-day tour of the Madrid office, she'd felt her heart nearly leap out of her chest. The secretary who'd been tasked to orientate the new recruits, took them past an occupied conference room and Ali saw someone who looked like Tony, the Tinder guy she'd hooked up with twice the previous week. Turning her head away from the glass-sided room so he wouldn't see her, she'd casually asked their guide about the people in the meeting, and she found out the man at the head of the table was Antonio Garcia Fernández, a partner in the firm. As soon as discretion allowed, she looked him up on the company website and studied his picture and biography; it was definitely him. The deep-set, hooded eyes, square jaw, patrician nose and firm lips that had made her shiver with lust just last week were the same – what was different was his style.

In his work garb, he looked to be in his forties, stern and professional, clean shaven and wearing a snowy white shirt, tie and exquisitely tailored suit. Whereas, when they'd met in the hotel bar he'd said he was younger and looked it in jeans and tight tee-shirt with a day's worth of stubble darkening his jaw. The app had handled the basic details of what they both desired from their hook-up; and she'd known they were well matched from the moment they set eyes on each other in real life. His dark gaze made her tingle in anticipation as it morphed from curiosity into delight, then un-restrained lust, as he devoured the sight of her in a tight, black body-con dress and high red heels. More than satisfied with her first impression of him too, she'd let 'Tony' buy her a drink and, after taking the measure of him over a glass of red wine, deduced that the only thing she didn't approve of was his lack of ink. A complaint that was rectified later in her hotel room when she found a black and grey, highly realistic lion tattoo on his right shoulder blade. Recalling that tattoo, and how she'd traced its outline with her lips, while reading his impressive resume at her new desk in the office of the firm that his forbears had founded both scared her silly and gave her a sexual jolt. Was she the only person in the building to have seen Antonio Garcia Fernández's, *león*?

She managed to avoid bumping into him at the office and the following week he messaged her again on the app, still not knowing who she was. She knew what she was doing was madness and *had* planned to come clean, but when he arrived at her hotel animal attraction trumped good sense. It was intoxicating that a man of his calibre had emerged from the morass of tolerable, rarely more than fit-for-purpose men she usually met through various dating apps. The illicit thrill of doing what she knew was wrong made him even more appetising – she found she couldn't help herself and fell on top of the bed, and onto the floor, and then into the shower with him. Later that night, as he was leaving, he asked how much more time they had together before she had to go back home to England, and she fessed up she wasn't a tourist staying for a few weeks in Madrid, rather a trainee lawyer at his firm.

She expected him to be angry, but he caught her off guard again. Antonio found the improbability of their meeting amusing rather than alarming, and suggested that as long as no one else knew, that they didn't interact at the office, and she played by the rules they could continue to meet. She'd grabbed onto his 'rules' like a drowning sailor. Allowing her fears to sink and get buried deeper than the Mariana Trench. But now those fears had risen to the surface.

She'd done a bad, bad thing, and she wasn't sure yet what she was going to do to protect herself and her career, but she knew one thing for sure, she couldn't deal with it on her own anymore.

It was time to talk it through and Charlie, though pissed at her for not telling her before, wanted to help. The girl was an angel, supportive and kind as always and she'd been a shitty friend in return: lying to her about why they were in Mallorca and then leaving her alone at that restaurant with no explanation. But Ali was determined to make it up to her.

She felt the bile of repressed guilt rise in her throat as she thought about the other big, noisy, impatient elephant in the room: the cruel and meddlesome things she'd said to her brother on the evening of her dad's birthday. Anyone with half a brain could see that Simon and Charlie had liked each other for a very long time and that they would make a great couple. But their connection had always pissed her off, and she knew why. It wasn't as noble a reason as she'd convinced herself – protecting Charlie from further heartache – it was the most selfish of reasons: jealousy.

She was absurd. Not only had she been having an affair with her married boss, but she had also managed to get herself into a love triangle with her brother and her best friend. It was time to set things straight and as soon as they got back to Palma, she'd tell Charlie what she'd said to Simon that night and why. And, if the two of them still wanted to pursue something, well then, they'd have her blessing, and she'd just have to suck it up.

And feeling a little bit happier with herself, she drifted off.

CHAPTER 31

It had been a crazy 48 hours. Not quite the relaxing sun and fun holiday she had anticipated, but perhaps it was all for the best. Ali had been forced to come clean about Antonio and now she could support her friend as she figured out what to do next. And they were in the perfect place to do it as there was still another week of holiday to go!

"You know, Simon, I'm very proud of our Ali. She did great today. I admit she gave me a scare, and I was quite upset with her at one point, her behaviour was very odd, and I'm so glad you came to help. But it all makes sense now. I know she only didn't tell me because she loved him and she promised *him* she wouldn't. She's so loyal. That's a hell of a burden to carry."

Simon moved his head noncommittally; he was halfway through his beer and was gazing at the twinkling lights that decorated the harbour in front of them. Looking at him looking at the view, made her happy. His presence and the knowledge that Ali was safe and recovering from her ordeal upstairs comforted her. It gave her the strength to ask something she was dying to know.

"Why did you go to Australia, Simon?"

"I guess it's time to come clean."

"Not on a cricket trip, then?" she asked pointedly.

"No. Not as enjoyable as that." He darted a nervous glance at her. "I went to see Sandy."

She nodded sagely. She'd guessed right. It was best that he told her.

"So, you're giving it another go?"

"No way." He nearly spat his drink out in disgust. Then turned to her with a hurt expression on his face. "What on earth made you think that? You know how I feel about y—"

She glared at him, so he stopped short of saying you. "Why did you go to Australia, then?"

"Can I go and get another drink?" He was just as evasive as his sister when it came to getting down to the nitty gritty, she noted grimly.

"No! Stay here and spit it out."

He sighed deeply. "A few days before the summer solstice ball, Sandy emailed me." She started doing mental arithmetic, that would have been in the week when he'd started behaving oddly with her, "she said she was six months pregnant and implied that…" He looked as if he was in physical pain.

"You were the daddy?"

He nodded his head sadly.

"Were you?" She couldn't believe how calm her voice sounded, considering there was a symphony of pain reverberating around her brain.

"I did the maths and realised that there was a very slim chance, so…"

And just then, her phone rang. Discombobulated by Simon's news, and wanting a distraction, she picked it up.

"It's Chix. I need to take it."

Simon acted like she'd shot him. Flinching away before falling back towards her and saying in a tight, urgent voice,

"No you don't Charlie, you need to listen to me first. Call him back."

Something snapped – how dare Simon boss her around like that?

"Don't tell me who I can talk to." She looked away from him, took a deep, calming breath and said sweetly, "Hey, Chix, what's up, my darling?"

By the time she'd finished the greeting, Simon had stormed off to the other side of the room. She watched his back, rigid with tension and saw him gesturing impatiently at the bartender, then at the shelf behind the bar. How like his sister he was!

"Hey beautiful, just checking in to see how my girl Ali's doing." Chix's mellow voice recharged her batteries like the sunshine he always seemed to bring with him.

"Oh, that's so kind of you." And she filled him in quickly. All the time she was speaking, she watched Simon. She noted how the barman poured him a huge shot of brandy, which he downed half of before he got back to their table. As he approached, and just because she knew it would wind him up, she started crooning into the phone. "Chix darling, you really are the sweetest. I don't know what I'd do without you. Speak tomorrow. Love you. Mwww."

She looked up and saw that Simon's face was puce with anger and decided to rub salt into the wound. "So, you were saying ... Sandy's pregnant, you're the father, and—"

"I didn't say that," he snapped at her. "I was *trying* to explain why I had to go to see her." He shook his head in frustration. "But no, you don't listen, you'd rather talk to that bloody Chicken fellow or whatever his stupid name is." Simon looked as angry and as ruffled as a Rhode Island Red being chased by a fox. She was enjoying his discomfort, truth be told. How could he be so jealous of Chix? All he had to do was ask what was or *wasn't* going on between them, but he never had.

Glaring at her he demanded, "Do you love him?"

She could have reassured him they were only friends, but Simon was annoying and she was enjoying making him suffer. "You know what, Simon, I do." It wasn't a lie. She *did* love Chix. Just not in the way Simon thought she did.

Her words knocked the stuffing out of him. She watched as his powerful six-foot three frame seemed to shrink, getting smaller and smaller until her big strong vet looked like a little old man slumped in the burgundy leather bar chair. She'd been mean, had gone too far and was just about to take pity on him and tell him the truth, because it had finally dawned on her that if he was this jealous of Chix, then he must really care about her, and then he said something that changed everything.

"I never thought I'd ever say this, Charlie, but I'm glad now that my sister warned me off you."

CHAPTER 32

Travelling cattle class is another punishment for fucking everything up, she thought. She'd failed to change her first-class return ticket on BA so she and her brother were on the last EasyJet flight of the day out of Mallorca, heading to Bristol. The plane was her cramped and smelly penance.

Simon, who'd bagged the aisle, because his legs were too long to put under the seat in front, was equally uncomfortable. He looked like death warmed up and every person who made their way along the narrow corridor to the toilet either tripped over his feet or kicked him. Ali, who'd got stuck with the middle, Simon on one side and another enormous man on the other encroaching onto her limited space, was both bothered by their hulking proximity and dismayed to find her bottom only just fitted the narrow seat. She felt as flat as the proverbial pancake and the thought of going back to her flat in Bristol was already filling her with dread. Despite sitting next to her brother, she'd never felt this lonely in her life.

"I've never seen that side of her before."

"What side before?"

"Vengeful! She slammed into our room in a terrible mood. You should have seen her. She was so cold, I could feel the chill coming off her in waves. First time I ever saw her like that."

"First time? What about that time you borrowed her precious CD and Tarzan got hold of it and buried it in the garden and we found it a few days later, all chewed up and slobbery?" Simon joked, humour having always been the way Hobsons dealt with painful issues. But not even a Tarzan story could raise a smile.

"She was so angry, Simon. And said that I had disappointed her, really disappointed her, which is the worst thing she's ever said to me. All I did was make a comment about her disturbing my beauty sleep while you two were getting all cosy downstairs and she bit my head off!"

Simon winced. "You shouldn't have done that."

"Well, she'd turned on all the lights and woke me up," she said defensively. But then recalled the look of utter disgust on Charlie's face when she'd complained. "She also told me to grow up and that she was fed up with both of us! And that we had to make our own way back to Palma because she was going to take the rental!" She looked at Simon accusingly.

"I didn't have any choice but to give her the key. She demanded it, but I was worried about her driving in that state," Simon said, "did you hear—"

"NO and I'm not likely to, until we get this mess sorted out. How could you tell her I'd spoken to you and warned you off her *for her own good*? You really dropped me in it."

"Because she wouldn't listen to me about Sandy," he hissed. "I was trying to explain to her, and she just wouldn't listen and it just popped out."

"You've really fucked things up for me, Simon, I was going to tell her."

He looked at her like he didn't believe her.

"When we got to Palma. I was going to thank her for everything she's done for me over the last few days and tell her I understand I have 'issues' around Antonio and that I'm going to talk to someone professional about my relationship – prove to the two of you that I'm not a bunny boiler."

"Good for you. She'd like that."

"Then we'd have a few days in Palma, go to some nice restaurants, enjoy the hotel, have a proper holiday this time and when she was in a good mood and all relaxed, I'd break the news about how I'd kind of interfered in 'youse touse' budding romance."

"Kinda interfered? You did interfere!"

She remembered watching Charlie in total bewilderment. She didn't recognise the tight-jawed, rigid woman, moving like an automaton as she put her few possessions together on the bed, and packed her overnight bag without acknowledging her attempts to talk to her.

"I assumed she was still cross I hadn't told her about Antonio, so I begged her not to rush off, said I knew I'd been a crappy friend recently but that I'd make it up to her." She felt sick when she thought about the way Charlie looked at her. "But she said she knew I was only being nice because I 'felt guilty about warning Simon off a clinging, needy person like me'. And that's when it hit me – you must have told her!"

Simon nodded, looking grim. "What else did you say?"

She felt embarrassed by his scrutiny. "Well, first, I tried to wiggle out of it by saying I hadn't said that – I'd just told you you'd better be 100 percent sure you wanted a commitment … and she basically said 'bullshit, Ali'." She felt a fresh bout of shame. "Then, because I was feeling backed into a corner, and sometimes rather than apologise I argue back…"

"Oh, Ali…" Simon was looking pityingly at her.

She glared at him. "I told her it was *her* fault because *she'd* never told *me* about the fact that you two started getting all kissy-kissy."

"Just to clarify, we didn't actually do anything, we just…"

She shuddered in disgust. "Yuck. No details, please." Warding off his words with her hands. "That backfired, because then she shouted at me about not telling her about Antonio which she said was much worse."

"I still don't understand that, to be honest. Why didn't you?"

"I wanted to, but I couldn't. I'd promised him," she said truthfully.

He took his time processing her response. "Funny. Charlie Girl guessed it would be something like that. About you having to be loyal to that prick. Even when she's upset with you she finds an excuse for your behaviour."

Ali wanted to cry. "My sister from another mister." The feeble joke went nowhere near expressing the feelings of guilt and regret she was experiencing for hurting someone who knew her so well. "Bet I seem stupid to you, now. You both saw the terrible side of him."

"I thought he was a complete tool to be honest, sis, but as the song goes, 'no one knows what goes on behind closed doors'," Simon quipped.

Ali rolled her eyes, but affectionately, at her brother's lame but well-intentioned attempt to sound understanding. "She was furious – I had nothing to lose by then, launched in about *her* secret – about you two getting close." She felt tears prick in her eyes, and she glared at him, "Because that hurt me, you know, and do you know what she said?"

"I don't but I guess you're going to enlighten me."

She gave him a Paddington Bear stare. "She said she was too scared to tell me. That she'd been working up courage to say something but because I'm so scathing and opinionated, she'd chickened out!" she finished, omitting to tell Simon that her own behaviour had been so distant and uncommunicative that she hadn't given Charlie the opportunity.

"Well, we make a pretty pair, don't we?"

She looked at her brother quizzically.

"The only reason she lashed out at *you* is because she's fed up with me, too."

"Go on."

Simon sighed, then confessed in a quiet voice, "You'd got it right back in the summer. I *did* like her and I was going to ask her out properly, at the ball. But then after Dad's birthday, I was kind of freaked out by what you'd said – and to make things even worse Sandy emailed me out of the blue and told me she was pregnant."

Ali was horrified. "Oh, that's a shocker. Did you tell Mum and Dad?"

"No! I didn't tell anyone. Because I'm not bloody stupid *and* by that time I'd found out she'd been having it off with the guy she worked for…"

She nodded sagely. "Charlie said."

Simon looked outraged. "You both knew about the affair?"

"Yep. For ages. Kitty told Charlie and she told me. Kitty found out at the ball," she explained helpfully.

He sighed then shook his head in exasperation, "Bloody gossipy lot. Anyway, even though I was ninety-nine-point nine percent positive the baby wasn't mine, because, well, I won't go into details…"

"Please don't," Ali quipped.

Simon glared at her then continued. "I wanted to be one hundred percent sure, so I spoke with Ed."

"I thought you said you hadn't told anyone."

Simon rolled his eyes in annoyance at yet another interruption, "Shut it, clever clogs. I had to talk to someone, I was going mad, so I spoke to him, no one else, about the email and he said best to admit to nothing, bide my time and if Sandy was still insisting the baby was mine after she had it – make her do a paternity test. Then, I told him I'd sort of asked Charlie Girl out…"

Ali did a double take; Simon was full of surprises today, too.

"You did? When?"

"The day after the ball. She turned me down."

"She did?" Before she had time to obsess over the fact that Charlie hadn't told her about any of this Simon blurted out the rest of explanation.

"It was terrible timing to be fair. Ed, who'd been quite sympathetic up until that point, called me an idiot and told me I should have waited." He shuddered. "Trouble was, I wasn't thinking with my brain. I was thinking with my—" Ali put her hand up to stop him saying any more. Just because Simon was attracted to her friend didn't mean she had to listen to him imagining them doing it. "When I saw that letch Davide slobbering all over her at the ball I knew I didn't want…"

"You didn't want anyone else to have her," Ali finished his sentence, understanding his motivation even though she'd never thought of her brother as the jealous type. She didn't want Charlie to have someone else, either. Was that creepy of her? Probably. Did she harbour romantic feelings for her friend? No! She'd never considered that as a possibility – but maybe that was something else to talk to her shrink about when she found one? Which she would have to do. An image of the dreaded pink jumpsuit lying crumpled in the waste bin at the Hotel Brismar flashed across her mind. She hadn't made the best decisions recently. Simon neither.

"That's not a good enough reason to be with someone."

"I know. I know I fucked up. So, I've been 'giving her some space' over the summer." He put the corny words in air quotes. "But then she called *me* about you, and she wanted my help and that made me feel …"

"Like a hero?" Ali injected sarcastically.

Simon looked hurt, "Well I was worried about you too, and it meant that Charlie and I were on the same wavelength again. So last night, after we'd dissected the whole el Prick situation…"

"El Prick. I like it." It suited him she decided.

"I tried to explain my trip to Australia, but then Chix called and she picked up when I asked her not to and we ended up rowing and long story short she told me to go back to Sandy! And that we deserved each other."

"Ouch." She picked up on the paranoia that had ruined everything. "Simon, why do you get so jealous when she talks about Chix? She's not interested in him, you know."

"But she was…"

"Maybe a little, and for a short time, Simon," she said gently. "He really helped her through her breakup with Graham."

His face screwed up and he said petulantly, "He sounds too bloody perfect. It's Chix this and Chix that. She calls him all the time for advice. Says he's good at *listening*. He's good with women, apparently. Seems like I'm only good with animals."

"It's probably true you're better with animals than you are with women. I mean if Sandy was a horse or a pet of some kind, you'd have liked the look of her, but you'd never have picked her with that temperament, right?"

Her lame joke failed to rouse even the tiniest of smiles. She looked at her big handsome brother, the brilliant vet, the perfect son, the current squire of Puddlington, and all she could see was a sad little boy when he said,

"I fucked up *again*, Ali."

She slipped her soft little office job hand into his big, rough farmwork one and squeezed. They didn't always see eye to eye on lots of things but they were quite similar in some ways.

"I fucked up too, Simon. Do you know what she said that hurt the most?"

He shook his head.

"She said she loved us, me, you and the Parentals from the moment we met. From the day the posh Hobsons from Puddlington Manor asked the lowly Pierces from Ivy Cottage for drinks. That we had welcomed her and her family into our lives and made our village feel like home and everything was better after that. And then she said she'd put us all on a pedestal for too long." She sighed. "She was sad but so strong you know, Simon. She said there'd been too many secrets and lies between us and we'd drifted so far apart that she didn't know if we can make it back to each other – and I'm worried she's right."

PART FOUR

SEPTEMBER 2015
MYKONOS, GREECE

CHAPTER 33

A pretty, plump blonde-haired woman with sparkling blue eyes and glowing skin was shouting and waving her hands energetically – trying to attract her attention and succeeding. She had a warmly welcoming smile with a touch of the cheeky in it and she looked vaguely familiar.

She called out, "So you're the famous Charlie! Come and take a seat in the shade by me, babe. Been dying to meet you." And she moved a couple of feet to the right to make room for her. The invitation *was* inviting. She looked perfectly cool and comfortable nestled into the huge white sofa. There was lots of lovely shade, being as it was positioned under a gigantic cantilevered white umbrella, from where you could look over the lake-like swimming pool onto the unmistakable mass of white boxy shapes that was Mykonos town, then up and out to the limpid blue waters of the Aegean.

Charlie was glad to be told what to do. She was shellshocked by the glamour of the vast villa where Chix had invited her to hide out while she dealt with her feelings about the bloody Hobsons. It was nice of the older woman to welcome her so effusively, but she was a little confused as to who she was and why she was here too. The woman must have read the question on her face and helpfully introduced herself.

"I'm Tracy, Chix's half-sister, and this is my other half, Dr Clinton Derrick," she smiled proudly, gesturing to her partner, who stood up, extended his hand in welcome and said in a deep, warm voice,

"But please call me Diver. Everyone else does."

Diver was a tall, well-built and friendly looking man with a charming gap-toothed smile. The couple complemented each other. Both were dressed in colourfully casual attire and the two of them really 'popped' against the elegant white décor of their surroundings: Tracy in her massive black cat-eye Gucci sunglasses and a hot pink sundress that was straining a little at the seams and Diver in a sunny yellow baseball cap and a turquoise tee-shirt with the words CHERISH ZEPHYR in curly white letters emblazoned across his chest.

"Chix's sister. How exciting to meet you." She was intrigued! So this was the mysterious half-sister from the UK. Chix had only found out she existed the year before. "He's told me all about you."

"I bet he hasn't!" she retorted, then cackled to show she was making a joke. She had a husky estuary-English accent and reminded Charlie, who loved vintage comedy, a little of Barbara Windsor, the diminutive actress made famous by the *Carry On* films and, more recently, *East Enders*. She had the same sort of mischievous sex appeal. Charlie tried to spot a family resemblance between her and Chix but couldn't. Apart from maybe the sex appeal and the easy confidence.

"Are you on holiday from England?" Charlie asked politely.

Tracy laughed again. "No, Zephyr. We live there. But we had to leave for a bit. Did you know the island got hit by a hurricane last week?"

Charlie nodded, and looked concerned. "I heard." She felt awful! Chix had mentioned it on the phone earlier but absorbed in her own personal drama she'd selfishly forgotten to ask about it. "Is everyone OK?"

"Our house got a bit of a battering and the pole went down so we don't have current – that's why Chix invited us here."

Current? she thought, but didn't say anything, unwilling to show her ignorance. *What on earth would dried grapes have to do with moving out of a house?* Her confusion was written clearly on her face.

Diver laughed and came to her rescue. "Current is how we describe electricity in Zephyr. My English lady is on her way to becoming a local," he teased and ruffled Tracy's blonde curls.

She laughed. "Well, that clears that up. Sorry about your house. Will it be OK?"

"It's actually fine." Tracy smiled, looking quite happy about it. "We're taking the opportunity to add A/C to a few rooms, aren't we, babe?" Diver nodded, looking less enthusiastic about that development than Tracy. "Zephyr is too blinking hot in the summer without it. So it was a blessing that Chix said he was coming here to spend time with his girlfriend and there was lots of room for us too."

Diver jumped in. "And it's quite fortuitous timing, as we're working on a project we need Chix's help with." He pointed at his tee-shirt.

Tracy took over, "And being in Greece means we can work on it away from certain nosy parker people in Zephyr." The couple exchanged pointed looks.

"And I *finally* got to visit Delos." The big man sighed like a lovestruck teenager and pointed a hand towards the great blue yonder. She tried to see what he was aiming at but couldn't. "Birth place of Apollo and Artemis? One of the most important mythological, historical and archaeological sites in Greece?"

Charlie was still drawing a blank. Tracy rescued her.

"Don't worry, love, I didn't have a clue either. But this one here, my museum man, he's a top archaeologist," said Tracy proudly, and looked at her guy with so much love and respect, it made Charlie catch her breath.

A lump formed in her throat at their evident togetherness and mutual besottedness – throwing everything she'd lost into sharp relief. She needed to change the subject, otherwise she'd start bawling about Simon and Sandy and the whole bloody Ali debacle.

"What a nice tee-shirt," she said brightly. "I really love it. I certainly cherish Zephyr! Where can I get one?"

"I'll give you one," Tracy answered promptly, "as long as I can take your pic in it looking gorge, and we can share it on social media."

"Of course. Are you selling them, then?"

"Not exactly. It's for a campaign we're working on – to raise awareness about this huge tourism project on Lower Shell Bay that a bunch of us concerned citizens think will ruin Zephyr."

"The same project Chix and Dwight and Marvel are involved in?"

"The very same. BeachLuxe." Tracy spat the name out with the force of a cat coughing up a fur ball.

"Oh. Is it bad news for the island?" she asked in a worried tone.

Turns out it was. Tracy and Diver spent the next ten minutes outlining the BeachLuxe team's evil plans for a mega resort they were convinced was too big for Zephyr and would threaten the beauty and sustainability of the island.

It sounded awful. And as they talked, she felt worse and worse, because now it seemed that not only had she fallen out with her best friend and rejected the love of her life, but she was also the one who'd introduced her ex, Graham, to Zephyr and his stupid development was going to ruin that too.

CHAPTER 34

It was her brother's idea for her to come home with him to Puddlington. He was right, the old manor house was cosy and familiar – infinitely preferable to being on her own in the soulless flat. She'd poo-poohed the idea to start with, because she couldn't face talking to the Parentals yet, they'd be so ashamed of her – then Simon had reminded her she wouldn't have to; they were away again, in Cornwall this time, for an Agatha Christie themed murder mystery weekend.

She didn't think anyone would miss her in Bristol or anywhere else either, so she'd taken his advice and decided to hole up at home. The idea was to work her way through the huge selection of ready meals in the Hobson family freezer and try her best to avoid decimating her dad's wine cellar, while she attempted to figure out what to do next.

The first morning back in Wiltshire, she woke from an unsatisfactory sleep feeling unsettled, unrested and deeply sorry for herself and only dragged herself out of her pit of misery when Flopsy's hand-licking and whining to be let out became too much to ignore. Simon had gone to work and had left the dog with her for company.

Luckily Puddlington Manor had huge grounds for Flopsy to get a bit of run around and do her business, because she couldn't risk taking her out for a walk. She might get spotted by a nosy Puddlingtonian who would likely say something to the Pierces, who, if they knew she was here would be curious and concerned and would come looking for her – which would be a disaster. She still had no idea where Charlie had gone, or if she'd even told her parents she was no longer with Ali in Mallorca.

In the morning, she sent three texts to Charlie asking her to please call, ate two slices of toast and marmite, drank copious amounts of tea and fed the ever-present and adoring Flopsy so many treats she started farting every time she wagged her tail, which was often.

In the afternoon she sent two more texts to Charlie and a long rambling voice message and then started googling Antonio – she didn't want to but she couldn't seem to help herself. She did a deep dive into his life in the upper echelons of Madrid and Mallorquín society, something she'd never done before as, brainwashed by her love, she'd created a little world for the two of them and hadn't looked far outside it. A few pointless hours and many hurtful discoveries later, feeling thoroughly disgusted with herself, like she'd consumed pages and pages of the worst sort of pornography, she erased her search history – then went to the wine rack and opened a bottle of her father's Claret, reasoning that Simon would be home in a few hours to help her finish it and it would go well with the M&S steak and mushroom pies with a rich gravy she'd earmarked for dinner.

She hoped the wine would help her focus. She needed a plan! She had a few more days before she was due back in the office to face the music. On the positive side, she still had a job. She knew that because in her line of work there was never ever a complete break and she'd been dealing with a few bits and pieces at her client's behest, even though she was officially on holiday. There had been no more threatening emails either, which didn't really surprise her as they didn't really have a legal leg to stand on.

On the negative side, she couldn't see how she and Antonio could possibly continue working for the same firm. One of them was going to have to go and as he was an equity partner it wasn't likely to be him. Her feelings towards her ex were quixotic. One moment she was grieving deeply for the loss of the love affair of her life, the next she felt overpowered by anger and disappointment. She imagined snuggling into his chest one minute and slapping his face the next.

Her brain was being unreasonable, trying to hold on to the good things, despite the cursedness of the situation. The recalcitrant organ was stubborn and didn't want to admit she had been hoodwinked. Thank goodness Charlie had saved her from making an ever-bigger ass of herself than she could have. She needed to thank her and tell her that she'd come to her senses – but she couldn't because the stubborn woman wouldn't return her calls.

The kitchen door opened, and her brother walked in – shoulders slumped and looking as tired and fed up as she felt. Flopsy, insensitive to his sombre mood, bolted joyfully over to meet him, squiggling and shaking in excitement. He stepped back automatically and managed to avoid her signature greeting, which missed his feet and instead pooled on the ancient flagstone floor in a delicate pattern.

He shook his head and asked, "Do you think she'll ever grow out the golden shower phase?"

Ali snorted and made a feeble joke in response. "I don't know. You're the vet. Maybe when she's the dog-years equivalent of a pensioner?"

"Rather than having an excitable bladder she'll have a prolapsed one by that age." He sighed dramatically and reached for the kitchen roll, placed a couple of sheets on the puddles and put his boot down on top to dry the mess. "I think we may be stuck with it." Gingerly picking up the sheets with his thumb and forefinger, to avoid the damp bits, he placed them in the kitchen bin while the culprit looked on innocently. He bent down and gave her silky reddish-gold head a stroke.

"Can I have a glass of that?" indicating the bottle in front of her.

"Sure." She poured a glass and pushed it over the kitchen table.

"Did you call Dr Ellen?"

"Yes, Dad." Rolling her eyes. "She said she'd fit me in tomorrow." Simon grunted in approval. "Any news on Charlie yet?" she asked anxiously.

"Eventually. Took me all day to find out. Kitty has banned Ed from talking to me – she's in a filthy mood with yours truly, too.".

"Poor you." Everyone knew Kitty could say terrible things when riled.

"Tell me about it. This morning she called me every word for 'stupid' under the sun and then instructed the Posse to send me to Coventry." He sighed and said tiredly, "They are forbidden from making me drinks, wouldn't give me a piece of Shirley's birthday cake, and everyone went home early, so there was no one there to help with the mucking out." She murmured in sympathy. That was a lot of small pony shit to deal with. "Anyway, Ed took pity on me eventually and told me what Charlie had told Kitty – that she needs another week off to think about her next move, not to say anything to her mum and dad, but also not to worry because she's safe and happy where she is."

"Which is?"

Simon looked positively green around the gills. "Greece. Bloody perfect Chix invited her to Mykonos."

CHAPTER 35

Turned out that Tracy, like her half-brother, was easy to talk to.

Last night she'd enjoyed getting to know Tracy and Diver over a splendid starlit dinner in the fig-scented gardens. Chix had hosted the delicious meal in his girlfriend's absence. He was in an expansive mood and told them that Ambrosia sent her apologies and hoped they would all enjoy their stay. He looked happy and relaxed – as completely at home in his girlfriend's villa as he was in his own bar. They talked about Mykonos and then Zephyr and the recent hurricane. She learnt how petrifying – and at the same time exciting – experiencing a major storm is, and how each one is different. Tracy enlightened her on how different life on Zephyr was when you lived there all year round, as opposed to being a tourist. Curious, she asked how Tracy and Diver had met (Diver gave them the PG version apparently) and then Tracy in turn asked her how Charlie and Chix had become such firm friends. She entertained them with a short version of her honeymoon breakup story on Prickly Pear and how Chix and Marvel had been amazing and saved the day; and she would love them for that forever. Diver then told her that he'd recognised her when she'd turned up at the villa.

Puzzled, she'd asked them how, and Tracy filled her in on how they'd seen Charlie and Chix dancing at Shell Cay, and how they'd made an impression on her because they made such a striking couple. That led on to discussing the incredible coincidence: that Tracy had no idea the handsome, golden loc'd man she was studying was, in fact, the brother she'd come to Zephyr to find! Diver then added they'd seen Charlie a second time – dancing with Chix again – but on this occasion at D'wine and commented she'd looked much happier then than she did the first time.

Charlie understood now why Tracy had looked familiar. Zephyr was a small place indeed!

"I was! And I remember you at Shell Cay! I was watching you two also! And I was jealous! I imagined you were having a hot and heavy holiday romance because…"

"We were all over each other – like a rash?" Tracy supplied helpfully. Charlie giggled, remembering the two of them dancing sexily and making out like teenagers.

"Yes! And because you looked so much happier than I felt and I was the one that was supposed to be having the time of my life – as I was on honeymoon."

"And Diver and I noticed you because not only were the pair of you gorgeous but you looked miserable as sin most of the time," said Tracy bluntly.

Charlie went on to tell them how Graham had ignored her for the entire lunch and confessed then it was quite likely that when she was drinking lethal rum punches and dancing with Chix to cheer herself up, the seeds of the dreaded BeachLuxe Project had been sown. She explained how Graham, a property developer in London, spent lunch chatting to Dwight and a fellow called Chad about real estate opportunities.

Charlie found out that Chix had also been part of the BeachLuxe team at the beginning, before he knew the extent of it, but he'd swapped sides and was against it now, hoping to find a way to get Dwight, his best friend and one of the major players, to back out too. She also found out that her friend Marvel, who'd got involved in the PR for the project, was also trying to extract herself from the contract without too much damage to her career, which Charlie was happy to hear.

Unfortunately, horrid BeachLuxe had already won outline approval from the government and secured the money from a huge financial backer from the USA but the Cherish Zephyr team were determined not to give in and were currently working on presenting a 'high-value, low-volume' alternative in the hope the development team could be encouraged to change it to something that would have less environmental impact. Diver and Tracy were passionate about 'their island' and Charlie was sure they'd come up with something fantastic. They were too clever and good not to.

This morning they all met up again for breakfast. Diver and Chix had gone into a huddle and Tracy, after consuming two slices of country bread with cheese, olives and tomatoes followed by a huge bowl of glossy Greek yogurt, pistachio nuts and local honey, rubbed her tummy contentedly, let out a little tiny burp (which Diver gave her the stink eye for) and said that she was going to leave the men to their 'teeny, tiny turtles, stinky salt ponds and septic setbacks' and go to explore Mykonos town. She invited Charlie to come with her and she leapt at the chance, having had enough sunbathing for a bit, keen to get out and do some shopping and sightseeing.

Tracy drove confidently down the steeply sharp and winding road that linked the villa compound to the famous pirate town and was happy to answer more questions about her decision to move to Zephyr. Charlie was enthralled by her story and thought Tracy was really brave to have taken such a chance on a 'holiday romance', she was also dying to know more about Tracy and Chix's mum, but the subject didn't come up and she didn't want to pry.

Half an hour later they were wandering companionably around the confusing but incredibly picturesque streets – trying to find their way to the famous windmills, but getting distracted and disorientated by the beauty of their surroundings and the plethora of shopping, art and other gorgeous things to look at. Tracy told Charlie she was a cat person, and had her eye on a rescue cat at home in Zephyr, a mature fluffy black and white tom who was still boarding at the shelter but who she planned to take home as soon as they returned to Zephyr. She wasn't sure how their dog, a spoilt little ginger madam called Sweetie Pie would feel about it but as they were currently living side by side at the same shelter, which doubled as a kennel, she was pretty sure it would work out fine. Neither of the women could stop taking pictures of each other or the slender felines that positioned themselves artistically on the steps and walls – posing beside pots of ruby red geraniums or the traditional blue wooden paintwork.

After an hour of meandering, chatting and shopping, they agreed they were both thirsty and peckish so when they spotted a long slither of blue at the end of a narrow, winding street, they struck out towards it in the hope of finding an opening to the sea and somewhere to have lunch. They were in luck. Just before the entrance to the water, the narrow passageway opened up into a wide square with a traditional church at one end and taverna at the other. It wasn't much of a sea view, as the church took prime position, but the square was charming and cool, with plenty of shade from the midday sunshine provided by a big orange awning that generously covered the eatery's blue and white tables and chairs. They agreed it looked like the perfect spot for refreshments and people watching.

"Oh it's so good to take the weight off. Those cobbles are hard on the tootsies," moaned Tracy.

"Agreed." Charlie flexed her toes in sympathy. She looked round the square and grinned at her companion. "Thanks for inviting me, Tracy. I'm having a lovely time."

"Me too, babe. To be honest, I'm loving spending time with you. Living in Zephyr is great, but I've missed my girlfriends. It's not so easy to make good new friends at my time of life I've found."

"Don't say that, please." Charlie's voice broke as she said, "My best friend…" and unable to stop herself, she started crying. Tracy looked concerned.

"What's up, love?"

"Didn't Chix tell you why I'm here?" She pulled herself together.

Tracy scoffed. "Chix? Tell someone, someone else's business. No. He just said you needed a holiday."

"Oh, he's so good. I do." She sniffed and said, "I'm <u>supposed</u> to be on holiday with my best friend in Mallorca right now…" And she found herself relaying the whole sad story of the disintegration of her two most important relationships, while they both drank lemon Fanta and Tracy ate most of the calamari and Greek salad and all the bread.

It was such a relief to unburden herself to someone who had no prior knowledge of her or her relationship with the Hobsons. Their lives were so intertwined it made everything complicated. She talked for a long time and Tracy listened carefully, then said,

"I've got a redhead as a best friend, too. They are the best. My Cheryl, she's a bit of a firecracker. Like your Ali?"

"She is that."

"And stubborn. And opinionated. Always thinks she's right?"

Charlie laughed. "Yep, that's her."

"Quite often is, to be fair. And she's really good company. Everything's more fun when she's around, you know?"

Charlie nodded. She did.

"Cheryl really believes in me, too. Always got my back."

Charlie sniffed. Ali was always boosting her confidence. "Ali always says she's my number one fan and that I'm my own worst enemy."

"That's lovely, that is. My life wouldn't be complete without my best friend. Sounds like yours wouldn't be, either? Can you forgive her?"

Charlie gulped. Life would be awful without Ali. Even bad mad Ali was better than no Ali.

"I don't know. I want to," she wailed, "it would be rubbish without her. But she's been so crap."

"There will be a reason for that," Tracy said sagely, "and you will want to hear it eventually, but it's OK to make her sweat a bit for a while." And smiled.

Charlie quite liked that idea. Ali *had* left an awful lot of messages.

"Why is she so dead set against you and her brother getting together? What's it to do with her if he's into you and you're into him?"

"She doesn't want me to get hurt again."

Tracy had heard her entire romantic history. "Well that's not her decision to make. Simon sounds like a solid bloke to me. One of those fellas that's good to animals and kind to his parents and old ladies – but hasn't got the emotional vocabulary so he gets all tongue tied around women." Tracy sounded like she knew what she was talking about.

Charlie's attention was piqued. "Emotional vocabulary? That's insightful. Are you a psychologist? Or is it a psychiatrist? Always get those two confused."

"No a hairdresser! Same difference," Tracy joked. "We hear it all. And then some."

"Simon reduces most serious conversations to a joke."

Tracy nodded sagely. "Lots of men do." And they sat in silence for a bit, digesting their long conversation.

Charlie thought Tracy might have hit the nail on the head and was just about to say so when the older woman distracted her with another interesting observation.

"It seems like you want to be swept off your feet, probably because that ex-husband of yours did a number on you. But what if that will never be Simon's style? Is it worth losing a good man, who you get on really well with and who you love to bits over that? Not all men are like my Diver," she said complacently.

"What did he do to woo you, then?"

"He found my long-lost brother for me."

CHAPTER 36

After their long lunch, Tracy and Charlie were too tired to carry on sightseeing and decided to head home for a swim and a siesta. Despite Tracy's self-proclaimed excellent sense of direction, they got lost on the way back to the car. Just like the pirates of old that the town was designed to repel, their journey seemed to take them in circles, and they were getting frustrated when Tracy spotted a landmark – a very classy-looking shop with replicas of ancient Greek artefacts in the window.

Tracy had noted it earlier, as it was on the same street they'd parked the car, and said she'd made a mental note to return to find a gift for Diver. Relieved, they stepped into the cool white interior of the shop to have a quick look at the exhibit-like contents before they drove home. Tracy, who admitted she was a magpie, gravitated to a case filled with glittering gold jewellery but it was something else that caught Charlie's attention. There, on a pedestal, perfectly lit like a precious ancient artefact, stood a replica of the little statue Penny Hobson had given to her for her 21st birthday!

"Tracy, look at this! Come please!" calling out the words crisply, in the same tone she would use to attract Ted's attention.

Golum-like, her companion, reluctantly dragged her eyes away from the precious golden delights and crossed the room to look at the sculpture.

"It's amazing! I have this exact funny-looking dog sculpture at home!"

"It's not a dog, love," said Tracy patiently.

"Yes, it is. Isn't it?"

Tracy was laughing. "Nope. Good job Diver isn't with us. He'd give you a right lecture."

"What is it, then?"

"That, believe it or not, is a lion."

Charlie was aghast. "I always thought it was a greyhound. A funny-looking one. That had lost its ears…" Her voice trailed off. The white marble animal had skinny legs and a long back, was sat on its haunches and had its mouth open in a howl or maybe a pant.

Tracy squinted at it. "I agree, it looks more domestic animal than lion. I think it's more like a cat because these Greek cats are skinny – maybe their ancient lions were skinny, too. Back in the day."

"But it hasn't got a ruff."

"Maybe they didn't have them then."

"How do you know it's a lion anyway, clever clogs," she said, already confident enough in their new connection to tease her.

Tracy looked cocky. "You know that island Diver was talking about yesterday, Delos? There's an avenue of those little beggars over there. Pretty impressive, actually. Maybe go for a day trip if you have time? I know Diver would love the excuse to go again."

"I think I will." It would be cool to see the original in real life. She loved her statue even more now she knew where it came from. I'll take a picture with it for Penny and Ali. Well, maybe just Penny.

Feeling sad again, she carried on browsing while Tracy made some expensive purchases (she'd tried not to take note of the total but couldn't help it – it was a lot!): a heavy gold signet ring for Diver and a gold coin necklace and some bangles for herself. All of which were a bit over the top for Charlie's taste, but suited Tracy's full-blown style perfectly. Tracy also bought her own replica of the lion-cat-dog, as they had now decided to call it. She said it would remind her of Charlie and their lovely day out together – which was so sweet of her.

When they got back to the villa, she went to her all-white, monastery-like but incredibly stylish – in a Mykonian way – room. She checked her phone for the first time that day and saw the usual barrage of texts and two missed calls from Ali, as well as a text from Ed, acknowledging her request to extend her holiday. There was nothing from Simon.

Sweet, kind Ed had told her to take her time and enjoy whatever she was doing. She was grateful, she would go back to work, of course. Brown's was where she belonged, but she couldn't face going back just yet and apparently she could stay here in Mykonos as long as she wanted. On the drive home Tracy said she and Diver were going to be there for at least another week, so she wouldn't be alone. Also, she was dying to meet and spend some time with the extraordinary woman who'd tamed Chix and who was clearly equally besotted by him if she'd let his ragtag friends and family seek shelter at her incredible property. Tracy thought she might come to the villa later in the week, news from a guy called Clyde – a man who the staff referenced with awe and who seemed to be a combination of bodyguard, property manager and close personal friend. Tracy hadn't met Chix's girlfriend either and was in a bit of a tizzy about it.

Still not ready to talk to Ali and in desperate need of a swim, she slathered on the sunscreen, slipped into her favourite white swimsuit and made her way out to the pool deck, stopping only to pick up an ice-cold Fuji water en route.

She waved over at Tracy, who was already ensconced on what she had named 'her' sunbed and waded into the pool, shivering with pleasure as the silky water coolly caressed her legs. The enormous crescent-shaped pool hugged the natural contours of the mountain it had been carved out of. It shelved beach-like towards the infinity edge, and was lined with glass mosaic tiles, sparkling like the waters of Zephyr. Last night she'd found out the pool was the way it was because it had been designed for socialising rather than exercising. Apparently Chix's girlfriend had never learnt to swim and preferred pools and rivers to the sea, so she'd made it a condition of the design that she could stand in the water at every point. Tracy had told her that the villa and its pool were sometimes used as a nightclub. She could only imagine how gorgeous it would look. In its natural state, it was the most theatrical and luminescent space she'd seen, it's design somehow enhancing the perfection of the setting. She would have loved to have taken a picture of herself there, not for social media, just for memories and maybe to boast a little to Ali and Simon, but not enough to break the confidentiality agreement she'd had to sign when she arrived at the villa!

She dipped down to wet her shoulders and, feeling refreshed, made her way to the infinity edge and slipped onto the submerged shelf that ran the length of the curve, pulling up her legs to rest along it and turning a little to make the most of the incredible view. She drank her water contemplatively as she counted the islands laid out in front of her, marvelling at the beauty of her surroundings and setting a task for herself to ask Diver which one was Delos. Once again, Ali came to mind. She couldn't help herself thinking how much her friend would love this experience. The combination of staying in this outrageous place combined with the fierce partying opportunities of Mykonos town, and the intellectual stimulation from all the ancient history everywhere, would delight her.

Or would have, she thought glumly, *when Ali was her usual self – before fucking Antonio. Or rather, before she fucked Antonio.* And she growled, angry with herself for letting that awful man corrupt such a gorgeous moment.

"Should I be scared?" It was Chix, heading towards her with a fake wary expression on his handsome face. His signature golden locs were in a messy man bun to keep them out of the water. He had on a wet Cherish Zephyr tee-shirt that did everything for his well-defined torso and was pushing a floating bar. *You are every heterosexual woman's dream*, she thought. *But not mine. Now, if that was Simon, in a wet tee-shirt…* She shook herself.

"You? Scared of me? Never."

"But you were growling? I heard you."

She bared her teeth at him. "Grrrrrrrr. I was thinking about the you-know-whos"

"Hmm. And? Did you come to a conclusion?"

"Yes, that I don't want to think about either of them, because it will ruin my holiday – now I'm finally having one," she said a tad petulantly. "I want to forget about them but Ali keeps calling and leaving messages."

He nodded. "No surprise there. Heard from the veterinarian?"

"Radio silence. I think he's pissed off with me. I've never shouted at him before."

Chix didn't comment. Just listened. It was so soothing how he never offered an opinion unless asked. As he always knew what to do in every situation, he reached into the ice-filled centre of the floating device and pulled out a frosty Mythos, uncapped it and offered,

"Beer?"

"You're off duty now, mate! I should get you a drink," she remonstrated but swapped her empty water bottle for it anyway, then took a refreshing swig. "Oh God, that tastes so good."

"I'll push the boat out and have an Orangina, bar keep," chimed in Tracy who'd followed Chix into the pool, her cerese and black leopard print bikini top creating havoc with the otherwise neutral aesthetic. She looked a little shy when she said, "Well, this is the life, isn't it?" And Charlie understood, instinctively, that the confident woman she'd had lunch with was feeling unsure about her welcome. She could sympathise, it was horrible not being sure what someone thought of you, but Tracy had already turned away and was staring at the view, her huge black sun hat barely skimming the water.

Charlie peeked around the brim at her, Tracy's cute face was in shadow, protected from the sun, but that didn't stop her from noticing her expression was serious and her eyes were wet when she said in a tight little voice,

"Thanks, Chix, I want you to know Diver and I really appreciate this. I know it's been hard, me turning up in your life like this, but coming here, getting to spend some time with you and your girlfriend, and your lovely friend, it means the world to me."

Charlie, who understood she was witness to a special moment, held her breath as the scene unfolded. She couldn't help but wonder if Tracy had picked this time to say something to her half-brother *because* she was there, because she needed the moral support. What would Chix say back? She had her fingers crossed for her.

Chix was such a cool customer, and he'd confessed to her when he was in England, that he had ambivalent feelings towards his half-sister and had been avoiding her. It seemed possible that he'd had a change of heart. He'd invited her here, which was huge. Perhaps it was only because of the project, but she doubted that. Far more likely, she thought, was that he'd mellowed – because he'd fallen in love. And he could see, like she could, that Tracy, to coin a Marvel expression, was 'really good people'.

She held her breath as he placed a gentle hand on his half-sister's shoulder, causing her to turn, then pointed his Mythos towards her Orangina, indicating they could clink vessels. As he did so he smiled at Tracy, a lovely genuine Chix smile, the smile Charlie loved, the one where his green eyes glowed like a tiger's, the smile he only used on his special people then said, man of few words that he was,

"It's my pleasure."

CHAPTER 37

Ali paced around the apple orchard while Floppy zoomed around her, chasing insects, pink slimy tongue lolling out the side of her dripping, happy jaws. She picked up a fallen apple and hurled it for the goofball to chase. Even the look of shock on Flopsy's silly face when she bit into the rotten apple didn't raise a smile. She was worried! She had so many important things that she needed to discuss with Charlie, but she couldn't because she still hadn't answered her texts or calls.

It was almost a week since they'd argued and Ali's guilty-as-hell feelings were now fully fledged, loaded with fear-and-frustration-what-if-we-never-talk-again feelings. If the stubborn bloody woman didn't answer or call her back, how could she ever apologise? And she knew it wasn't fair of her to be so, but she was feeling jealous too – Charlie had run from her and Simon straight into the arms of her 'new' friends.

The first thing she wanted to tell her was that she'd been officially signed off work – for the first time *ever*. Dr Ellen, the Hobsons' family doctor, had fitted her in to her packed week as a favour. After promising Ali their conversation was completely confidential and that she wouldn't say anything at all about her visit to her parents, Dr Ellen checked her blood pressure and weight, then listened intensely as Ali vomited out information about her energy levels, sleeping habits, diet and alcohol consumption, lack of exercise regime and work demands – concluding with her recent erratic behaviour. Dr Ellen had declared her 'remarkably physically fit considering how badly you look after yourself' but clearly suffering from depression and stress. She recommended 'counselling and addiction therapy', then said she couldn't go into the office or work from home for 'at least a month'.

Faced with the longest time 'off' she'd ever had was daunting. The thought of not achieving, working or studying for something left her fearful, and she knew she wouldn't be able to sit around on her arse for weeks in Puddlington or Bristol without going even madder. So, after batting around a bunch of ideas with her brother, like: going to the outback to help at one of Simon's friend's sheep farms (never going to happen), or going to Hong Kong to take a language course and hang out with an old uni friend who'd settled there (but who was a big boozer, too, so that was a no-no), or a luxurious-looking sex addiction treatment centre in Palm Springs (which Simon suggested as a joke but she thought had potential). They'd concluded that relaxation and wellness with a healthy dose of mental activity was what was required. Therefore, she was focusing her research on exercise-rich, organic, vegetarian (she couldn't do vegan), alcohol-free, activity-stroke-counselling-heavy retreats. The type that would normally make her gag but which, she hoped, would test her mettle and give her time to think and figure out if she needed professional help or not.

Currently, it was a toss-up between a month-long yoga and kick boxing retreat in Thailand, an intensive poetry workshop with daily Pilates and coastal walks in Crete, or a lengthy stay at an old-fashioned but effective-looking mineral waters spa in Poland, which included regular colonics (apparently a great way to 'lighten up') and counselling. With so many options to choose from, she was going round in circles and she needed Charlie to help her decide.

Hanging out with her brother hadn't been all bad. They'd talked a lot over their nightly 'mystery freezer' dinners. Mutually happy to avoid discussing serious stuff, she and Simon had told each other tales – anecdotes from their years away from Puddlington when he was in Australia and she was in London and Madrid. The stories had taught them both a lot about each other. He confessed he had never enjoyed cities, that he felt out of place and very much a country bumpkin on his rare visits to London. As he had been working the other side of the world when she lived in Madrid, he knew nothing about her life there and surprised her by being interested enough to ask why she loved the city and its culture so much, and listen to her wax lyrical. She came clean to him that despite the Parentals offering to pay and begging her to come with them on one of their trips to Australia, she'd never wanted to visit the country. A sheep farm in the outback held zero appeal, but she admitted that after hearing about some of his adventures she was beginning to regret that decision.

She decided her brother was an excellent companion – funny, wise, practical, kind and interesting; he seemed to be enjoying their time together too. It was cool rediscovering each other. From the time they had left the family home, and gone to their respective universities and careers, the bulk of their adult interactions has been through the lens of their parents' rose-coloured glasses: Ali would hear of his daring deeds in the outback and slew of gorgeous girlfriends; he would hear their admiration of Ali's top grades and mastery of languages. It seemed the Parentals had done such a very good job of bigging up each of them to each other they hadn't made the time to connect themselves.

She wouldn't go as far as to say she was glad the whole mess with Antonio and Charlie had happened, but it was refreshing to spend so much time with Simon as a 'grown up' – and she'd shaken off some assumptions about him she'd carried over from their youth.

Apart from how much he'd mucked it up with Charlie, which she could now admit was pretty much due to her, and the rest down to him being a bloke and therefore crap at expressing how he felt, she'd had a newfound respect for him. Simon the adult had built an enviable life – the one he wanted. He was proud of being a vet, was content living in Puddlington and seemed to have the time to do things other than work. It made her think there may be more things than her love life she needed to fix.

She loved the law with all its intricacies and challenges and couldn't imagine not using her training to progress in her chosen field – but did she love the way she lived her life in law? Was it the best use of her talents and traits – or was it exacerbating her competitive streak, her need to be the smartest person in the room, to her detriment? She was earning a shit tonne of money for a twenty-five year old and had an incredible home, but what was the point if she never had a moment to enjoy it? Were the crippling hours, the struggle to be taken seriously by her older male colleagues, the bitchiness of her peers – the ones who weren't 'succeeding' as quickly as she was – turning her into a person she wasn't?

Yesterday evening, to her surprise, Sebastián de la Cruz had called. He'd rung the hotel in Mallorca to find out how Ali's stay was and had found out she'd checked out early and wanted to know why – concerned she hadn't liked it. She'd had to reassure him the place was amazing and came up with a suitable reason for her premature departure, citing family health issues and the need for a few weeks off work, all the while keeping her fingers crossed to offset the lie.

Even though their relationship was strictly professional, she'd found him so *simpatico* and easy to talk to that she'd ended up thanking him profusely and gushing about how much she admired his acquisition strategy and enjoyed their work together. He'd thanked her and said how much he appreciated what she'd done for him and asked a few questions about her ambitions and her career progression plans.

Simon, who'd heard the tail end of the conversation, had assumed it was a job interview, which she assured him it was not, but then it dawned on her that it could have been. De la Cruz plc had a big in-house legal team, based in Madrid, and she wondered if he might have been feeling her out. The thought was intriguing – going client-side might be a good solution for her.

She called Flopsy, went back into the kitchen and fired up her laptop. Just as she was looking at a picture of the bedrooms at the Thai retreat and figuring out if she could bear to stay in such a basic room for a month, a Skype call ringtone interrupted her. Her heart leapt. It was Charlie! Her fingers scrabbled over the keyboard and nearly pressed the red button instead of the green in her haste to answer.

Her friend's unmistakable profile came into view. She was framed by the unfiltered blue of the Greek sky. With her bare tanned shoulders, neat features and masses of hair tied into a messy bun with tendrils escaping, she looked beautiful and serene and bore a remarkable resemblance to a cameo brooch.

"Hiyah," she said, stomach in her boots. Then blurted out, "How are you?"

"I'm fine. Having a lovely time with Chix's sister and his girlfriend – who is amazing – at this place, which is just incredible," she said quickly while gesturing behind her.

"Where are you?"

"I can't tell you that." Charlie's tone was not encouraging. To Ali she seemed as stiff and distant as the image she conjured. "What did you want to talk to me about?"

Her heart sank. Charlie was having a brilliant time with her new friends and wouldn't even tell her where she was staying! What did she need Ali for anymore?

"I just wanted to explain," she said desperately, "and apologise. I'm so sorry."

Charlie turned to face the screen, looking into the web camera intently. Ali could see a softening in her golden-brown eyes and, in that moment, it felt like they weren't so far apart after all. It felt like they were sitting opposite each other at the Lamb, drinking cider, chatting shit as usual, especially when Charlie said,

"I know you are and I'm ready to listen to you now, Ali."

CHAPTER 38

There was something restful about Diver's company, Charlie decided as they sat side by side on the Mykonos to Delos sea bus.

Diver alternated scanning the deep indigo water of the channel between the two Cyladic islands (he was looking for fish) and glancing with barely suppressed excitement at the rapidly approaching slither of white rock that was the uninhabited island of Delos. He had said little during the thirty-minute journey but, when he opened his mouth, what came out was interesting, and he'd given her the salient facts about the living museum they were about to visit and even offered to give her a quick tour if she wanted.

Sensing he was offering to show her around out of kindness rather than a desire to do so (according to Tracy he was actually dying to 'geek out' alone) she thanked him and said she was happy to explore a little on her own.

This was her last full day in Greece. Considering the mood she'd been in when she arrived, her time at Ambrosia's villa had turned out better than she could ever have imagined. She loved meeting and spending time with Tracy, and was looking forward to (possibly) seeing her famous hostess in the flesh tonight, although the diva had cancelled on them twice already, so she wasn't holding her breath. If her visit had been under any other circumstances, it would have been an amazing holiday. But she missed home so much and couldn't wait to sleep in her own bed, cuddled up with Ted.

She'd been tempted to forfeit what she worried would be a boring trip to Delos because she wasn't a museum person, and spend another day lunching and shopping in Tracy's easy company but felt she owed it to Penny Hobson and herself to visit the dog-cat-lions of Delos and take a selfie or two given they were just a short boat ride away. Diver had prepared a small day pack for her, and a huge pack for him, which included sunscreen, water and snacks enough to feed an army – he was going to spend the whole day there.

She wanted some alone time to process the long conversation she'd had with Ali – she still had some thinking to do on the whole Hobson family situation and hoped Delos would be just the spot.

Life was complicated. She let out a little sigh. Her travelling companion picked up on it and surprised her by saying,

"Tracy and I nearly messed it up before we got started, you know?"

She knew something about that because in one of their lazy, hang-by-the-pool sessions, Tracy had told her there'd been a stormy start to her seemingly perfect relationship. Something to do with her thinking Diver was a fisherman when in reality he was this professor genius type.

"Really?" she said non-committally. She was intrigued to hear his side of the story.

He carried on talking. "We had this huge row and she went back to England thinking that I thought she was an awful person. But it wasn't that at all. I was furious with her because she'd assumed something about me that hurt my pride."

Something to do with the fisherman-professor thing she guessed, not understanding but nodding anyway.

"But then I talked to my brother about it and he told me to think about it from her side." He laughed at himself. "I needed him to help me understand she'd just made a silly assumption. A mistake, and we all make mistakes, and she felt terrible and had tried to apologise, but I was so mad at her that I didn't want to listen. He asked me if I was going to let my pride and a stupid misunderstanding ruin the best thing that had ever happened to me, saying I would lose her before it even started. So I reached out to her, and we figured it out and, well, here we are now."

Charlie realised he was trying to explain something to her about her own situation in his rather convoluted way.

"What are you trying to tell me, Diver?"

He smiled and shrugged his shoulders. "Just that even good people make mistakes sometimes and we need to get over ourselves and forgive them."

Could it be that simple? When she'd finally spoken to Ali, they'd talked about many, many things – including Simon. Ali had actually admitted to envying her relationship with her brother and with the Browns, and with Chix and the Zephyr crew, because they got to spendtime with her when she didn't. She said she knew that was unfair, because Charlie had always tried to include her, but confessed she'd allowed herself to get so absorbed by her affair with Antonio and her relentless pressure to prove herself at work, that the fun had seeped out of her until she wasn't good company anymore and she'd started to think that Charlie didn't want to be around her.

She'd also admitted she'd been drinking way too much to compensate for how crappy she was feeling about herself and asked Charlie for her help and support with that. When Charlie heard the doctor had signed Ali off work for being physically and emotionally stressed, she grasped just how low her friend had sunk and burst into tears.

Her tears set Ali off and both of them sobbed and snotted into their respective screens, until one of them, she couldn't remember which, blew their nose in the most trumpetty way, breaking the tension and they started laughing instead at how ridiculous the whole situation was.

There was so much to catch up on, the conversation went on and on. Ali answered her questions about Antonio and work, reassuring her she had the beginnings of a plan in place. Charlie's fear for her subsided and relief took its place. That awful man had put her girl through hell, but she was putting herself back together, stronger than ever.

Then it had been Charlie's turn to apologise for being so wrapped up in her own life she'd failed to notice Ali's troubles. She admitted that she'd had a feeling something was off but she'd selfishly pushed her worries aside. When Ali told her how upset she'd been on the day Charlie stood her up for lunch and had gone to help Simon instead she felt incredibly guilty and started crying again at the thought of how much hurt she'd inflicted unknowingly. And she admitted she should have found the words to tell her about Simon but had been too worried about her reaction to do it.

After an hour and a half of chatting, interrupted only by wee breaks on either side, a cup of tea for Ali and a dash to the fridge for water for Charlie, they concluded they had both been guilty of keeping secrets and taking their friendship for granted – but the root cause of their 'breakup' was neither Simon nor Antonio, rather one cataclysmic event: Ali moving to Spain.

"It was awful when you went, Ali. You realise it was the first time we didn't live within five minutes of each other since we met? We'd hardly had a day apart before then."

"I know. I wanted to go to Madrid, but it scared me, too. Not that I showed that, of course. And then I had work, too, and then pretty soon I had Antonio."

"I gave you space to settle in and enjoy your adventure. I didn't want to be clingy. I knew we had to have some time apart at some point, that's natural, but back then it felt like I'd lost a limb. I think that's why I fixated on Graham when we met. Why I got serious with him so fast." She shuddered thinking about it. "I can't believe I moved into his flat after only knowing him for six months – all because I didn't have *you* there to talk sense into me."

"Don't beat yourself up, love. Same at my end. If I'd met Antonio in London, you would have sweetly but firmly pointed out he was poison. And told me to swipe for the next one."

"You've always had my back – from that day we started at secondary school, when you faced down those mean girls."

"Oh, those mean girls." Ali's eyes glinted with glee at the memory. "Nothing I hate more than a bully. I enjoyed putting them in their place. Bloody little snobs. The only reason they wanted me to sit with them was because we have a big house and they fancied Simon."

"You sat with me that day, Ali. You could have sat with them. They wanted you in their gang. But you chose me."

"I knew they were bitches," Ali scoffed. "Anyway. We were best friends by then and we still are – so that was a solid choice by me," she joked.

"Like I said, you've always stood up for me."

"But I don't need to anymore, because you've learnt to stand up for yourself, Charlie, and that took some getting used to, but I love that! And I love you. You're the best friend anyone could have and I'm glad, really glad you have your fabulous country life now and, well, I understand I can't be the only Hobson in it. So I think it's time we talk about Simon. He's been moping around something rotten since Mallorca and I said to him—"

There was a bang and a clang, as the boat came up against the worn stone of Delos's ancient harbour and she was flung against the boat's metal railings and back to the here and now. She looked at Diver and smiled. The big man was so keen to get on the island he was already out of his seat, shrugging one shoulder into his bulging backpack, while cradling the clunky old camera hanging round his neck to keep it from swinging and hitting something and getting damaged. His kind face was lit up like a kid in a candy store in anticipation of all the Delos delights he had to look forward to. She guessed her face would look like that, too, when she finally got home and gave Ted a snuggle.

CHAPTER 39

"Come on in, fellas, come on in," Ali chirped, holding back the door of her Bristol flat, ushering them inside and accepting hugs and kisses of welcome and the deliciously fragrant aroma of three well-groomed men.

"Love it!" trilled Kris, as he walked towards the floor-to-ceiling windows, eyes darting between the vista and the interior, clearly liking what he saw. Ali smiled. Kris, bouncing on his Prada trainer clad toes and enthusing about her apartment, was living up to every gay man stereotype she could imagine. "Love, love, love it! Why on earth do you spend all your time at the Blind Pig when you could gaze at that?" He gestured towards the captivating view of Bristol, twinkling merrily in the orangey-pink dusk light.

"I agree. It is fabulous, thanks for having us," chimed in Darius. "And welcome home, by the way."

It didn't feel like home. Yet. But maybe it will one day, she thought. It certainly looks more homely today – thanks to the addition of a few jewel-like embroidered cushions and soft woollen throws, requisitioned from her mum's stock of soft furnishings.

"Thanks for coming," she said, feeling equal parts pride and shame. Proud that these lovely, stylish men thought she had a beautiful home and embarrassed they were the only guests outside of her parents, Charlie and el Prick who'd ever visited it.

Digging deep and channelling the Parentals' legendary hospitality skills so her guests wouldn't know what a big deal this was for her, she smiled graciously and gestured to the sofa, and the two armchairs arranged cosily around her coffee table.

"Sit down. Make yourselves at home."

She'd rather overdone it on the snacks – the table was literally groaning with Marks and Spencer's luxury nibbles, laid out tapas style. But the murmurs of appreciation were enough to make her feel she'd done the right thing. And three men and a hungry Ali could eat a lot. Darius and Mario sat down in the two armchairs and Kris came towards her bearing a luscious bouquet of peonies – velvety purple and deep red, nestled in glossy green leaves.

"Put these in a vase quickly before they droop."

"We don't like droop do we," chimed in Mario.

"Definitely not, guys. No droop around here," said Ali, carrying on the banter. "These are absolutely gorgeous. Thank you."

Kris looked at her carefully. His kind, dark brown eyes meeting hers deliberately.

"We thought we'd bring something you could enjoy for a few days rather than a bottle of fizz, which goes down too quick."

It was a graceful way to acknowledge the issue of her drinking. But he didn't need to have worried. She was facing it head on. She popped the plug in the sink and ran a couple of inches of water and left the flowers to drink, then turned to look at her guests.

"Thank you, that's really very nice of you. Now, let me get you all an adult beverage. I'm not drinking myself at the moment, taking a little sabbatical, but I have something chilling for you to enjoy … ta da…" She produced a bottle of pink Laurent Perrier from the fridge, then took three frosty champagne glasses out of the freezer. Kris, you're the pro here, could you do the honours, please?"

"With pleasure, my lady." He moved to join her at the kitchen island, expertly popped the cork, poured and served a glass for the two other men and then one for himself, then took a seat on the sofa. Ali fixed herself a 'fake' gin and tonic (just tonic, lots of ice and lots of lemon) and joined him on the sofa to enjoy the snacks and a gossip.

Ali had got back to her flat late the previous evening after dropping Simon at the airport. When she'd messaged to say she was back in Bristol, Kris, who'd been keeping track of her the whole time she'd been away, invited himself over to keep her company on her first day alone in the flat, and, feeling so much better after finally talking to Charlie, she'd been the one to suggest they turn their reunion into a small party and asked him to invite his friends Darius and Mario along too.

Her talk with Charlie had been *everything*. The lightness she'd experienced after being able to fully confide all that she'd hidden from her had lifted her spirits enough to give her the confidence to head back to Bristol and make some plans. She hadn't spoken to her parents yet, but she would next weekend, and she and Simon had reached a mutual understanding. She hadn't thought about Antonio (apart from an I'll-get-you-back-one-day-you-bastard kind of way) for a few days now. For the first time in ages, she was content in her moment, not longing for someone who wasn't there or something she couldn't have. It felt like a huge step forward.

It was so nice hanging out with her new mates at the flat. Yes, she would have liked a drink or two, but knew it wouldn't have stopped at that; and she was determined not to give in to temptation so easily. Being entertained helped, and she was happy with the way their conversation meandered from topic to topic in the comfortably relaxed way that easy friendship allows. Once the subject of which snack was the most delicious had been exhausted, and Ali had been caught up on the most recent developments for Nu Greek (Kris had shortlisted two potential venues he wanted her to take a look at and briefed a graphic designer on the branding and was waiting to see first concepts), the talk got round to the concern that had been occupying Kris's mind.

"So, did you finally discover where Charlie's staying in Mykonos?"

She knew all three of the guys had a thing for the island and she had some gossip for them. The best gossip.

"Yep."

"And?" said Kris, encouragingly.

Ali smirked. It was such fun making him wait.

"Can you guess from this?" She showed them a screen grab of a balcony with two blue chairs and a small round table on a white-walled balcony, with bushes of magenta bougainvillea overlooking a shimmering sea and islands in the distance. She'd taken the photo when Charlie took her crappy phone outside to show Ali the view.

Kris huddled over the picture, zooming in. "Well, it's quite high up. Very high up, I would say. And I think that's Delos and probably Rhenia in the distance, so it's probably in the hills above Mykonos town."

"Very good. Any more ideas?"

"Ali!" Kris said impatiently.

She couldn't hold out any more. "OK. But you all have to promise you won't breathe a word. This is top, top secret."

"Mum's the word. Now spill the beans."

"I can't believe I – a lawyer – am doing this. Anyway…"

"Ali…" Kris sounded almost threatening.

"It's OK because Charlie is the one that signed the non-disclosure agreement, which means we're in the clear, but we would get her in big trouble if we say anything."

The words 'non-disclosure agreement' had a thrilling effect on the rest of the room. Ali smiled as six round eyes stared at her as intently as a pack of meerkats on the lookout for trouble. There was a hushed silence before they all started talking over each other.

"Anything you say absolutely stays here," said Mario at the same time as Darius said,

"Cross my heart and hope to die."

"We are an unbreakable circle of silence," confirmed Kris, "but please get on with it and it better be worth the wait."

"It is fellas." She grinned and rubbed her hands with glee. "So, remember you told me about a nightclub you two went to a few years ago, and a certain diva made an appearance?"

"Ambrosia?" breathed Kris darting a look at Darius, normally ultra-cool art expert, but who at this moment looked like a little boy trying not to wet himself.

"That's the one. Well, it turns out that my best friend's new friend Chix, the barman from Zephyr…"

"Yes?"

"Turns out he and Ambrosia were childhood sweethearts."

"No way."

"Yes way." She nodded complacently. It was way cool to share news like this. "Carrying a torch for each other for years and they got back together recently. Very recently. Which is why no one in the media knows about it – or can know about it – until it becomes public knowledge. It happened just after he was here in the UK. So they're back together and Charlie says it is *lurve*."

"That's incredible. I'm so happy for her. Ambrosia's had some shit in her life to deal with." Kris was talking like he knew her personally. "But I don't understand why Charlie's in Mykonos with them?"

"All very random. Apparently there was a hurricane in Zephyr, so Chix and Ambrosia came to Greece to avoid it. Around that time, he found out about Charlie being all broken-hearted and apparently Ambrosia overheard a conversation and said *mi casa es tu casa* – and let him invite Charlie and a bunch of other people to come stay in her incredible home." As the boys absorbed the news, Ali thought, but didn't articulate because it would have been uncharitable of her, that Ambrosia was doing the thing most women do when they first get together with a guy: being terribly nice to impress him. She wondered what Ambrosia would think when she caught sight of Charlie and saw how good-looking she was; the diva had a reputation for being jealous and smothering with her men. Something she could never see the cool, laid-back Chix putting up with. The three men, however, were in awe of her generosity – they could only see the good in their goddess.

"Soooo lovely of her."

"I always knew she was a sweetheart."

"I don't care what they say about her. I've always adored her."

"She's a queen, an absolute queen." Ali watched and listened, highly entertained, to a long discussion and dissection of all Ambrosia's best qualities until something occurred to Mario and he said,

"Oh my God! Did *you* see her?"

"No. Sorry. Charlie hasn't even met her yet. Charlie is at Ambrosia's enormous villa with Chix's sister and her partner, who also needed somewhere to stay. It looks incredible and, as she says, it doubles up as a nightclub. I imagine it's the one that you went to. But Chix settled them in, stayed a few days then left yesterday to join his beloved. Right now he and Ambrosia are cuddled up in her *other* luxury villa, in a secret location on another island somewhere – from which, I was told, Ms Diva comes and goes by helicopter or speedboat depending on her mood. Sounds super James Bond villain."

"So your Charlie is really mixing with the rich and famous," said Darius wonderingly, choosing to ignore the villain reference.

"Yes, which is hilarious, as she has zero interest in any of that. She'd rather be at home with her dog and Simon."

"Speaking of which, how's that relationship panning out now you've decided to give it your blessing?" asked Kris.

Ali started giggling. "I should get an update soon."

"What's so funny."

"I'm just thinking about the last time I spoke to my brother."

CHAPTER 40

Charlie couldn't believe her eyes. There, wearing a gladiator costume, walking purposefully in her direction between the sculptures that made up the Avenue of Lions, was Simon Hobson.

He was clinking and glinting like a pile of golden pennies in the sun, sporting a helmet with a stiff red mohawk-like fringe sticking out of the top, full chest and back pieces, a short pleated skirt, belt with dagger and leg plates. The overall effect was spoilt a little by his footwear; a pair of dirty old Blundstones took the place of the more traditional strappy sandals. Her first thought was that he must be boiling under all that gold plated plastic; the second that she hoped his codpiece, if he had one on, didn't chafe.

"What are you doing here?" she asked when he reached her side, trying very, very hard not to laugh, "and how did you find me?"

"Hi, Charlie Girl. Nice to see you, too. Well, Ali told me where you were staying – even though she said she shouldn't. But when I got to the villa, they wouldn't let me in. I was just about to get back in the rental when this nice blonde lady rocks up in a natty little sports car and tells me you'd gone to Delos to see the lions and very kindly told me how to get here."

He looked up at one of the bleached white marble statues, its iconic shape darkly drawn against the cloudless sky.

"Doesn't look much like a lion, more like a dog, possibly a greyhound?" he said conversationally.

"Shut up, Simon," snapping at him because it was crazy that he'd just shown up here – and it was really irritating how similar to her own thoughts his were. "Why are you wearing that ridiculous outfit?"

"This old thing?" he joked in a camp voice, then said in a more serious tone, "Because I'm not good with words, Charlie Girl, but we need to talk and I thought this might get the ball rolling?"

Even though she was excited to see him and hear what he had to say, she gave him what she hoped was a haughty look. Not put off, he began speaking in the passionate tone of voice he usually reserved for describing a particularly good manoeuvre on the rugby field.

"Charlie Girl, I've messed things up, so I thought I'd go back to the beginning and try to explain why."

The moment she'd seen his get-up, she'd figured it was something to do with the time they'd got together all those years ago. The outfit was a close replica of the costume he'd worn to the fateful party. She didn't have a toga on today but she was wearing a white baseball cap, white shorts and a long-sleeved white linen shirt, which, she congratulated herself, was much more suitable for sightseeing one of the world's archaeological marvels than what he had on.

She was trying to assimilate the knowledge that Simon was here, that he'd managed to track her down to Delos! For such a homebody he'd racked up some impressive airmiles in the last few weeks, back and forth between the UK, Australia, Mallorca and now Greece! The whole situation was bizarre in the extreme. She wondered if he'd had the outfit on when he'd talked to Tracy and what she thought and what the boat crew had made of it, or if they were used to crazy British tourists by now.

"Simon, if you did this to get me to come back to the practice, it's OK – you didn't have to dress up as a gladiator to make your point. I like my job too much to leave. I've already messaged Ed and Kitty to let them know. I'll be in next Monday."

"It's not about work, Charlie Girl. It's about us."

"I think we've said all there is to say," she said firmly.

"I'm so sorry about rowing with you in Mallorca, if you could just give me the chance to explain." She expected to hear yet another jokey excuse, but the seriousness of his tone took her by surprise. Simon's voice was husky and deep as he confessed, "I lied, all those years ago, when I said what happened between us at that party meant nothing, but I was scared. I was such an immature idiot." She dropped her eyes to the ground and studied her sandal-clad feet, feeling the truth in his words this time.

"It's OK, Simon. It was a long time ago. It's all in the past."

"But it isn't." He looked at her pleadingly, wanting her to understand. "When I came back from Australia, and I saw you again, it was … like … wow … I couldn't take my eyes off you. But the timing sucked. You'd just got divorced. I'd brought Sandy to live with me. .. so I did my best to ignore my feelings. Then we started working together, and it was brilliant seeing you every day, but then you went to Zephyr and Ali and my mum both mentioned how you had this guy there you were checking out and it drove me crazy, but how could I say anything because I had a girlfriend?"

"Despite the fact you were clearly unhappy with her."

"And that's why I finished it, but by that time you'd started dating Ryan. And we were hanging out as mates. Then when you split up with him, I thought, here we go and I was getting the courage up to make a move."

She didn't believe his shy boy act, and it showed.

"Honest. I wasn't sure how you felt. I knew you liked me as a friend, but I didn't know if you fancied me, you'd been dating all those guys."

"All those guys?" she scoffed, "I dated *one*, you silly sod." Charlie looked at his gorgeous face and muscular body, perfectly complemented by the revealing gladiator costume, and raised a sceptical eyebrow. *How could he envy anyone? Who wouldn't fancy him?* "<u>You</u> were the one who said I was always looking at you!" Which, to be fair, she was.

"I wasn't sure, though. Don't forget, you once told me I wasn't anything special in the bedroom department?" he responded in a hurt voice.

"Well, I was just protecting myself, you idiot. Anyway, you should have just asked me out."

"I felt…" He looked embarrassed and struggled getting the next words out, "…unworthy of you."

"Unworthy?" Had she heard him right?

"Yes. I'd heard you tell Kitty about all the romantic stuff Ryan got up to, let alone all the things you did with Chix, the mega yachts and God knows what else. Then there was the fact that you and Ali are always so scathing about men – how crap we are at knowing what you want." He was making excuses, but he did have a point, she conceded. "I thought that if I wanted you to take me seriously, I needed to make a grand romantic gesture." He looked shy and said ruefully, "I *was* planning to ask you to be my girlfriend at the summer solstice ball and sweep you off your feet. But…"

"But then you had the chat with Ali."

He looked fed up. "I did. My drunken, highly opinionated, very protective sister."

"That's the one. And she warned you off me."

"She did, forcefully."

"Why didn't you fight for me? If you were so into me?" she questioned. "Were you *that* worried you'd lose the cheapest office manager you'd ever had?" She knew she was being unfair but she was feeling hot and cranky.

He looked most offended, his helmet fringe quivering with indignation. "Of course not. My conversation with Ali actually clarified things – I knew I wanted to get serious with you and I was all set to ask you out at the ball, when…"

Charlie reminded him of his odd behaviour around that time. "We were supposed to go together."

"I know and I'm sorry about that, but I didn't think it was a good idea because the day after Dad's birthday, I got this email from Sandy—"

She cut him off sharply. "I know Simon, you shared the delightful news of her pregnancy with me in Mallorca."

"But I never got to tell you the full story and – by the way I'm definitely not the father."

"Well, that's a relief," she answered sarcastically. Not indicating that she already knew, – both Ali and Kitty had previously confirmed he was in the clear.

"So I'd decided I wasn't going to say anything to you that night, but you looked so bloody beautiful in that dress, and it felt so right when we were dancing, that even though I knew I shouldn't, I was about to say something when…"

Charlie's heart softened at his compliment, then hardened up again when she thought about what happened next.

"When Kitty came over and you left for work," she supplied, remembering all too well how bereft she'd felt when he'd abandoned her on the dancefloor.

"Sorry about that, too, but it was a good job I went, I delivered twin Limousins that night. The first one had breeched and the second one was stuck behind her brother. Saved them both." He looked very pleased with himself. "Do you know how much those babies sold for?"

"No, tell me," she asked instinctively.

"Over a thousand each!" And he carried on talking about the birthing complications he'd miraculously navigated.

She was just about to ask who'd bought them, because this was the stuff they talked about and it was interesting, then caught herself. This situation was out of control! She was, by some chain of coincidence and connection, visiting the island that was reputed to be the birthplace of the gods Artemis and Apollo. And instead of exploring the antiquities, she was talking to a Wiltshire vet about his pregnancy scare, a breech birth and breeding lines.

It struck her that she'd had enough of trying to figure out whatever point Simon was attempting to make, he needed to make it. It had been amusing enough when he first appeared, but honestly, why was he here dressed like a porn star gladiator, bronzed arms dripping with sweat under the cloudless Delos sky? Not to talk about calving! And why did he still make her feel the way she did now? Anticipatory, frustrated and very hot!

She looked at him, and felt a pooling of heat inside to rival the sun warming her skin on the outside. He really did look the part: a Greek god surrounded by all the other idols.

Exasperated with her imagination for running in a certain direction, she concluded she should hydrate and cool herself down. She reached into the portable ice bag that Diver had so thoughtfully insisted she walk with and took out two bottles of water, one for each of them, even if she wasn't sure the ridiculous man-child in front of her deserved it.

He thanked her and gulped it down greedily. And something struck her with the force of cupid's arrow. *Why were men always declaring their true feelings for her in the burning hot sun?* Graham on Prickly Pear and now Simon on Delos. She felt her frustration and anger erupt so violently she expected he might see steam coming out of her ears! She hoped so, because she'd had enough of the hot sun and Simon bloody Hobson beating about the bush and she said in a deeply sarcastic tone,

"Well. I'm happy to hear you're not a daddy and I'm also delighted you saved the farmer's investment. Sooooo pleased the baby cows are worth more than me."

Simon attempted to stutter a denial, "C-c-calves, actually, as you well know … and I don't think—"

She cut his excuses off. "If you've quite finished with all your stories, I'm going to get the ferry back to Mykonos. I suggest you wait for the next one. It goes in three hours. Give you plenty of time to enjoy the history."

"No, Charlie, I'm nowhere near finished yet. You must hear the whole thing."

"This conversation is so epic, it's turning into Simon's odyssey," she said snarkily, then smiled proudly, rather pleased with her Greek joke.

Simon looked impressed. "Classical reference. Simon's odyssey. Good one, Charlie Girl."

"Go on, then. Get to the point."

"OK, well, you know what happened the day after the ball—"

She interrupted, impatience flaring again, "Knowing you may have got another woman pregnant, you took me for a walk and asked me if I'd like to bonk occasionally, as long as it didn't interrupt the office dynamic too much."

He looked shamefaced. "Not the ideal proposal. I can see that now. I was nervous, and I tried for a kind of jokey banter approach, but it backfired."

"Certainly did."

"To be fair, I did have a really nice speech lined up, but it all came out wrong!"

"What you said was awful, but I've chalked it up to experience and, of course, managed the situation so we could continue to be friends."

"Because you're brilliant," sounding like he meant it. She didn't respond. "So this summer was awful. I'm on tenterhooks, worried about the baby even though I didn't think it could be mine." He shook his head in frustration. "And then your friend Chix blesses us with a visit and I hated the fact you were so eager to see him and everyone was going on about what a great guy he was."

"Because he is, which you'd know if you'd ever met him!" She stamped her sandal in frustration. "I had to send Ali to the airport to collect him because you wouldn't give me the morning off!"

He looked shamefaced. "That *was* petty of me. But I was jealous," he said pathetically.

She raised her eyebrows. "Jealous when you were worried you had another woman up the duff? Hypocritical much?' she pointed out, but her words had lost their sting and he sensed it.

"And then, of course, there was the Mallorca episode."

She paused and looked him in the eye. "Where I will admit you did good, coming to help me with Ali."

He beamed at her. "Because we make a great team."

"But then you went and blotted your copybook again!"

He sighed. "I know. I fucked up after the showdown with el Prick, but I was in the clear by then and I felt like all I needed to do was set the record straight about Sandy and we'd be on the same page and then Mr Perfect called *again*, and interrupted the moment and I'd been under a lot of strain and I just saw red."

She shrugged. "When you had absolutely no cause or right to."

She was trying to sound tough, but she wasn't angry with him anymore. In fact she was beginning to find his endless excuses endearing. He was right, his timing had been terrible and his communication skills worse, but his intentions were true.

They looked at each other for a while before he said quietly, "I felt so awful on that flight back to the UK, I wanted to die. Ali and I talked, really talked, and we said we'd both taken you for granted and agreed that the worst thing in the world would be to lose you."

"Hmm." She liked the idea of the two of them worrying about that. They did take her for granted, but life would be dull without them.

"She set me straight about Chix."

"Good. Carry on."

"And she apologised for telling me to break up with you."

"We weren't going out," she corrected.

"Nearly," with a hopeful grin.

"Whatever. Carry on."

"She said she was envious of our closeness." Charlie felt a flower of affection bloom inside. That would have been very hard for Ali to admit to Simon. "But since we got back from Spain, Charlie, she's doing great. No more bunny boiler talk, she's taking some time off work and she's rethinking her life." She knew this already, of course, knew everything that Ali and Simon had talked about since Mallorca, too.

"She said the best thing she can do to make amends is to give us her blessing."

"Cheeky cow. We don't need her blessing." But a warm and tingly feeling was growing inside her, because that was exactly what she wanted. Had always wanted.

"That's what I said," he agreed.

"Not that there is any we," she back-pedalled, not ready for him to assume.

But he'd spotted the crack in her defences and, sensing victory, his voice became serious. "There is a 'we', Charlie Girl, and you know it. I was just too stupid to tell you how I really feel about you."

She felt a ripple of excitement. "So how exactly do you feel about me?" she asked, although she could tell from the way he was looking at her, from what Ali had said and from the long confusion-filled story he'd just told her.

Smiling like a man who had the Holy Grail within reach, he removed his helmet and put it on the ground as he sunk heavily to one knee, making his armour clatter and creak under the strain. He raised both hands in supplication and his grey eyes looked at her soulfully as he delivered his words slowly and carefully, like the lead in the school play:

"Beautiful vestal virgin of my dreams. I've travelled thousands of miles from a far western land, by car, plane and a stinky ferry boat wearing this gladiator outfit, with one purpose in mind: to find you and ask you…" His voice was husky and his face crumpled as if he was in pain. "I'm very dry, do you mind if I get up?"

She smirked, enjoying the power she had over him. "No, you can stay there." And she used a firm hand to push his shoulders back down. Taking a little pity on him, she handed over her water bottle. He took a small sip before he passed it back to her to finish and seemed ready to continue his speech, but before he could say any more, she interrupted.

"Simon, I don't need grand romantic gestures, although this one will entertain me for years. I need you to know what I want."

"I think I do."

She glared at him. "You'd better tell me, then. And get it right this time. No more friends with benefits talk. This is your last shot."

He gulped, looked panicked at first, then she saw his confidence return along with a sweet smile as her words sunk in and he sensed he hadn't blown it yet.

"I know what you want and I know I can give it to you." Then he stood up and placed his hands on her shoulders, all the time gazing at her intently. "Because I love you, Charlotte Pierce. With every inch of this sturdy body."

She smiled at him in satisfaction. He'd called her Charlotte. He must be serious.

"And I'm so very sorry if I didn't make it clear before – but I want to be the Ed to your Kitty and I want to live, work and play with you every day, even if it means dealing with deranged middle-aged volunteers and sharing you with my sister and the rest of my family."

"Go on."

"I think you are the kindest, funniest, most beautiful person I have ever met or will ever know. I want to have kids with you and to raise Ted as my own and we can get a bunch more dogs, too." She raised one eyebrow at him for clarification. "Rescues, of course. I want us to live together at Orchard Cottage until we find our forever home. I want to walk the lanes and play golf and watch rugby and eat food and run our practice together until we are old and grey or the ponies stampede us to death – whichever comes first."

She took his hands from her shoulders and pressed them between hers, smiling in encouragement. He was doing really well so far. He took a deep breath and the next words tumbled over each other in his haste to get them out.

"Will you marry me, Charlotte Pierce?" She held her breath and watched in fascination as he rummaged under his gladiator skirt for something. "I didn't have time to get a proper ring, but I have this – as a sign of my devotion."

She looked down at his big, weathered, upturned hand. In the middle of his palm was one of the yellow plastic livestock identifiers he always carried around in his vet bag. He'd sealed it closed to roughly the size of her ring finger; the finger she presented to him seriously as her lips twitched in suppressed laughter.

As he slipped the gaudy band into place, he said slowly and with gravitas,

"With this livestock identifier I thee wed."

She held out her hands to admire it. She loved it more than if it were a two-carat diamond solitaire from Tiffany's – it suited her hand perfectly. Grinning so widely that she thought her face might break, she gave him his answer.

"And, with this body I thee worship, Simon Hobson, but with one condition: I need you to wear that outfit every year on our anniversary."

And with that, she reached up and grabbed the back of his neck, pulled his mouth to hers and kissed him under the true blue sky.

THE END

Previously in the Live, Love, Travel series:

Book One: *Endless Turquoise* Two women travel separately to a tiny Caribbean island with wildly different expectations.

Book Two: *Deepest Aqua* Dive deeper into island life with Tracy and Diver

JOIN MY MAILING LIST – PLEASE!

Dear reader friends,

If you have enjoyed *True Blue* and would like to read more of my writing, I would love you to join my mailing list. As an encouragement to do so, I will send you my favourite rum punch recipe – a drink so inherently sunny and potently delicious it has the power to transport you back to the beach.

My mailing list members will also be the first to know about any new books, be offered the opportunity to join my Advance Readers Club *and* be invited to special book signing events.

To receive your rum punch recipe and other benefits, please sign up here: www.trudynixon.com

I look forward to getting to know you,

Trudy

PLEASE LEAVE ME A REVIEW

If you enjoyed *True Blue* please help me get it noticed so others can enjoy it too. Reviews are one of the most powerful ways to help an author like myself get noticed.

Reviewing the book benefits me in two important ways. Firstly, your review will bring my writing to the attention of new readers that I may not otherwise reach. Reviews add credibility and increase visibility. You will improve my ranking in the algorithm and may even help me to become a best-selling author!

Secondly, my dream is to build a team of readers who look forward to the release of my books – to do this your feedback is essential. I want to know what you loved (and did not love so much) about my characters and their stories, as well as who or what you would like to read more about.

By spending a few minutes leaving an honest review, you could make a difference to my writing career and I would really appreciate it.

Thank you, Trudy

OTHER BOOKS IN THE LIVE, LOVE, TRAVEL SERIES

Book One *Endless Turquoise*
Does your life need the Caribbean? – theirs did.

Two people travel separately to a tiny Caribbean island with wildly different expectations. Tracy, a funny, feisty businesswoman in her forties, comes to paradise to investigate a shocking family secret. Expecting the worst, she instead falls madly for a charming fisherman. Is it Just a holiday romance or could it – should it – last?

Beautiful Charlotte should be having the time of her life on her dream honeymoon – but isn't. And when she finds out why, her self-confidence and faith in the future are destroyed. Will the island help her heal?

Endless Turquoise is a delightful, inspirational beach read and is the first book in the Live, Love, Travel series – colourful, humorous and inspirational romance novels set in gorgeous destinations.

Book Two *Deepest Aqua*

What happens when you meet the love of your life and follow him to paradise, is it everything you dreamed of?

Dive deeper into real life on a Caribbean island in this sunny, funny and intriguing follow up to *Endless Turquoise*.

Tracy's taken a career break and is determined to concentrate on her man, but when he gets a big promotion and she finds out the truth behind his late nights at the office, will the reality of small island life be enough for an independent city girl?

Meanwhile, Zephyr's favourite playboy, Chix, is used to loving and living life to the fullest, until two women from his past arrive on the island to mess with his head and his beloved home. How will he keep his Caribbean cool?

ACKNOWLEDGEMENTS

Dear reader friends,

We all dream of falling in love, but to my mind the gift of lasting friendship is equally precious. I hope this book does that gift justice.

As of the publication date of this book, I still haven't met 'the one' but I like to imagine there is a Diver or Simon out there for me somewhere. In the meantime, my life is full and happy because I've nurtured friendships. I've met amazing people and fallen in love many times, sometimes romantically but more often and more lastingly with the outstanding individuals I get to call friends.

So, this book is really a love story about friendship, and that is why I've dedicated it to my Aunty Dorothy (Dorry) and Aunty Gemma, dear friends of my mum's, two amazing women who have been in my life since I was born. Both are perfect examples of 'the family you choose'.

I also want to make special mention of some of my friends – redheaded and otherwise (it's true that I have a thing for 'gingers' and have several of them in my life). For this book I am immensely grateful to two school friends. The first a redhead, Louise Wallace, who in real life is not only a fiercely loyal friend but also a super, duper, incredibly successful (very proud of her) lawyer who loves a glass of champagne. For the record, Louise is *not* Ali (she is much kinder, even more intelligent, very well adjusted and has a lot more friends); but she also did me the honour of reading an advance copy of the manuscript (even before Alex my editor saw it), bravely battling all the typos etc. and she checked Ali's meteoric career success as a young lawyer so I had my facts straight. And the second, a brunette, Sarah Brunskill (nee Hues), who, for the record is *not* Charlie, but whose enviably long legs, super model figure, love of a good chinwag, wicked sense of humour, self-deprecation, kind-heartedness and brilliant listening skills inspired parts of her.

While I'm on the subject of reader friends, I'd also like to thank my developmental readers Alice, Beth, Kevin, Sarah, Sheelagh and Susan for their feedback on the earlier drafts – you made this book better and I truly appreciate your time and input. And, of course, my eternal gratitude goes to my dream team – editor Alex, illustrator Esme, cover designer Andrew, coach Beth, assistant Lily and proofreader Lisa – for giving me the practical tools and support I need to get my stories out there into the world. I couldn't do this without you.

True Blue is the third novel in my **Live, Love, Travel series** and completes the story arc I'd imagined when I first sent Tracy and Charlotte to Zephyr and set their adventures in motion. It finally gives Charlie the happy ending I'd imagined for her years ago, when I came up with the characters for *Endless Turquoise* and realised she had to love and value herself before any man would. Tracy clearly had no problem with self-image from the get-go, so it was easy to give her hers.

I'd always intended for my main characters to meet – just not in the first book. They are very different women – in age, background, appearance, dance skills and self-esteem – but what they have in common is that they are both good people: open minded, optimistic, great friends and generous listeners. I really enjoyed writing the final chapters of the book – using Zephyr as the connection between all the various storylines but setting the denouement in Mallorca and Greece. These are places I adore and which, in a period where I didn't travel out of the Caribbean, I was able to revisit in my imagination.

Because this story focuses on Ali and Charlie, we also spent a lot of time in Wiltshire, which was bitter-sweet for me. I think this may be why the book took me longer to finish than I had anticipated. I got pretty emotional when I was writing about village life, as I still miss my parents every day, but it made me happy, too, because when I was writing about Puddlington they were there with me again.

And finally, some of my early readers have said that they love the book but miss having Zephyr in the mix – did you? Don't worry if you did, the Caribbean will star again in the next stories in this series:

Ultramarine Dreams – can Ali overcome her addictions and help the Cherish Zephyr team foil corrupt Minister Everett and the dreaded BeachLuxe development?

Green Flash – will perennial bachelor Chix handle the unwanted media attention and Ambrosia's diva-ish ways after their love affair becomes front page news?

Thanks for reading and, if you get a moment, please drop me a line or post a review and tell me what you thought of *True Blue*.

Love, Trudy

ABOUT THE AUTHOR

Photo credit: Kevin Archibald, KSharp Media.

I am a British-born writer who grew up on a dairy farm in Wiltshire, studied art and English at the University of Lancaster (even though that would never get me a job), worked and partied hard in London for years, then had a life's-too-short experience and crossed the Atlantic to live in my forever home – Anguilla, British West Indies.

I would love to hear from my readers and am easy to find and reach – either in person, on the beaches and in the bars and restaurants of Anguilla, or online.

www.trudynixon.com

Facebook @TrudyNixonBooks
IG @TrudyNixon
info@trudynixon.com

Printed in Great Britain
by Amazon